DEATHWATCH

The word spread like a raging forest fire across the torn nation: Ben Raines is dying.

Sam Hartline's spotters reported large groups of Rebels gathered around Ben's command post, standing quietly. Waiting.

Then the word came, buzzing out of the radios: *The Eagle is dead.*

Hartline sent in a team to check it out. They reported back with grim satisfaction. Ben Raines was dead. The Rebel movement was in chaos.

Sam Hartline leaned back in his chair and howled his laughter.

"Get the boys ready," he ordered. "We're gonna kick those damn Rebels into the sea!"

WIND
IN THE
ASHES

WILLIAM W.
JOHNSTONE

PINNACLE BOOKS
Kensington Publishing Corp.

http://www.kensingtonbooks.com

PINNACLE BOOKS are published by

Kensington Publishing Corp.
850 Third Avenue
New York, NY 10022

All Kensington Titles, Imprints, and Distributed Lines are available at special quantity discounts for bulk purchases for sales promotions, premiums, fund-raising, and educational or institutional use. Special book excerpts or customized printings can also be created to fit specific needs. For details, write or phone the office of the Kensington special sales manager: Kensington Publishing Corp., 850 Third Avenue, New York, NY 10022, attn: Special Sales Department, Phone: 1-800-221-2647.

Pinnacle and the P logo Reg. U.S. Pat. & TM Off.

ISBN-13: 978-0-7860-1962-5
ISBN-10: 0-7860-1962-X

First Pinnacle Books Printing: January 1998

10 9 8 7 6 5

Printed in the United States of America

Me, comprenez-vous?
Non, je ne vous comprends pas!

I bend but do not break.
                    —Jean de la Fontaine

Book One

One

Ben stood in the deep timber that surrounded his camp and listened to the sounds of nature returned to pure nature. Was earth's destruction the work of God? hc pondered. Back in '88, when the world's leaders finally decided upon the ultimate answer to everything—war—was God's hand guiding the human hand that pushed the button?

Had He tired of it all? Had He so wearied of humankind's continuous screwing-up that He, not mere man, decided upon the ultimate response?

Ben didn't know. But he strongly suspected his suspicions were correct.

I am facing so many problems, he silently mused. And not the least important of them is the matter of getting back to God. If this shattered and battered land is to ever pull itself out of the ashes and back to some degree of normalcy, the land and its people are going to have to have some divine help.

Not a very religious man, and certainly not a praying man, Ben felt impotent in his lack of ability to communicate with The Man.

He thought of Gale. He smiled. Or The Woman—

whatever the case may be.

But, he thought with a sigh, I firmly believe the age of miracles is long past. And since God so loved His warriors, perhaps He is looking to warriors to aid Him. So—he touched the butt of his shoulder-slung Thompson—let us give God a helping hand.

But, he mused, looking heavenward, it is a two-way door, Lord. I can't do it alone. So don't leave me alone. Lend me a hand.

Amen. Or whatever.

Ike and Colonel Dan Gray stood several hundred meters back from Ben, watching him.

"I do believe the general is praying," Colonel Gray remarked.

"Probably," Ike agreed. "Ben never wanted the role of leader. He damn sure never asked for it. Everybody just thrust it at him without giving him any options. I'll say this, though: a hundred years from now, when this nation is once more functioning, and historians are writing about how it pulled itself out of the ashes of war, that man standing right over there will be the man they write about."

"Most assuredly. I do wish he'd carry a more modern weapon, however. That damned old Thompson has to be fifty years old."

Ike grinned. "There isn't an original part left in that thing. It's been reworked so many times it's practically brand new."

They watched as Ben touched the stock of the Thompson submachine gun and turned, looking at the men looking at him.

"Does Ben know that weapon is nearly as revered and feared as he is?" Gray asked.

"Yes. But he doesn't know what to do about either."

Ben walked toward his friends and fellow warriors.

"If he pulls this off," Gray said, referring to the upcoming confrontation with the Russian commander of the IPF, Striganov, and the mercenary, Hartline, "Ben will be more feared and revered than before."

"He knows that too. He also knows he doesn't have any choice in the matter. He's just got to do it, and he's going to."

Ben was fast approaching them.

"He's fully recovered from his wounds," Gray observed. "And you know what that means."

Ben settled it. "Assimilate all the recon intel thus far received," he ordered. "Ike, get on the horn and tell your motorized battalion to push it. Get here. Both of you meet me in my CP in one hour. We're jumping off in forty-eight hours."

Ike grinned. "Yes, *sir*!"

"It's going to be a bloody son of a bitch!" Ben told the Rebels gathered in his command post. He pointed to a spot on the map on the table. "Striganov and Hartline control everything, and I mean *everything*, from the Nevada line west to the coast in this area of California. In Oregon, Hartline's people control everything west of Highway Ninety-seven. Now both men have their people spread pretty thin. But even at that, we're going to be badly outnumbered."

"Ain't we always?" a young lieutenant muttered, caught herself, flushed, and glanced at Ben. "Sorry,

General."

Ben smiled. "That's all right. And you're right. But right, I think, is the key word here. We're right, and they're wrong. Now, our recon intel shows that Striganov and Hartline have beefed up their own people considerably by enlisting a lot of these local warlords. Their people are, for the most part, ill-trained with a noticeable lack of discipline; but they're very savage. As much as I despise Hartline and Striganov, I will give them credit for having professional soldiers under their commands. But we must not discount the warlords. Bear that in mind—always!

"I hate to split our forces. But under the circumstances, I don't see any other way to accomplish our mission. We're not going to stand and slug it out, people. We try that, and we'll get creamed. As good as we are, we can't survive against these overwhelming odds in a stand-up, conventional type of war."

Ben paused, noting the grins of Ike and Gray. "You two apes find something amusing about all this?" he asked.

"Oh, quite, General," Gray said.

"Oh, just ducky, lovey," Ike mimicked the Englishman's precise manner of speaking. Something the Mississippi-born Ike had been doing for years.

The two men were very close friends, although that was hard to pick up from listening to them.

Dan looked at Ike. "Cretin!"

"Smartass!" Ike popped back.

"Barbarous pirate!" He was referring to Ike's belonging to the famous, or infamous, Navy SEALs.

"Stuck-up snob!" Ike told him. Dan had been a member of England's famous, or infamous, depend-

12

ing on one's point of view, SAS.

"Illiterate redneck!" Dan countered.

Ben let them have at it, knowing that when soldiers stop bitching and joking, you have a very bad morale problem.

Colonel Dan Gray drew himself up to full height and sneered at Ike. "Of course, *my* Scouts will lead the way into this upcoming fray."

"That' *your* ass!" Ike popped off. "Your Scouts couldn't find their way to the bathroom. SEALs go in first. *My* people will spearhead."

Ben put an end to it and brought everyone in the tent to full alertness and shocked silence. "*Rangers* lead the way," he said. "I'm picking a team and we'll jump in."

"Now see here, General!" Gray said, his tone shocked. "That is totally unacceptable. *Generals* do *not* lead the way. Why . . .!" he blustered.

Ike pounded on the table. "I'll be goddamned, Ben!" he shouted at his closest friend. "You'll jump in over my ass!"

The lieutenants and captains in the room stood and stared in shock at Ben Raines. The general's hair was salt-and-peppered with age. He had to be fifty years old. And he'd just been hideously wounded during the battle with Hartline.* If something happened to Ben Raines . . .

No one even liked to think about that. General Raines was the Rebels. General Raines was the

*Alone in the Ashes

13

very core of the movement to pull the ailing country out of the ashes. Many people throughout the war-ripped nation thought the man to be a god. The underground people worshipped him; altars had been built around the nation, erected to Ben Raines. The man was a living legend.

"I lead the way," Ben said quietly, calmly. He stared Ike into silence. "There will be no more discussion on that topic. Those of us who will be jumping in will use steerable dash chutes. See to them, Lieutenant Barris," he said, looking at the young woman who had spoken earlier. "You will lead a team in with me."

"Yes, sir." Like every woman she knew, she was in love with Ben Raines. Like every person her age, the young Rebel could not remember when the nation had been whole; when there were schools and factories and law and order and places of safety and productivity. She had been eight years old when the world exploded. As so many had done, she had forced the past from her mind, not wishing to relive the horror.

"Now, as to why these two jokers"—he cut his eyes to Dan and Ike—"were insulting each other. We will fight a guerrilla war once inside the areas controlled by the enemy. We will carry in as much as we can stagger with. And we're going to be heavily loaded. We're going to be forced to live off the land. I suspect this operation will take a long time. I'm looking at six months, minimum. We are not going to leave the enemy-controlled area until the Russian and Hartline are dead. They are the main stumbling block in getting this country on the right track back to nor-malcy. Dan, we'll go over the maps, then you'll send

Pathfinders in to lay out the DZ."

"Yes, sir."

"Ike, get on the horn and tell Cecil to get out here. He's going to have to take command of the battalion kept in reserve. We've got to pull all the stops out, people. All right, get cracking!" He glanced at Lieutenant Barris. "Stay."

"Yes, sir." She felt a flush of sexual excitement as she looked into Ben's eyes.

Perhaps they could . . . ?

Two

"If you weren't good at your job, Lieutenant," Ben said to her, after the command post had emptied, "Ike wouldn't have picked you."

"Thank you, sir."

"What is your first name?"

"Sylvia."

"Sylvia it is. How old are you?"

"Twenty-three, sir."

Jesus! Ben thought, suppressing a grimace. He suddenly felt every bit of his age.

"Where were you born, Sylvia?"

"Michigan, sir. I mean, I guess I was born there. That's where I was when . . . everything fell apart."

"You were about eight or nine." Not a question.

"Eight, I think, sir. I've . . . uh . . ."

"Suppressed it," Ben said gently.

"Yes, sir."

"I don't blame you. There was a lot of human filth prowling around back then. We had a way of dealing with them back in the Tri-States."

"Yes, sir. I remember."

So she had been one of the survivors of the old Tri-

17

States, Ben thought. One of the few to escape that bloody time. Ben tried to at least know the faces of those who served under him, but sometimes it was impossible.

He looked at Sylvia. Brown hair, worn short for the field. About five five. Slim, but with an aura of strength emanating from her. Pale green eyes. Pretty, with a sassy sort of look about her.

She met his direct stare.

"All right, Sylvia. Thank you."

"Will that be all, sir?"

"For the time being, Sylvia." He left the unspoken open.

She left the command post, conscious of General Raines's eyes on a certain part of her anatomy. She knew, as did everyone else, that the general liked the ladies.

That was fine with Sylvia; all Ben had to do was ask.

Walking away from the command post, she wondered how Ben Raines survived the initial shocks of war – way back when she was just a little girl.

Wasps, probably. Although Ben would never know for sure. He had been a writer, living in the Delta of Louisiana. A loner, people called him. He had been a member of the super-secret Hell Hounds. That small and highly elite branch of the U.S. Army; its ranks filled with Green Berets, Rangers, A.F. Commandos, Marine Force Recon, Navy SEALs and UDT. They were the most highly trained battalion of men in the world.

Ben had taken his experiences in dozens of tiny brush wars around the globe and put them on paper, becoming a widely read author.

On the first day of the germ-warfare attacks on the U.S., Ben had been hit by dozens of yellow-jacket wasps and stung into unconsciousness. He had been told by medical people that that had probably saved his life, counteracting the biological warfare that floated invisibly around the globe. Then the bombings had begun, and Ben had drifted in and out of consciousness, unaware of the horror that was taking place around the world. He was sick for many days, barely surviving the venom from the wasps.

When he was back on his feet, he discovered the terrible fate the world had suffered.

His sole goal had been to travel the U.S., transcribing on paper and tape recordings, and then chronicling the events in a book, a book that, hopefully, would tell the why and how of it all.

But it was not to be.

He discovered that he had been picked to lead the nation back from devastation, to bring it out of the ashes.

But Ben didn't want the job, and had told the people he didn't.

They insisted, and in the end, Ben found himself the leader of thousands.

Tri-States was formed. A country within a country; a place where crime was virtually nonexistent, where everyone who wanted work found it. It was not a Utopian society, for the laws in the Tri-States were harsh if violated. And it did not matter how rich or how poor one was; the law was the law. Outside the boundaries of the Tri-States, the rest of the nation was picking itself up and trying to function, and Ben Raines's critics were many and vocal. Ben Raines became a hated and feared man.

He was so hated his own brother tried to kill him.

A member of a neo-Nazi hate group, the elder brother had slipped past the closed borders of the Tri-States and tried to assassinate his brother, almost succeeding.

Probably the darkest day in America history came when the government sent troops in to smash the Tri-States. They'd destroyed the small nation, but could not kill the dream of Ben Raines and his Rebels.*

But Ben, with a handful of survivors, had escaped, and waged a guerrilla war against those in power in America.

A decade after the bombings that ruined the world, a plague had struck the world, and civilization was no more.

The world's population was reduced to roving gangs, warlords, dog-eat-dog savagery and barbarism.

Raines's Rebels grew in size and number as people realized that Ben was the key to bringing back — if that was possible — some degree of stability.

Then the Russian Striganov and his IPF — International Peace Force — entered the U.S., teaming up with the mercenary Sam Hartline. Striganov's dream was a pure white nation. He began systematically destroying human beings. Until Ben Raines stepped

*Out of the Ashes

in to stop him.

They had been at war ever since.

New territory, Ben thought, sitting alone in his command post. We'll be going into new territory. And we have so few planes and pilots, most of my people will have to come in by truck. Or on foot. The pilots will have to make many, many drops, resupplying us. And that will put their lives in very high risk.

He minutely shook his head, thinking: Can't be helped. There is no other way. Striganov and Hartline must be stopped, once and for all.

Ben rose from his chair and walked out of his command post, getting into his pickup and traveling to the airstrip. There, he walked around the planes, visually inspecting. They were old, but in fine shape. The pilots, many of whom had been with Ben from the outset, years back, were in one of the buildings, going over maps, plotting their course.

Ben walked to the largest of the buildings still standing. Lieutenant Barris was using that for her riggers to inspect and repack each chute.

The clock was ticking. Jump-off time was fast approaching.

Ben wondered if Rani was still alive.

In his command post in northern California, General Striganov wondered when the attack would come. He now knew for certain, through his recon teams, that Ben Raines was indeed alive and massing

21

his people for attack.

The war to end all wars, the Russian thought, humor touching his mind. How many times have men repeated that phrase?

There never will be a war to end all wars. Not as long as there are two people remaining on earth with two opposing ideas and there is a club or a stone handy.

It is the nature of humankind to fight, Striganov mused. Men fighting over women, women fighting over men. Both sexes fighting over territory, or religion, or whatever one has the other wants.

Sam Hartline was the perfect example of that. Sam Hartline was the universal soldier. And he really didn't give a damn which side he was fighting for, or on.

But the Russian was glad Hartline was on his side. The man was a savage. A fine soldier; a good, if not brilliant, tactician. And he could take and carry out orders.

As long as he was supplied with women.

The man was the epitome of a satyr. Completely insatiable. And he liked to inflict pain on the woman of choice. But then, the Russian thought, so do I.

His thoughts turned bitter as he thought of the woman Hartline had kidnapped from Ben Raines. Rani. The Russian had been unable to break her. He had beaten her, abused her mind and body, and raped her.

Then, in disgust, he had given her to Hartline.

It seemed she had screamed for days after that decision.

Before she died.

The Russian turned his chair, looking through the window toward the north. He hoped Hartline and his men were in place. And he hoped neither of them would underestimate Ben Raines. He didn't believe the man loved Rani. But he was quite certain Ben had been fond of her.

Ben Raines would be very irritated when he learned of Rani's death. But that would not make the man careless. Raines was too fine a soldier for that. The Russian had thought about digging up the body of Rani and having it airlifted and dropped into Raines's territory. He had rejected that idea. Knowing it would accomplish nothing; just waste fuel. Ben Raines was not the type to be angered into any careless move.

Striganov knew the upcoming battle would be costly in terms of human life. But that was unimportant in the final analysis. Just as long as the Russian came out victorious.

And he felt he would.

"Come on, General Raines," he muttered. "Let us finish this."

Sam Hartline sat in the den of the house he had chosen as his own. He had recovered from the wounds Ben Raines had inflicted upon him. And because he was a professional soldier, he did not hate Ben Raines. Indeed, Hartline respected the man.

In his own peculiar way.

His one regret about the whole miserable affair was Rani dying on him.

Not that she was dead. Hell, he didn't care about that.

He never could get the woman to renounce her faith in Ben Raines and betray him.

Right up to the end she had sworn Ben Raines was the better man.

That pissed Hartline off.

For the life of him, Sam Hartline could not understand what pulled people to Ben Raines. Long, tall drink of water was just a man, goddammit. Not a god. Just a man. Not a god.

Hartline had to keep that thought in mind. Ben Raines was a mortal, flesh-and-blood man. That's all.

Wasn't he?

All those damn fool people erecting monuments to Ben. Those people thinking he was God. That was stupid. There was no God. Never had been. When you were dead, you were dead. That's all she wrote.

Right?

"Ben?" Ike walked up to him.

"Ike."

"We just got word from our deep recon people." He seemed to hesitate.

"Give it to me, Ike. We're both old soldiers, buddy; we've buried too many friends."

And wives, Ike thought, thinking of times past. "Rani's dead, Ben."

"I felt she was. How?"

"Hard. The Russian gave her to Hartline."

"Well try to take Hartline alive," Ben said.

Ike suppressed a shudder. He did not like to think what Ben had in mind, for he had seen Ben operate too many times. The man could be totally ruthless.

"We'll try. But no guarantees."

"None asked. What's the word on your motorized battalion?"

"They're pushing hard. Cecil is on his way out. That doesn't leave too many back at Base Camp One."

"Keep me advised." Ben walked away.

Sylvia walked up to Ike's side. "What's the matter, sir?" she asked.

Ike ignored that. Ben's personal business was his own. At least the dead personal business. "In a few hours, General Raines will need someone . . . just company, probably. Stay close by. He likes you."

"Why?" Her question was honestly asked.

"Beats me, honey," he drawled. "With Ben, you never know."

"I'm sure not the prettiest girl in camp."

"Pretty ain't got nothin' to do with it, Sylvia. Ben was a writer before he became a general. I never in my life met a writer that wasn't weird."

Three

They talked deep into the night, with Ben doing most of the talking. Sylvia was content to just listen. Even though she didn't know, sometimes, what the general was talking about. He spoke of things she had never heard of, but she never let on. She felt he knew her education was spotty, at best. She reached the conclusion that Ben Raines was a lonely man. Had been a lonely man for a long time. There were questions she wanted to ask of him, but felt it was best to wait.

"Any family left, Sylvia?"

"No, sir. Not that I know of."

Ben looked at her. She noticed his eyes were a mixture of sad and hard. She had never noticed that before. But then, she had never really been that close to the general.

"Thank you for coming by and talking with me, Sylvia," Ben said. "I needed someone close to me this night."

Was that a dismissal? Damn! she didn't know. "I

enjoyed it, General."

"All the chutes repacked?"

"Yes, sir. We're sittin' on go."

Ben smiled at her. "Going to be a tough one, Sylvia."

"Yes, sir. I know. But I've been fighting seems like all my life. I'll probably be fighting when I die."

Is that the sum total of it all? Ben silently wondered. Will we ever know peace? No, he answered his own question. We will know moments of peace, perhaps weeks or a few months of peace, but never know it as my generation did. "I'm afraid you're probably right, Sylvia. And for that, my generation owes your generation a deep and profound apology."

"I don't understand, sir."

She really doesn't, Ben thought. The girl has no concept of what life was like Before. Only After. How sad. As pretty as she is, Sylvia would have probably been a cheerleader or pom-pom girl; perhaps a majorette. Steamy kisses in the dark-darkened seat of a boy's car while the radio played what passed for music back in the 1980s.

Before civilization was destroyed at the hands of power-hungry men with domination uppermost in their minds.

"Penny for your thoughts, General?" she asked, smiling.

"I was thinking of better times," Ben said. Not quite a lie.

"For you?"

More astute than I first thought. "No," he said honestly. "For you."

"How so?"

"What all you have missed."

"But if I don't know what I missed, how can I miss it?"

Ben chuckled. "Good point, Sylvia. So we won't talk of what might have been."

"Why not?" She became a little bolder. "You gettin' sleepy?"

Was that a dig at his age? Ben thought not, but he wouldn't have taken umbrage. Ben enjoyed joking and kidding around as much, or more, as the next person. But people treated Ben with more than respect — awe. It got a little wearing at times. "Oh, I imagine I can keep these old eyes open for a while longer."

Sylvia grinned, and with that action years were wiped from her face, making her look more childlike.

Made Ben uncomfortable as hell, and brought back memories of Jerre.

He fought those memories away. Damn, but he had a lot of memories piling up on him.

"I've lost you, Ben," Sylvia said, moving closer to Ben on the old couch he had had moved into his command post.

"I do that occasionally. When you get my age you get a bit senile."

"I know what that word means. So don't be pullin' my leg. Sir," she quickly added.

"You can knock that off, too, Sylvia. Here, alone with me, keep it Ben."

"Ben," she tried the word. "I guess I'd better get used to it. General would be kind of formal and out of place in bed, wouldn't it?"

"Yes," Ben said softly. "It damn sure would."

Sylvia stood up and took off her tiger-stripe fatigue shirt. She wore no bra. Her breasts were small and perfectly shaped. The nipples jutting out, hard and erect. Whether from the coolness of night or sexual excitement, Ben didn't know.

He sat on the couch and watched her.

"A stripper in combat boots," Sylvia said, smiling.

And Ben had to laugh.

He held out his hands. "Come here, Valkyrie."

She came to him, sitting on his lap, moaning softly as Ben caressed her smooth skin, kissing her breasts.

"What's a Valkyrie, Ben?" she asked softly.

"I'll tell you some other time."

Then fire met ice and melted.

She had left his blankets sometime during the early morning hours. He did not stir when she gently kissed his mouth and slipped away into the coolness of the Northwest. He knew she was leaving as much for her sake as for his, even though both knew the entire camp already knew what was going on.

And Ben knew, while she probably did not, that things were going to change in a very dramatic manner for her. She was no longer just Lt. Sylvia Barris. Now she was Ben Raines's woman.

After passions had cooled, he had patiently explained what she was letting herself in for . . . should this continue.

She had looked at him through those pale green eyes. "I didn't come here because you're my general, Ben. I came here because . . . well, Ike said he felt you liked me."

"And you came here because of that?"

"No. I came here because I felt you needed me."

He had pulled her close to him, enjoying the feel of her warm skin next to his. She was much closer to the truth than she realized.

Ben stepped out into a cool spring morning in the Northwest. Walking across the busy compound area was Sylvia, carrying two cups of coffee and her pockets bulging with Rebel-produced field ration. She smiled at him.

"Morning, General. Sleep well?" The question was very innocently phrased.

"Like that much-written-of baby, Lieutenant. I'll welcome the coffee. But if those cans are breakfast rations, I'll pass. I can't stand green eggs."

It seemed that not even the Rebels, with all their vast energy and talent, could better the old military's efforts at producing a canned breakfast.

"They are full of vitamins, General."

"I'll take a pill."

"You need to eat!"

"Coffee will do."

She lowered her head and narrowed her eyes. "How would you like for me to plant a lip-lock on you that'd blister your hair, and then grab a quick feel of your ding-dong—right out here where everybody can see?"

Ike and Dan had started over when they saw him leaving his command post. Now the two men had stopped and were busy inspecting the overcast skies . . . and both of them grinning.

"You wouldn't *dare*!" Ben said.

"Try me!" she said, a wicked note to her reply.

The bustling, busy camp had suddenly come to a halt, although no one was looking directly at Ben and Sylvia.

Ben leaned close to her, towering over the young woman. "I will not eat those goddamned eggs!"

She smiled sweetly and licked her lips.

"Gimme the goddamned eggs!" Ben said.

A few moments later, Ike and Dan wandered over and took a seat outside the command post.

"Enjoying your early morning repast, General?" Dan inquired.

Ben glared at him.

"Yeah, Ben," Ike said. "Them eggs sure do look good."

"You want to eat them?" Ben asked.

"Oh, no, Ben! I've already had a can. Thanks, though." He winked at Sylvia.

"When?" Ben challenged. "Back in '85?"

"That's . . . close," Ike admitted.

It misted all that day. Never a full rain, but always a light mist. Ben often glanced up into the sky, knowing he could not, would not, jump his people into a driving rain. They would be going in low. Five hundred feet, with no reserve. No point in it. If the main didn't open, they would not have the time to pull the rip cord on a belly pack and claw the silk out in time for it to open.

At noon, those that were going in by truck pulled out. Ben had originally planned on a mass assault on the sixth of June. But he soon realized he could not wait that long. Ben Raines and his Rebels had to move, and move now.

The battalion that was moving out by truck had a most unenviable assignment: they would drive as far as possible, and then force-march to the coastline, leaving a thin line of Rebels along the border separating what had once been California and Oregon. They were to be resupplied by air drops, and eventually would be beefed up by another battalion of Rebels. Their job was to contain Hartline and his men and the warlords.

And more Rebels were on the way.

Ro and Wade and their savage bands of woods-children were on the way. Those kids, under the leadership of Ro and Wade, had helped defeat battalions of the best IPF troops that Striganov could hurl at them. The woods-children, most of them, had never known their parents or the security of any type of home life other than the woods. But they all shared one common point: they worshipped and would willingly and knowingly die for General Ben Raines.

For despite Ben's lecturing on the subject, they all felt him to be a god.*

The Orphans' Brigade, as Ike called the woods-children, were as furtive and dangerous in the timber as killer pumas. They were expert with bow and arrow and knife and small axe. They could rig booby traps as well as and better than many of Ben's Rebels.

As Wade had said, when Ben asked him how he and his bands of woods-children had survived all the years alone in the timber, "We know the ways of the

*Anarchy in the Ashes

33

mountains and the deep timber, Mr. Raines. We are as much at home in the wilderness as you are in your house. Have you ever tried to capture sunlight or a moonbeam and hold it in your hand?"

And the dangerous children were on their way west to assist the man they believed to be a god.

Ike walked up to Ben and said, "Just got off the horn with Cecil. He's comin' out with his people."

"I knew he would."

"You could order him to turn back, Ben."

"You seem to forget, Ike. I put Cecil in charge."

"He just resigned. Left Dr. Chase in charge. Chase told him to kiss ass. The old bastard is comin' out with Cecil."

Ben could but shake his head.

"There's more." He waited until Sylvia had walked up. The young lieutenant had staked her claim and wanted, by God, everybody to know it. Ike hid his smile. "Deep Scouts report that underground society we've heard about . . . you remember?"

"Those that live in tunnels and caves," Ben said. "Yes. What about them?"

"They're going to fight with us."

Ben sighed. "We are certainly going to have some strange allies, Ike."

"You shore right about that," Ike drawled. "But there's more."

"The *underground* people?" Sylvia asked, her eyes wide.

"Get Ben to tell you about it."

"He's already promised to tell me about Valkyrie," Sylvia said.

"Who?" Ike looked puzzled. "When'd you run that one by me, Ben? I don't remember her at all." But his eyes were twinkling.

"*Ike!*" Ben said. For his bullshit, Ben knew Ike was a highly educated man.

"Them underground people, they been buildin' shrines in the deep timber. And you know to who, whom, whatever."

Ben sighed. He had warned Cecil, in a rather heated discussion, that he did not wish to discuss the matter of various peoples worshipping him.

"Ike . . ." he warned.

"I'm just tellin' you what's goin' on, Ben. Don't get your ass up at me."

Sylvia suppressed a giggle and Ike had to grin, the grin taking years from his tanned and rugged face.

"How are these people armed?"

"Clubs and bows and arrows. Just like Ro and Wade, I reckon."

"I wish I had known about this before the trucks pulled out. We need to have some way of marking our people."

"They know, Ben. We're all in tiger-stripe and lizard camo. They'll know us."

"How about Ro and Wade and the woods-children?"

"Them people know all about them, too. Everybody's all right."

"I'm curious about something, Ike. Ever since I got here, I've had the damnest feeling of being watched. Has that feeling touched you, too?"

"Yeah. I think it's . . . them underground people, Ben. Both of you come with me. There's something I

35

got to show you. I wasn't goin' to. But you're gonna see it sooner or later. Or one like it," he added mysteriously.

With Rebels flanking the trio, for nobody was going to let Ben Raines get too far out of sight—not again—they moved out. About a mile from the compound, in the deep timber, there sat a crudely carved wooden monument; the carvings were very fresh. A thick tree had been felled, the stump about five feet tall. There, the woodcarver had gone to work with knife and axe.

Ben stood and stared in shocked silence.

It was his face carved into the wood. His face, and the outline of something else.

"Jesus, Ben!" Sylvia blurted.

The Rebels seemed very nervous as they gathered about the wooden monument.

Then Ben recalled how nervous Wade and Ro had been looking at his Thompson. And that day when he confronted many of his young Rebels with the weapon, telling them it was *only* a weapon. Nothing more.

Beneath Ben's profile, there was the outline of his old Thompson submachine gun.

Four

Back in '88, when the world exploded in war, every nation around the globe, including the U.S., went through a period of disorganization and confusion. And for a time, it appeared the battered nations, most of them, would recover. But the gods of Fate continued to laugh darkly, and through the laughter, hurled thunderbolts of destruction at the world.

First came a deranged President, Hilton Logan, who was instrumental in ordering the wiping-out of Ben Raines and the Tri-States.

Hilton Logan paid dearly for that decision.

With his life.

A full decade after the bombings, the world still seemed unable to pull itself out of the ashes. Only one man and one grouping of peoples had managed to rebuild and pick up their lives: Ben Raines and his Rebels.

Then came the rats, carrying their deadly cargo of fleas, spreading death all over the world, further reducing the earth's population.

Still, Ben Raines and his Rebels survived and grew in strength. Ben's dream seemed impossible to kill:

He would bring law and order back to America; he would rebuild from out of the ashes of war.

And the man did not, really, seem to age. That phenomenon only served to heighten the myths and rumors about the man.

Ben Raines was indestructible.

Ben Raines was more than flesh and blood.

Ben Raines was a god.

Nature, as surviving humankind was finding out, could recover much faster than so-called superior humankind. Nature was rapidly reclaiming its own, now that humankind was not fighting her with chemicals and axes and chain saws and bulldozers and choking smoke from millions of cars and trucks and other types of human-produced and often needless pollution.

The trillion-dollar mistake called the interstate highway system now lay like great twisting snakes throughout the land, broken only by the rushing waters of creeks and rivers.

And nature was slowly but steadily reclaiming much of that, too.

With no maintenance for almost fifteen years, the superslab was rapidly deteriorating. For the first time since its inception, the 55 mph speed limit made sense.

More than 25 mph now.

And if the interstate system was in bad shape, the two-lane highways could best be classified as awful.

Trees were blocking many of the two-lanes, bridges were out, abandoned vehicles squatted like rusting old time machines, mute memorials to an age long ago and far away; an age that would nevermore exist.

And the people. The survivors.

What about them?

Many had forsaken the various religions they had once embraced, believing that if indeed there ever had been a God, He would never have allowed this . . . this *awfulness* to have occurred. Hell, you couldn't see Him; you couldn't really talk to Him and expect any reply; there never was really any proof that He existed. So . . . all we have is our wits, our strength, our own two hands. Let's stop this other foolishness and survive.

Inhabited towns either became haven for thugs and outlaws and perverts and lawlessness, or they became walled, barbed-wired, bunkered-in fortresses, with the people finally learning to pull together.

Of course, the people now did not have to contend with Big Brother Government and the mumblings of the Supreme Court interfering in their lives.

And many thought that was a blessing. Something good came out of the horror of war.

Now, there was no sign, anywhere, of factory smokestacks, no humming of machinery, no assembly lines, no commuting to work in car pools . . .

. . . and no lawyers.

But there was silence.

Sometimes the silence, for those who knew what went on Before, was loud. Too loud. They would wander away from the safety of fortress, and never be seen again.

Women became rare prizes, to be taken and used and then traded for a gun or a horse or a car. It was not an easy time to be a woman.

Or a child. Of either sex.

It was as if law and order had never existed. Now, there was no law—only the law one was strong enough to enforce. Despite all his efforts, the country that Ben Raines held in his dreams was slowly sliding back into a dark abyss, an abyss that many felt was too deep and too dark to even consider crawling out of.

This, then, was what Ben Raines and his Rebels faced—discounting the Russian and Sam Hartline.

"What is God, Ben?" Sylvia asked.

They were sitting outside the command post as dusk softly gathered her skirts around the land, casting purple hues, creating a false illusion of peace.

"Haven't you ever read the Bible, Sylvia?"

"Yes. Sure. But I can't make any sense out of that, Ben. It's too . . . well, contradictory for me. And I don't know what a lot of the words mean. Besides, if God is all-powerful, He wouldn't have let this happen. He could have stopped it, right?"

"I guess he could have. But if you're asking for my personal opinion as to why He didn't . . . I think He just got tired of it all. I think He became weary of humankind's pettiness, greediness, cruelness, and inhumanity to fellow humans. So He started over."

"He created a flood the first time, didn't He?"

"Yes. And said He'd never do it again. And He didn't."

"You think God did this, don't you?"

"I think He had a mighty hand in it. He just let

humankind destroy itself. There are those of us who always maintained our priorities were always wrong. I wrote about them, as writers are prone to do. Didn't do any good, as far as I could tell."

"I've read all your books. You sure wrote a bunch of them, Ben."

"Yes, I did."

"Some of them were pretty sexy, too."

Ben grinned. "Sure were, Sylvia." He hoped she was not leading up to what he thought she might be.

She was. "Every Rebel has at least one copy of a book you wrote, Ben."

"When they should be carrying a pocket Bible, Sylvia. My words are not chiseled in stone, babe. I wrote paperback books for the mass market."

"You never had a book done in them stiff covers, Ben?"

He thought for a moment. By God, he couldn't remember. "No, I never did, Sylvia. I wrote to entertain, not to change the world."

She didn't understand that; and Ben really wasn't sure he did, either.

Ben took a sip of water from his canteen and rolled the liquid around in his mouth for a moment before spitting it out on the ground.

"What's the matter?" she asked.

"I can't get the taste of those goddamned eggs out of my mouth."

In the gathering darkness, Ben leaned over and kissed her laughing mouth.

In his command post, General Striganov sat behind his desk, gazing at a map of the United States. He had just received intelligence that some of Raines's command had moved out in trucks, heading west. But only a part of Raines's command had left.

What was the man up to now?

It didn't make any sense to Striganov. He had Raines heavily outnumbered as it was, so why would the man split his forces?

Curious.

Striganov sat quietly, puffing contentedly on his pipe. Georgi Striganov was a strikingly handsome man; tall and well-built, with pale blue eyes and blond-gray hair. A very intelligent man, Striganov liked Ben Raines. Of course, that would not prevent him from killing Raines when the time came. Well, perhaps *like* was too strong a word . . . but he did admire the man. As to his intelligence, that sometimes worked against Striganov, for he thought himself to be brilliant, when he was merely very intelligent.

Why would Raines cut his forces? Why?

He rose from his chair and walked to the huge wall map, studying it more closely. He shook his head. Possibly some of Raines's Rebels were airborne qualified, but Raines was too smart to jump in with them, for the man was about the same age as Georgi. And when one gets to fifty years of age, combat jumping was not only reckless but foolish.

And Raines had not left with the truck convoy. His deep recon people were sure of that.

So, Striganov thought, that meant Raines was going to wait awhile before launching his attack.

Good. Then he could take his time about setting up

defenses; go slowly and make certain of each and every detail.

But where in the hell was that one battalion of Rebels going and what did they hope to accomplish when they got there?

Obviously, he would not know the answer to that for some time. And he couldn't order an attack against a force that large; didn't have enough people out in the field. And another bad point was that his deep recon scouts were on foot, with no way to keep track of the truck convoy once they passed their position.

No matter, he brushed that away. He had enough force to crush a battalion like a dry piece of toast.

The Russian turned away from the maps and returned to his desk, picking up the latest photos of the babies born to human mothers, mutant fathers.

"Ugly bastards," Striganov muttered, gazing at the enlarged photos. It would be at least a year, probably longer, before their intelligence could be truly tested and the Russian could know for sure if he had succeeded in producing a worker race; a select breed to serve as servants and houseboys and field hands.

But his scientists were sure they had done it.

"We'll see," Striganov said. He pressed a button on a panel on his desk. An aide stuck her head inside.

"Sir?"

"I need a bath. Send a girl in to assist me."

"Yes, sir."

Striganov waited patiently until there came a timid knock on his office door. "Come!" he called.

A girl, no more than fourteen, at the most, entered the lushly appointed office of the supreme commander of the International Peace Force.

"Sir?" she said, keeping her eyes downcast.

"You're new," Striganov said. "When did you arrive in camp?"

"About two weeks ago, sir. I have been tested by the doctors."

Which meant the young girl was free of any disease and ready, if not willing, to be on call to General Striganov. The general had developed some rather curious sexual habits over the past few months.

He attributed that to his association with Sam Hartline.

"What is your name, girl?"

"Jane."

"Jane, *sir*."

"Yes, sir. I won't forget again."

"Fine. Remove your robe."

Jane unbelted her robe and let it fall to the thick carpet. Striganov licked suddenly dry lips at the sight of her nakedness. The girl was a rare blooming flower, he thought. No doubt about it.

Her pubic hair was thick and lush. Her breasts forming up nicely, centered with brown-cherry circles. Her little nipples looked delicious.

Striganov had long ago given up on finding a virgin. Any girl over six who still had her virginity would be a rare find, indeed.

But his men were still looking.

"Come to me," he said, his voice thick with growing passion. His trousers bulged with his erection.

He pulled her onto his lap and began stroking her flesh. Georgi Striganov felt this was going to be a good year. He had a full complement of willing young girls to satisfy his sexual needs, and very soon he would see Ben Raines die.

Yes, a good year indeed.

Five

The morning broke to a gray sky and a hard-falling rain. It was just as well. For Ben had made up his mind to cancel the jump anyway. By doing that, he would give his first battalion more time to get in position, and the Rebels coming from the east more time to arrive.

Leaving Sylvia to sleep amid the warmth of their blankets, Ben dressed and pulled a poncho on and stepped from his command post. He walked over to Ike's quarters and knocked on the door.

"Come on in, Ben."

Ben shucked his poncho and hung it up. He moved to the coffeepot at Ike's wave of his hand and poured a cup.

It really wasn't coffee, but a mixture of coffee and chicory and other things that Ben would just as soon not know.

"You and Sylvia decided to just shack up and to hell with what the others think?" Ike asked, a grin on his face.

"Might as well. Her idea. But fine with me. Ike, we both can't buy it on this run. Have you given that any thought?"

"Sure have. And I think you ought to stay back here and—"

Ben waved him silent. "You can take that thought and shove it, pal. Ike, after Sylvia went to sleep last night, I couldn't sleep . . . "

Ike paid him back for cutting him off. "I'm sure you couldn't. Probably laid there and wondered if you was goin' to have a heart attack."

Then the ex-SEAL roared with laughter at the expression on Ben's face.

Ben unsuccessfully fought to hide his grin and took a sip of the awful-tasting brew. At least it was hot. "I've got to be thinking of a successor, Ike."

"When you finally buy it, Ben," Ike said, "the movement goes with you." There was a flatness, a finality, in his voice that Ben did not like.

"Ben, I'm an ol' curly wolf; not an administrator. Cecil is one of the finest men I have ever known in my life, but he'll be first to tell you: he won't be able to hold it together. No, Ben, it's your show all the way. Hell, partner, it always has been. I knew that when you showed up down in Florida . . . Christ, how many years ago was that?"

"More than I care to recall," Ben said with a sigh. "Okay. We'll talk about that later. Let's get down to business. You're sure you want to take your people in from the south?"

"You bet."

"You're going to have some hot area behind you,

buddy. No backing up for your bunch."

Radioactive areas.

"I don't intend to back up, Ben. Just go forward and sideways and every other whichway."

It was to be the type of war that Ben and Gray and Ike were trained to fight: a cut-and-slash, hit-and-run, guerrilla-type action.

Ben nodded. What deep recon intel they had been able to receive showed that Hartline had few planes. He could not escape by air. And since the nuclear blasts, the tides had been affected; the oceans that hammered the coasts on both ends of the United States had become a raging torrent of fury. Scouts reported gigantic waves crashing against the shoreline; the seas bubbled and roared, creating a nonsurvivable maelstrom.

No one was coming in by the sea along the California coast.

And Ben was not sure he wanted to see the once-peaceful Pacific in such a rage.

Dan Gray entered Ike's quarters and poured a cup of what now passed for coffee. He sipped and grimaced. "So so, is good, very good, very excellent good; and yet it is not; it is but so so," Dan said.

"Shakespeare on a rainy morning, Dan?" Ben asked.

"It's the best I could come up with in describing this dreadful brew," the Englishman replied.

"Why don't you say it just tastes like shit and be done with it?" Ike needled him, knowing Dan would have a quick retort.

"I shall leave crude remarks to people of your ilk,"

Dan said.

Ike feigned great personal affront. "The man has cut me to the quick."

Dan set the coffee mug aside. "Doubtful." He looked at Ben. "To insult someone of his boorish nature would require a much more eloquent person than I."

"Don't he talk pretty, though?" Ike said, grinning.

The men joked and insulted each other for several minutes. They'd been friends, good friends, close friends, for years, and they were the type of men who did not, or would not, allow their feelings to show in any type of overt manner. This was their way of showing affection for the other.

The rain continued falling, harder now than before. Ben cocked his head and listened to the drumming of the raindrops. "Dan. Double the guards. Tell them 'heads up.' If we've got unfriendlies out there, this would be an ideal time for them to hit us."

"Right, sir." Dan left the small hut.

"Expecting trouble?" Ike asked.

"No. But I do wonder if all those eyes out there are friendly ones."

"Good point."

Dan returned in a few minutes. He had a small tin of tea with him. "Now we shall enjoy a gentleman's drink," he announced.

"Does that include me?" Ike questioned.

"Heavens no!"

The water boiled, the tea steeping, Ben said, "Ike and his bunch will be going in from the south, Dan, as we agreed. You and your Scouts still want to play it the way we planned?"

"Wouldn't have it any other way, General," Dan cheerfully replied. "We shall have a gay ol' time doing our bloody bit."

"Always knowed there was something funny about you," Ike said.

"Imbecile!" Dan told him.

"Flea brain!" Ike returned the cheerfully given insult.

Ben shook his head and took his mug of steaming tea, sweetening it with a bit of honey from a jug.

Sugar was very nearly a priceless commodity.

The men sat and sipped, enjoying the tea, as the rain drummed on the roof.

"Something puzzles me, General," Dan said.

Ike picked up on the serious note in the question and did not stick the needle to Dan. Yet.

Ben waited.

"In less than fifteen years," the Englishman said, "how could intelligent men and women revert from civilization back to the caves, as these so-called underground people have done?"

"You're asking me a question I don't have a ready answer for, Dan. Maybe they thought underground would be safer. With the roaming gangs of thugs and punks and assorted creeps prowling the land, these people returned to the caves, perhaps driven by some primal urgings. I just don't know. Maybe on this run we'll find out, since they've indicated they'll fight with us."

"And maybe they just gave up on the promise of civilization," Ike interjected. "A lot of folks have.

You both know that; we've all seen it."

"I shall surely never understand that kind of thinking," Dan said. "I do not understand people who just give up without a fight."

"And speaking of that," Ike said, after draining his mug of tea. "I'm gonna ask one more time, and then I'll shut up about it. Ben . . . stay back on this one."

"No. I'm taking my team in, dead center. We'll be jumping in as planned. And have you heard from your Pathfinders, Ike?"

"Only that they all made it. They're probably busy laying out the DZs."

Ben nodded his head. "Now comes the hardest part, boys."

And they knew what that was: the waiting.

The Rebels waited all that day, that night, and the following day. Still the rains continued. Ike's Pathfinders called in from their positions. The drop zones were laid out, the coordinates given. Yes, it was raining there, too. Had been for two days. It was a bitch!

The building where Sylvia's riggers had worked so feverishly leaked; the chutes would have to be unpacked, dried out, and repacked.

If it ever quit raining.

Another full day lost.

And the battalions coming in from the east were bogged down, having to make many detours due to the bad roads. More delays.

And Ben knew that Striganov was not sitting on his

hands. The longer his Rebels had to wait, the more time the Russian had to beef up his defenses. For Ben did not delude himself: he knew the Russian knew where he was. And the Russian would be wondering what his old enemy was up to.

And worse yet, the human suffering at Striganov's experiment stations would continue unabated.

Ben paced his command post and cursed.

"Goddammit!" Cecil cursed, standing in the rain beside his Jeep. "We're a hundred miles out and bogged down. "Son of a *bitch*!"

The Rebels maintained a respectable distance from General Jefferys. The almost-always-eloquent and soft-spoken black man—one of General Raines's closest friends—rarely used profanity. But when he did . . . stand clear.

Cecil Jefferys had been with Ben since the inception of the Tri-States, and, for a very brief time, Vice-President of the United States. Cecil was the man Ben Raines leaned on most heavily for support.

Cecil turned to an aide. "Bring a tank up here," he ordered. "And blow that goddamned bridge clear."

"Yes, sir!"

An M109A1 was off-loaded from a flatbed and rumbled into life. It roared up to Cecil's position. The commander of the twenty-six-ton vehicle spoke to Cecil through a headset. "I think we can push that crap free, General."

"Then do it," Cecil said tersely.

The commander reversed his howitzer and ordered

the massive machine forward, slamming into the rusting debris that blocked the bridge on the interstate. The tank backed off, allowing a truck with a scoop-mount to roll into place. The scoop shoved what remained of the blockage off to one side and the column began rolling.

"Hang on, Ben," Cecil said, climbing back into his canvas-shielded Jeep. "We're almost there."

Cecil ordered the hammer down. About fifty miles from Ben's base camp, Cecil's column caught up with Ike's motorized battalion. His Jeep skirted the front column and Cecil waved them forward, clenching his fist and working the clenched fist up and down; the infantry signal to *Go*!

By late afternoon, the sun began poking through the clouds, the air warming. Forward scouts radioed back that the road was clear and free of any obstacles all the way to General Raines's camp.

Just before dusk, Cecil's battalions rolled into the old Tri-States.

It was the first time Cecil had been back since the government assault against Raines's Rebels. The familiar terrain brought to the man a myriad of emotions. His wife, Lila, had died not too many miles from here, during the government assault on the Tri-States; she had stepped in front of a Claymore mine.

Then, all of a sudden, Ben was standing by the side of the road, tall and erect and seemingly ageless, his beret cocked on his head Ranger fashion. A young woman stood by Ben's side. Cecil recognized her. Lieutenant Barris.

He grinned, thinking: Ben and his women.

But he was glad for Ben.

The men did not shake hands. They embraced.

"Ugly bastard!" Ben told him.

"Old goat!" Cecil responded, cutting his eyes toward Sylvia.

"Ready for a war?" Ben asked.

"I'll follow where you lead, Ben."

"Then, let's do it!"

He never could get that woman to renounce her

Six

General Georgi Striganov's forward deep recon scouts would make no more radio reports back to the Russian. They would never do anything again. Ever. They lay motionless on the damp ground, widely separated, the earth soaking up their blood. And they had been unable to fire one shot in their defense.

None of the IPF people had ever gotten so much as a glimpse of the men who killed them.

They had encountered the underground people. Silent and deadly.

The first IPF scout to die had risen from his concealed position—a position he thought was concealed. He took an arrow through the head, the point driving out the other side, carrying with it bits of bone and brain and tissue. The scout dropped to the earth, only a bit more loudly than he had risen.

The scouts were widely separated; none of his comrades knew of his death.

The second IPF scout to die never heard the person

who crept silently through the brush and timber behind him. He felt only the eyes on his back. He turned to check the source of his concern. The hand axe bit deeply into his skull; blood and fluid splashed from the massive wound. The attacker grabbed the IPF scout before he could tumble loosely to the ground and make any noise as his body came in contact with the ground. The underground man lowered the body to the damp earth. The underground man, dressed in clothing of earth tones, turned and slipped silently back into the timber.

The third scout to die felt first the leather strap-loop around his neck and then the knee in the small of his back, pinning him to the earth. His head began roaring as life-sustaining air was closed off. His frantically clawing fingers could not slip under the tightly pulled leather strap around his neck.

The roaring in his head dimmed all other sounds as life began oozing away from the Russian. He could but vaguely remember his mother and father back in Russia. Most of his boyhood and young adult life had been spent in Iceland. But he thought, now, of his parents. He wondered what had ever happened to them?

And he thought too of the teachings of Marx and Lenin. Was there nothing after life? Only death? Were they wrong?

He knew he was about to find out.

His lungs began to collapse as his heart seemed to literally burst in his chest.

The underground man swiftly tied a knot in the leather as he felt the young Russian's body grow limp. He slipped away from the body, back into the timber, knowing that they would be back when all the scouts were dead. They would show Ben Raines they were sincere in their offer of help.

The last IPF member of this forward team tried to raise his comrades by radio.

He received no reply.

The team leader placed the radio on the ground. With a terrible feeling in his guts—a feeling that would soon be replaced by a terrible pain—he knew his friends would never again answer anything.

Not on this earth. Not in this life.

His own thoughts startled him, and for a few seconds, shamed him.

Then he turned to meet his fate.

A spear flew out of the lush greenery. The young soldier had but a few seconds to respond, but he seemed unable to do so. Or unwilling. He did not know which it was. He knew only a horrible pain in his belly as the spear tore open his guts. He dropped to his knees in the forest, in a vague praying position.

It was in that fashion that life left him.

The underground man who had hurled the spear stepped out of the timber, walking to the cooling body of the IPF scout. "Gather them up and take them to the camp of Ben Raines," he ordered. "Tonight. Leave them." He turned to face another man dressed in earth tones. "Send a runner out. Your very best. He must travel far and fast to warn the others that Ben Raines will need our help in this fight. Warn him to travel only at night. Our like kind will offer him shelter during the light hours. Go."

And then the forest was once more as silent and nature-controlled as it was ten thousand years ago.

With no sign of human life.

"I suppose," Ben said to Dr. Chase, "you're going to tell me you plan on jumping in with us?"

"I hope your leadership qualities are better than your wild suppositions," the doctor fired back. "I have no intention of hurling my body out of a moving airplane with only a few pounds of silk—if it opens—to float me to earth. Piss on you, Raines." Dr. Chase had never been one to tap dance around Ben. The ex-Navy doctor, now in his seventies, was yet another of the few remaining who had been with Ben from the beginning. And one of the few who would treat Ben as Ben wished to be treated: as a mortal man, nothing more.

"What are your plans, Lamar?" Ben asked him.

"There will be wounded to be cared for. I shall set up my field hospitals as close as is possible to the front. As soon as a front is established, that is." He looked at Ben and Ben knew what was coming. "I shall treat *all* wounded, Raines. But our allies will get top priority."

"All right. As yet, we have no communication with Striganov or Hartline. I suppose you'll want to lay down some sort of honor system with them concerning the treatment of prisoners and the wounded?"

"If at all possible, Ben, yes."

"We'll try. But don't expect too much, Lamar. For our part, we'll be engaging in a guerrilla war. There aren't too many amenities offered guerrillas."

"I am aware of that fact."

"Just clearing the air, Lamar."

"It's clear."

A sergeant stuck his head into Ben's command post. "General. Would you come see this, sir?"

Ben, Cecil, Ike, Dan, Lamar Chase, and Sylvia walked out into the cool, starry night of spring in the Northwest, following the sergeant.

He led them to a pile of bodies, piled in a heap on the outskirts of the compound. The bodies still had the arrows and spears and leather.

"Good God!" Lamar blurted.

Ben looked at the sergeant. "No one heard them being brought here?"

"No, sir."

"They're IPF scouts," Dan said, kneeling down beside the stiffening carcasses. "See the shoulder flash?"

"They were brought by those who live in the caves and tunnels," a young voice spoke from behind the gathering.

All turned.

Ro and Wade stood in the night. The young leaders of the woods-children had arrived with the motorized battalion, but this was their first public appearance. They chose to sleep in the timber, shunning tents and other shelters offered them by the Rebels. They carried their survival with them.

"Ro. Wade," Ben greeted them. "Did you see the bodies brought here?"

"Yes," Wade said. "The underground people are telling you, in their way, they are ready to fight for you."

"Why didn't they just come talk with me?"

"Because that is forbidden," Ro informed him.

61

"Who forbids it, Ro?"

The question confused both the young men, really no more than boys, and in the starry light their uncertainty was evident.

"It is forbidden," Wade ended it, reaching the end of his understanding.

"All right," Ben said softly. "We all have to accept some things on faith alone."

Chase and the others were looking at Ben strangely.

Ben said, "I want to meet with all commanders first thing in the morning. Wade, you and Ro be there."

"We shall be." The two leaders of the woods-children turned and vanished into the starlit darkness, leaving without a sound on footgear made of animal hide.

"Them kids spook the shit outta me," Ike said. "They woulda made fine SEAL instructors."

Dan grinned in the night; the opportunity was just too great to resist. "Indeed?" he said. "So would have the Boy Scouts, I should imagine."

It took about two seconds for that to sink in to Ike. He started jumping up and down and hollering, waving his arms and cussing. He looked like a large fireplug with a mouth, cussing the British SAS.

And Cecil told him he looked like a fireplug . . . a fat one.

Ike started jumping up and down with even more fierceness, cussing Cecil's old outfit, the Green Berets.

Laughing at his friends' antics, Ben and Sylvia melted into the night. It was getting late, and jump-off time was growing close.

Ben looked at Ro and Wade. It cut against his grain to commit children to war. But he knew there was no way he could keep the woods-children out of it. One way or the other, they were going in. Question was . . . how?

"Are you hesitant to use us, General?" Wade asked, picking up on Ben's thoughts.

"Some of those with you are children, Wade. No more than twelve or thirteen."

"The youngest one has, I believe, eleven years," Ro informed Ben.

Dan shook his head in disbelief. He said nothing. Cutting his eyes, he could see the other commanders felt the same way as he did.

But they all remained silent.

"Isn't that a bit young for combat?" Ben asked.

"Have you ever tried to grab hold of a young mountain lion, sir?" Ro asked.

Good point, Ben thought. "Would some of your people consider staying back and guarding the hospital area?"

"No," both young men said simultaneously.

There it was. Ben faced the young leaders of the woods-children and slowly nodded his head. "All right. Then tell me this: how can I best use you and your people?"

"We cannot jump from the skies to float to the earth as some of you are planning," Ro said. "We have had no training in that sort of thing. But you said just a few moments ago that you are going to fly in some of your people; land them on the earth in the plane. I would like that way to be our way in." He smiled, and he looked very young. "It would be fun, for none of us have ever been in an aeroplane."

Ben had no idea where the young man picked up the British pronunciation. Perhaps he was English. There was much Ben did not know about these strange, wild, elusive woods-children. But he knew firsthand they were savage, vicious, no-quarter fighters.

And the woods-children did not take prisoners.

That would not set well with the people they would be going up against. Ben pointed that fact out to Wade and Ro.

Both young men shrugged it off. Ro said, "We spoke of that with the others last night. None of us wish to be taken as prisoner by the Russian, Hartline, or any warlords. They would sexually abuse us, and then torture us to death. Believe me, we know."

"Then, get your people ready. You'll lift off with the second contingent this afternoon. Scouts report a deserted airstrip at Big Lake. That's where you'll deplane. A platoon of Gray's Scouts will be going in there, too. You'll take orders from the team leader. Understood?"

They understood.

"Draw what supplies you'll need and get ready."

Ro and Wade wheeled about and left without another word.

"To tell you the truth," Dan Gray said. "I rather feel sorry for any IPF people who encounter that bunch."

"They didn't say it," Ben said. "But I'm guessing they know where underground people live in that

64

area. That's the area they both told me they wanted . . . earlier this morning."

"They are so young," Sylvia said, her words gentle.

Ben looked at her. "How old were you when you killed your first person, Sylvia?"

"Eleven," she said very quietly. "After he raped me."

"They wanted in," Ben said. "They're in. And they know what is ahead of them — or have a pretty good idea. All right, now. Dan, you and the remainder of your people are dropping in when?"

"We'll be leaving straight away, General."

"Luck to you, Dan."

The Englishman saluted Ben and the others, then left the command post without another word.

Ike moved to the open door and called, "Hey, limey!"

Dan stopped and turned around.

"You bring your ugly face back here in one piece, you hear, you toy soldier?"

Dan grinned. "I shall certainly endeavor with all my might to comply with your request, swabby."

On the runway, the old prop engines were growling, warming up.

Ben looked at Cecil. The man's hair was almost all white now, but he still wore his beret proudly. And Ben knew the man was in excellent physical condition.

"Yet another battle for us, Cec," he said.

"And after this, there will be another, and another. We should be used to them by now."

"Yes. I know you don't like your assignment, but someone has to do it."

"That isn't the reason you gave it to me, and you know I know it."

"Yes. The belief that one of us must come out of this alive certainly played a part in my decision. I won't deny that."

Cecil nodded his head. Ben noticed for the first time that the man's face was lined with age. But Cecil wasn't that old, he thought. Fiftyish . . . but certainly not ancient, by anyone's standards.

"My people will form the eastern line, Ben. We'll stand in reserve."

Ben extended his hand and Cecil took it. "Luck to you, Cec."

Cecil smiled, nodded his head, and left the command post. A few moments later, the engines of his truck convoy coughed into life.

Ike stepped back into the command post, joining Ben and Sylvia. "Gettin' down to the wire, now, Ben."

"Your people ready?"

"Sittin' on Go, Ben."

Ben nodded his head.

"You're gonna be cuttin' it pretty fine, Ben, goin' in last."

"Can't be helped. We're short of planes and pilots. All my people have studied the terrain. If the winds don't screw us up, we'll be in good shape. And we'll be a hell of a lot harder to find at night."

"I never did like night jumps," the ex-SEAL admitted. "I made a whole bunch of 'em. But I never did like them."

"Keep your boots together, Ike," Ben gently needled the man, a grin on his face. "I don't want you coming back with a cracked spine."

"Yeah? Well, you do the same, skinny. And don't land in no damned tree."

The men shook hands. Ike looked at Sylvia. "You take care of the old man, now, you hear?"

Her reply was a smile.

"Geronimo, and all that crap, Ike," Ben said.

Ike smiled. "The truth now, Ben. Did you ever holler that leavin' a plane?"

"Not one time in my entire life."

Ike laughed and left the command post.

Seven

With his forward scouts no longer listed among the living, General Georgi Striganov had no idea when General Ben Raines might strike.

He just knew the man was coming at him. When, and how, was up for grabs.

And Striganov had accepted the fact that his forward people were dead. That bothered him. For those recon people were the best he had at that type of work.

It was those damnable people who lived in caves and tunnels and only moved about at night who ambushed his men. The same people who erected monuments to Ben Raines.

Which Striganov's people tore down whenever one was found.

And was promptly rebuilt the next day.

Goddamned little pockets of resistance could drive a person insane if one would let it, he thought.

Problem was, he mused, northern California was honeycombed with caves and tunnels and mountains and deep timber. It would take twenty divisions to rout them all out. And even that many might not be able to do it.

Striganov looked toward the east. "Come on, Ben. Come on. Let's do it!"

Sam Hartline was restless, and he did not understand the why of it.

Things, conditions, were better now than they had ever been for him. Well, at least since the world fell apart, that is.

He had the finest foods available; all the women he could ever hope for; more men than he had ever commanded. But still he felt . . . well, *odd*.

Like something was about to pop.

True, he knew, from radio contact with Striganov, that Ben Raines was going to do something. But the Russian didn't know when; only that Raines was going to strike.

Hartline again fought back that ever-growing feeling in his guts.

He could not remember ever being afraid of any living man in his life.

But he was afraid of Ben Raines.

The son of a bitch just wouldn't die! Jesus H. Christ! The man had been hit so many times he should have been dead ten times over.

Instead, he just kept on coming at you. And people kept on joining his ranks.

Hartline paced the den of his home. Stopping abruptly, he looked toward the east.

"Come on, you bastard!" he shouted. "Goddamn

you, let's get it over with once and for all."

Ben stood on the edge of the tarmac and watched the planes take off, circle, and then take a westerly heading. He lifted a salute toward the vanishing planes and the men and women in them.

He turned to Sylvia. "Let's check our gear."

Ben and his short battalion checked all their gear and laid it out in rows on the edge of the tarmac. They would wait for the return of the first wave of planes before suiting up for the drop.

For now, all they would do is recheck equipment, field strip and oil and reassemble weapons . . . and wait.

Something every soldier knows is a nerve-stretching ordeal.

The Rebels could but marvel at General Ben Raines. He laid down, his head on his pack, and took a nap. A picture of calmness.

Ben napped for an hour, then lay still, with his eyes closed, and let his mind roam free, settling on whatever issue came up. Memory, problem, or philosophy.

Take care of us from the cradle to the grave, and we'll give you one hundred percent loyalty. That was the Rebels' attitude and philosophy toward Ben Raines. Basically the same philosophy of the old-line, hard-party Communists of years past.

With notable exceptions, of course.

The Rebels were perfectly free to express their sentiments; live as they chose to live; be whatever they chose to be in the civilian aspect of their lives; defend life and property without fear of unjust penalty . . .

The sounds of plane engines cut into his thoughts.

. . . *Free* summed it up and closed the subject.

Ben stood up and stretched just as the planes lined up in the sky for a landing. The pilots would refuel plane and body, take a piss break, check engines and tires, then Ben and his people would climb on board.

"Platoon leaders!" Ben shouted. "Start forming up your sections. Secure gear."

Dr. Lamar Chase climbed out of a Jeep and walked up to Ben. "Don't break your damned legs in this insanity," the doctor said sourly. As was his manner of showing affection toward Ben.

"I'll do my best. Give us a full two days to get set up, and then try to contact the Russian by radio. Make your medical peace with the man . . . if possible."

"All right. I just heard about that woman . . . Rani? I'm sorry, Ben."

Ben nodded. "I intend to finish it this time, Lamar. If at all possible, I intend to settle the matter. Then we'll get cracking on the outpost idea."

"It's a good idea, Ben. If you can get the Russian and Sam Hartline off our backs, we can try to bring some semblance of order back to this land. Productivity will naturally follow that."

"You've got to include God in there somewhere, Lamar," Ben said softly.

"The first two will come about a lot easier than the latter, Ben," he was reminded.

"Don't you start on me, you old goat."

Lamar grunted his reply. Just before he turned walk back to his Jeep, he said, "Take care, General. God be with you all." Even though, he thought,

72

keeping it silent and to himself, many of the men and women with you think God is already here.

The Rebels were almost staggering under the weight of their loads. Ben knew they were going in too-heavy-loaded. But a lot of paratroopers had done so before.

He wondered, watching his people being boosted up into the planes: For how many would this be the last jump?

He shook that away and motioned the lead pilot over to him. "Give her all she's got," he ordered the woman. "I want to be over the DZ just before dusk. Then you people get back here, get a good night's sleep, and start ferrying in supplies to us first thing in the morning."

The woman opened a map and pointed to pre-marked locations.

"That's it. Thank you, Jean."

"Yes, sir, General."

He looked at Sylvia. The woman was almost buried under the load of equipment carried. "You ready to go head hunting, Lieutenant?"

She nodded, her eyes large under the protective plastic headgear. Once on the ground, that would be discarded and a black beret would take its place.

"Let's do it."

The cold winds howled through the open doors of the planes. Conversation was very nearly impossible. Some of the sticks of jumpers would be going out the side, others would jump from the rear. All would be on static line.

And Ben would be the first one out of the lead plane.

Using a headset, Ben stayed in constant communication with the pilot. "Anyone heard anything from the others?" he asked.

"General McGowen and his people are on the ground and moving," she radioed back. "Just got that word."

Ike had made it.

"Colonel Gray's people are down and all right," she continued.

Dan and his Scouts were okay.

"First Battalion is in position along the border. The Scouts and the woods-children were off-loaded. It all went without a hitch."

"Very good. How much further to the DZ?"

"Forty minutes, sir."

"Advise us five minutes before jump off."

"Yes, sir."

Ben looked up at the jumpmaster, James Riverson. The huge ex-truckdriver from the bootheel of Missouri was yet another who had been with him since the outset. Ben held up four fingers and then made a circle of thumb and forefinger. Riverson nodded.

The minutes ticked by. Those who wait for combat can attest to how tricky time can be. It can seemingly drag or speed up.

The sun was dipping dramatically toward the western horizon.

Ben's headset cracked. "Five minutes, sir."

"Stand 'em up and hook 'em up!" Ben shouted to James.

The red light came on.

"Check equipment!" James shouted.

Equipment was checked.

"Stand in the door!" James said to Ben.

The webbing was lowered; the door yawned into empty space.

James smiled and gave Ben the thumbs-up signal. Ben returned the smile and added a wink.

James grinned.

Ben positioned himself in the door, hands on the sides of the door, ready to pull himself out. His boots were together. His heartbeat quickened. The wind howled around him.

The green light came on. James slapped Ben on the butt and hollered, "Go!"

Ben left the plane, boots together, legs slightly bent. He grunted as the static line pulled him up short, jerked out the chute, blossoming above him. Another grunt as the slight opening shock seemingly pulled him back toward the sky.

The ground was coming up fast.

The sky was filled with chutes.

The ground met Ben's boots. He was too heavily loaded for a stand-up landing, even with the slitted dash chutes. He rolled and popped his harness free, running, gathering up the silk, trying to keep his feet out of the shroud cords. Shouts filled the dusky air as section leaders called for their teams to gather around them.

The drop had been very nearly letter-perfect, the Rebels landing some twenty miles east of Interstate 5, between Redding and Red Bluff.

"Scouts out!" Ben called.

The recon teams took off at a run, heading west.

"Points forward!" Ben called.

The point people ran forward.

Ben waited for three minutes, then called, "Force march, route step. Let's go!"

There was no silly, sophomoric growling or clapping of hands as the lines surged forward—this was not a game. The Rebels did not need cheerleaders. They were, to a person, professional warriors. Their arena was a battleground. The stands were filling with stars, silently watching; there would be no cheering when a Rebel died from an enemy bullet, or mine, or wire, or silent ambush. These were not paper tigers. And neither were their enemy.

Both sides were fully combat-tested.

The Rebels force-marched for fifty-five minutes, rested for five minutes, then moved out. That was the pattern they would follow until Ben called a halt.

They halted three miles from the Redding airport at a signal from the recon teams.

Ben keyed his walkie-talkie. "Talk to me."

"IPF personnel control the airport."

"How many additional people do you need to take them out?"

"None!" the terse reply came back into Ben's ear. Ben grinned. The recon team leader had sounded insulted that Ben would even ask that.

"Take them out, Sergeant. Silently."

"Yes, sir."

The IPF guard was bored. His boredom was about to end. So was his life. Silly having to maintain such security at this place, he thought. It was so secure a gnat couldn't penetrate their outside defenses.

He was still thinking that as a great gaping wound

appeared in his throat. His blood gushed hotly down his chest. The razor-sharp knife edge withdrew and his dying body was lowered to the tarmac.

Another sentry never saw the black wire looped around his throat. He felt only the panic as air to his lungs and brain was shut off tightly. He dropped his AK assault rifle. Other hands grabbed it before it could clatter to the cement and alert the other IPF members.

The guards on the east side of the airport were quickly and silently taken out, their bodies lowered to the ground, or to the tarmac, or to the cement. It was done with about as much noise as a soft summer breeze.

A deadly, knife-wielding, black-tinted wind.

The Rebels that stealthily performed their deadly, bloody work did not attempt to take any prisoners; they did not have the additional personnel to guard prisoners, and they knew the IPF people would go to their graves without giving up any worthwhile information.

And because of that, they died.

But the recon people knew, in all probability, their luck would not hold one hundred percent that night. And when they were discovered, the night would suddenly turn noisy and very bloody.

"Hapy—Haoer!" a voice yelled in Russian.

And the night rocked and rolled with gunfire.

A Rebel tossed a grenade into a room filled with IPF personnel. The large fragmentation grenade blew, scattering bits and pieces of IPF personnel all about the room. The Rebel stuck the muzzle of his M-16 through the screenless, open window and finished what the grenade had not.

Ben had started his people forward the instant he had given the orders to secure the airport. The Rebels at the point were running across the tarmac when the shouted Russian words reached theirs ears. The Rebels forced tired legs to churn a bit faster, to get them there a few seconds earlier.

"Try to contain the west side!" the recon leader shouted the order. He keyed his walkie-talkie and asked for Rebels on the north and south sides of the airfield. Box the IPF personnel in.

One IPF man made it to the radio room and got off part of a message to the IPF headquarters on the coast, near the King Mountain Range, some one hundred and fifty miles away.

"Rebels attacking airport. Need help. Almost overrun by—"

A bullet to the head ended the message before it could be completed.

Striganov was furious. *"What* airport?" he screamed.

"I don't know, sir," the radio operator said. "I'm contacting them all now."

Striganov waited, and paced the floor.

At the airport in Red Bluff, the battle was almost over. The small contingent of IPF personnel were overrun by Raines's Rebels. Half a dozen very valuable cargo planes were seized along with tons of supplies: food and weapons and ammo.

Ben stepped into the bloody radio room and slipped on the headset, sitting down at the radio. He could manage a few words in Russian, and hoped the upcoming transmission was brief.

"Red Bluff!" the voice cracked out of the speaker.

"Red Bluff," Ben radioed back.

"Are you under attack?"

"Nyet."

"Have you heard of anyone under attack by Rebels?"

"Nyet."

"Stay alert, Red Bluff."

"Da."

The set went silent.

Ben leaned back, a smile on his face. By the time Striganov learned the truth, the airport's supply depot would have been stripped bare and the planes ferried back to the forward base camp of the Rebels.

The speaker crackled again. "Red Bluff."

Ben recognized the voice. Striganov.

"Red Bluff," Ben radioed.

"This is General Striganov. Is everything all right?"

"Da, cynapb."

"Speak English, you fool."

"Yes, sir," Ben replied, muffling his voice with a handkerchief.

"The airport is secure?"

"Yes, sir. Very quiet."

Ben could hear the Russian's sigh. "Very well. Go to full alert for the remainder of the night."

"Yes, sir."

The set went silent.

Ben leaned back in the blood- and brain-splattered chair and laughed.

Eight

Ben told the radio operator to get on the scramble horn and order a planeload of pilots to be at the airfield by dawn, to ferry captured aircraft back to the base camp.

He ordered half his personnel to rest for an hour, the other half to start loading equipment on the planes and trucks and other vehicles found at the airport.

He called his platoon leaders together. "How many did we lose?"

"One dead, three wounded."

"Bury the dead. We'll send the wounded back with the planes in the morning."

Ben looked toward the south. He wondered how Ike was doing.

Ike was cutting a throat, the hot blood of the Russian IPF man bathing his right hand in thick stickiness.

"Yukk!" Ike muttered, lowering the body to the ground. He wiped his blade clean on the Russian's shirt, then wiped his hands clean.

The southernmost outpost of Striganov's IPF forces had been neutralized without a single Rebel getting so much as a scratch.

He turned to his XO. "We'll neutralize everything between 101 and Interstate 5," he said. "I don't wanna get trapped with the ocean to our backs and no place to cut and run. Six-man teams . . ." He looked at a woman sergeant and grinned. "Six-*person* teams. Get 'em moved out pronto. We're gonna be stretched pretty thin, but what the hell? So is everybody else."

"How about the civilians?"

"They're either with us, or agin' us," Ike drawled. "And if I have to explain that, you're in a heap of trouble, boy."

His XO grinned. He was just old enough to remember that TV commercial. He saluted and left.

Ike's eyes turned toward the north. He wondered how Dan was doing.

"My good fellow," Dan said, looking at the IPF colonel. "You must realize you are in a perfectly dreadful situation."

The Russian's eyes were as cold as his heart.

Dan held out the map his Rebels had seized from the colonel's quarters. "These outposts you have *X*'ed. They are still operational?"

The Russian said something terribly vulgar.

"How crude! And to the best of my knowledge, physically impossible. Is that all you have to say, Colonel?"

It was.

Dan turned to Tina Raines, Ben's daughter and a longtime member of Gray's Scouts. "Shoot him."

Tina shot the Russian between the eyes, the .45 slug swelling his head before it exited out the back, removing part of the man's brain as it traveled.

Dan spread the map out on a table and studied it. "This is going to make our mission infinitely easier." He began assigning teams to sectors. When he was finished, his teams fanning out, he turned to Tina. "We haven't got enough personnel to neutralize all these outposts, so I'm going to have to contact our northern teams. We test the mettle of the woods-children now."

"They'll stand," Tina opined.

"Oh, I have no doubt of that. It's these underground people I'm a bit uncertain of."

He was thoughtful for a few seconds.

"If I could just *see* them perhaps I'd feel better."

"You want to bet they're not looking at us?" she tossed the challenge at him.

"I think I'll pass, Tina." But he did look around him, at the dark forest with its deep timber.

Did something move in there?

Dan wasn't certain. But he thought his eyes had picked up a flash of earth-colored clothing flitting through the vegetation.

"I saw it too, Dan," Tina said.

"Yes. But *what* did we see?"

"A friend," she said, adding, "I hope."

Dan picked up his submachine gun. He looked at Tina. "Good luck, Tina."

She smiled and winked. "Yeah. Let's go kill a

commie for mommie."

Dan laughed, loud and long. "Where in the world did you ever hear that, Tina?"

"I read it, back when I was just a kid." Tina was every bit of twenty-three.

"Oh?"

"Yeah. In one of Dad's books."

The young IPF soldier was so frightened he forgot his English and spoke in Russian.

Gray's Scout looked at Ro and Wade and the other woods-children who had captured the young IPF soldier. The young people's eyes were as cold as a glacier.

"He's asking for mercy," the Scout said softly.

Wade glanced up at the Scout. "Mercy? Ask him how many children, both male and female, he has had sexually. Ask him how many men and women not of his race or color he has helped capture and transport to the Russian for butchering."

The IPF soldier could speak perfect English. He dropped his eyes, refusing to meet the eyes of Wade or any of the others around him.

"Ask him," Ro said, "how many times he's killed men and women and children who refused to accept the IPF's demands. Ask him how many of Ben Raines's Rebels he has killed. And ask him if he will tell us the location of every IPF outpost in our sector?"

The Russian soldier shook his head.

Ro met the Scout's eyes. "Would Ben Raines let him live?"

"No," the Scout replied in a low tone.

Wade reached down, jerked the soldier's head up, and with one quick cut sliced the man's throat. The body flopped on the ground and then was still.

The Scout's face and eyes remained impassive. He had been warned just how savage these young people could be, and that they all, to a person, had good reason to hate the IPF and any warlord.

"We'll rest here for a time. While we're taking a break, I'll assign sectors." He walked off.

A young girl stood off to one side, but close enough to have seen the entire execution and its method. She was among the youngest of the woods-children. She was eleven. The carbine she carried was very nearly as large as she. Her name was Lora. She did not know her last name. She did not know if she even had a last name.

She was dressed in patched jeans and a man's flannel shirt, way too big for her, the sleeves pinned back. She carried a .38 caliber pistol in a holster belted around her slim waist, right side. A very sharp hunting knife in a sheath on her left side.

She had joined Ro's group of woods-children when she was eight, after being seized and raped repeatedly by a gang of roaming outlaws. She had managed to escape from them after a particular savage night of drinking and lust. With her blood streaking her inner thighs, so sore she could hardly walk after being raped and sodomized, Lora had slipped away from the sleeping circle of men and made her way deep into the timber of Kentucky.

But not before she killed the man who had last taken her. She had calmly and viciously, with all her strength, driven a sharpened wooden stake through his right eye, penetrating the brain.

Lora shoulder-slung her carbine and walked off to sit by herself in the shade of a huge old tree. The butt of the carbine almost dragged the ground as she walked.

Seated on the ground, she ate some berries she had picked that morning and sipped water from her canteen. Then she opened her rucksack and took out a ragged magazine she had found back in one of the buildings at the airport in the old Tri-States.

It had such pretty pictures in it. Pictures, in *color*, of kids about her own age, she guessed. But they were dressed so fine, and all of them seemed so happy. And they were so clean, with shining hair and pretty rings on their fingers. They had little gold and silver and shiny things on the bottom part of their ears.

She wondered what those things were.

But what really grabbed her attention and held it, was the fact that none of the kids carried a gun.

Not even a knife.

That seemed very odd to Lora.

And some of the girls wore fancy dresses. Lora thought she might have had a dress one time in her life. She seemed to have that memory. But she couldn't bring the memory into full light of consciousness. But she thought she had had a dress on sometime.

Maybe it was Before.

No. She had been told that was . . . twelve years ago. And Lora only had eleven years. So it had to have been After.

Oh, well, she thought, suppressing a sigh. It didn't

matter.

She didn't know anything about Before. Just After. And now that could be called Here.

Sitting alone, she turned the page. More pretty pictures of smiling and laughing kids.

Lora could not understand why they would all be so happy.

She wished she could read the words.

She could make out some words. But she wasn't too sure she understood what they meant. She had seen the funny-looking word TV many times. She wished she knew what a TV was.

And a moving star. Or something like that. *Movie* star, that was it.

Now she wished she knew what a movie star was.

Stars were up in the heavens. Everybody knew that. Stars were far away and untouchable. Why would anyone want to be far away and untouchable?

Well . . . Ben Raines was untouchable, but he wasn't far away.

It was all so confusing.

The other woods-children had told her that when things were better, Ben Raines was going to have them all attend school where they would all learn many things.

Lora thought that might be fun. Maybe.

"Let's go!" the shouted command reached her.

Lora carefully replaced the magazine back into her rucksack and stood up, slinging her carbine. She looked down at her ragged tennis shoes. She'd have to find a new pair pretty soon. Soon as they came up on a house she'd look. Maybe she'd find a pair the rats and mice hadn't chewed on.

She took her assigned place in the short column and moved out.

The plane from the old Tri-States had landed and the pilots were busy inspecting the newly acquired aircraft. Jean walked up to Ben.

"They're in fine shape, General," she said. "And we found an old Puff—believe it or not—in the far hanger."

"All the guns operational?"

"They seem to be. We'll check them out when we test fly the plane."

"Fine. Get the planes back to a safe zone as quickly as possible. I've asked Dan's Scouts to hit every airport they can. Striganov seems to have set up posts at airstrips. That's good for us if it holds true. I'm taking my contingent straight up the interstate into Redding as soon as you people get airborne. We'll reconnoiter the area and if possible hit the airport just before dark. I sent recon teams out before dawn, in seized vehicles. They'll be reporting back any minute. Get cracking, Jean."

She saluted and turned to leave.

Sylvia walked to his side. "Recon teams just radioed back, Ben. They report only a small force of IPF personnel at the airport in Redding. And the airport has been cleaned up and is fully operational."

"Thank you, Sylvia. You heard it, Jean. Get the planes back and stand ready for my call to return." Ben grinned. "Pretty soon now, we're going to have more planes than pilots, huh?"

She returned the grin and said, "At last count,

General, we've got about a hundred and fifty people who are, or were, qualified pilots. Checked out in everything from props to jets. You're going to have an air force before you know it."

"I'll make you the first commander of it, then," Ben said.

"For the first time in history," Jean said drily.

"That may well be what we're all trying to do." Sylvia said.

"What?" Jean asked.

"Trying to keep history from repeating itself."

"Very profound, Sylvia," Ben said.

"Oh, I'm just full of surprises, General," she replied.

Ben glanced at her, smiling.

Jean left before it could get mushy.

Nine

Early that morning, before dawn, Ben had ordered the residents of Red Bluff—those that could be found—rousted out of bed. IPF sympathizers were quickly pointed out to the Rebels.

And just as quickly disposed of.

Ben and his Rebels had no sympathy for those who would willingly surrender their freedom. And no use for them. And no place for those types within the ranks of the Rebels.

The handful of survivors found in Red Bluff, less than two hundred in all, were armed with weapons taken from the IPF garrison and told they had damn well better get ready to fight. To the death if it came to that, and that it might just come to that.

Ben's Rebels pulled out, with Ben's Jeep leading the column, his Scouts ranging far out in front of the main column. Sylvia driving.

"Isn't this awfully brazen, Ben?" Sylvia asked. "Just driving right out on the interstate in broad open daylight?"

"No. We're driving vehicles with IPF markings. If Striganov has spotter planes out, the pilots will think it's a column of their own people. I would think our greatest danger would come from Americans along the road; maybe with a sniper rifle."

Sylvia muttered something under her breath that Ben ignored with a smile. It sounded suspiciously like, "Smart-ass!"

Ben halted his column on Highway 273, just west of the interstate, and waited for another report from his recon team. Redding was about five or six times the size of Red Bluff, so the airport would be much larger, and probably with a much larger contingent of IPF personnel assigned to guard it. While they waited, Ben studied maps taken from the slain IPF guards at Red Bluff.

"Curious," he muttered. "But typical of the arrogant bastard."

"Who?" Sylvia asked.

"General Striganov."

"What'd he do?"

"Put his back to a wall of raging ocean. He might have a spectacular view, as I'm sure he does, but he cut off a valuable escape route." Ben thought for a moment, then said, "No, he didn't."

"What do you mean?"

"If by some chance we do trap him in there, he can walk right out of there. He could put the women and children in front of him, knowing we wouldn't shoot through them to get him. Or he'd stay put and start killing hostages if we tried to rush him."

"He's ruthless enough to do it, too."

"Tell me." Ben's thoughts were flung through a mist of bloody events, back to when Hartline and the Russian had tied naked men and women to the front of tanks and trucks and Jeeps and APCs, and used the helpless men and women for cover while they advanced on Rebel-held positions. And mixed in with the advancing mercenaries and IPF forces were several hundred elderly people, stripped naked and forced to jog and trot ahead of and mingled in with the advancing forces.

If the elderly couldn't keep up and fell down, they were run down and crushed by the vehicles behind them.

Ben sighed and lit one of his rare cigarettes. "Yeah," he said. "Tell me about Hartline and the Russian."

"You say contact is poor from the Red Bluff end of the transmission?" Striganov asked his radio operator.

"Yes, sir. It's the atmosphere again. That radioactive belt must be dipping closer again."

"Then it would affect *both* ends of the signal, *fool*!" Striganov shouted. "Goddamn, I'm surrounded by *idiots*! Get Red Bluff."

With shaking fingers, the young woman operating the radio keyed her mike and called Red Bluff.

But in the time the IPF had occupied northern California, the Americans had learned a lot of Russian. And the man Ben had left in charge of the civilians in Red Bluff, George, had grinned and agreed when Ben had given him instructions as to what to do when his base was contacted.

George smiled and keyed his mike. "*Da* . . . Red Bluff . . ." He paused for several seconds between each word, as if his radio was faulty. *"Kaxkb . . . bce . . . tyt."*

He hoped the other end would understand that everything was quiet here.

Striganov cursed as he listened to the man's voice break up. "I don't like it. I just don't like it. Start contacting the others, all of them. Chart their responses and have it sent to me as soon as you are finished."

"Yes, sir."

Redding reported that everything was quiet. So did Yreka and Old Station. Yuba City, Marysville, Oroville, Paradise, and Chico all reported everything normal.

But when she tried to contact anything south of Highway 20 and north of Highway 299, she once more experienced that odd breaking-up of transmissions.

Strange, she thought.

But everything was all right in Susanville, Lake Almanor, in the Pumas National Forest, and Grass Valley.

She checked a few more locations and called her relief operator, walking to General Striganov's quarters in the newly built command post.

She could hear the gruntings and the whimpering cries before she reached his office door. She for certain was not going to interrupt the general's fucking. The general was getting as bad as Sam Hartline.

She felt certain that was the young girl, Jane, in there with him. He probably had her bent over a desktop and was screwing her butt.

The woman sighed. The general didn't used to be

this way, she remembered. He had always been such a proper man. A gentleman, even.

Except with the minorities, of course. But who cared a whit about them?

It was not until he became associated with that pig, Sam Hartline, that General Striganov became so . . . perverted with his sexual appetites.

The girls kept getting younger and younger.

The sounds of a blow reached her. The sounds of a hand slapping naked flash.

"Stop your whining, you bitch!" Striganov's voice carried to her. "You know you like it. Reach around. Spread the cheeks further apart. That's it. Good."

His gruntings picked up in tempo.

The radio operator shook her head and walked away, out of earshot. Walked to the secretary's desk and sat down on the edge of the desk. The two women's eyes met for an instant.

The secretary said, "It is not for us to criticize the general's activities."

"No one did."

"The look in your eyes did."

"I'll remember to be more careful."

The girl screamed and the secretary's hand shook as she lifted her teacup to her lips.

The radio operator smiled and put the needle to her friend. "You must remember to be more careful, Val. Your emotions gave you away."

"Watch your mouth, Hedda. I outrank you, remember."

Hedda laughed. "He'll be calling for the medics now. He probably split her."

The secretary's intercom buzzed. "Yes, sir."

"Call the medics to come get this stupid bitch," Striganov said.

"Yes, General."

"And where is that damned Hedda?"

"Standing right here, sir," she said with a wink at Hedda.

"Give me a few minutes, then send her in."

"Yes, sir." She looked up at Hedda. "Take a seat. He'll shower before he buzzes me again. He'll want to wash the blood away," she added bitterly.

"The radio room first," Ben told his people. "We've got to take those people out but leave the equipment intact. The longer we can keep up this farce, the better off we'll all be."

"About fifty IPF men there, sir," Ben was informed.

"All right." Ben spread a map of the airport — compliments of the IPF back in Red Bluff — on the hood of his Jeep. "This is how we'll go in."

"Have you made contact with the Big Lake outpost?" Sam Hartline asked the man in the radio room.

"Yes, sir. But it's very poor; breaking up badly. I can just make him out."

"Contact the Mount Shasta outpost."

"Yes, sir."

Mount Shasta was contacted, the signal clear and loud. Everything was five by five. Okay. Boring.

Hartline's cold green eyes held a thoughtful light

for a few seconds. "Get me General Striganov's CP."

The general came on the horn.

"Georgi? Is everything all right down your way?"

"So far as I can tell, yes. We've had some difficulty reaching some stations. But you're coming in very clear. It's baffling."

Hartline agreed. Baffling. But . . . maybe not. He said as much to the Russian.

"Explain, please?" Striganov radioed back.

"We know Ben Raines is on the move, right?"

"Yes. But there has been no sign of any Rebels in our sector. And our network of outposts would have picked up any unusual movements. No, it's too soon for Ben Raines."

"Don't be too sure, Georgi. I'm going on full alert; sending out recon."

"Very well. I'll do the same. Keep in touch."

Hartline turned to his radiomen. "Contact our people on the border. Tell them we're going to full alert. Tell them to be very careful. Ben Raines is on the prowl."

"In *our* territory?" the radioman was startled.

Hartline nodded his handsome head. "I think so. My guts tell me it's coming down to the wire."

Late afternoon began settling softly into dusk as Ben's Rebels, one by one, attracting no attention from the woebegone-looking people scattered about Redding, moved into position around the airport.

"Folks around here look like all the fight's been kicked out of them," a Rebel observed.

"Sure looks that way," his partner agreed. "I

haven't seen anyone so far I'd trust."

"I think what we're seein' is the losers; they'd be losers war or no war."

"Then where are the others?"

"Watchin' and waitin', I'd bet."

The Rebel's walkie-talkie, clipped onto his web belt, crackled softly.

"Go ahead," the Rebel spoke.

"This is Raines. I've just been informed there is a very active resistance force of Americans working out of Redding. They know we're here and will be linking up with you point people very soon. Leader's name is Harris."

"Ten-four, General."

"Over to your right, Mac."

Mac looked. A man was standing in the doorway of what had once been a drugstore. He waved the Rebels across the street.

They approached him cautiously.

"I'm Harris," the man announced. "Man, are we glad to see you people."

"Is that right?" Mac asked. "You look like you're big enough to kick ass and take names. Why didn't you?"

Harris smiled bitterly. "I've got about seventy-five people in my group. Seventy-five out of three thousand. That tell the story?"

Mac was sorry he had spoken so sharply. But while he knew what the Rebels were doing was necessary, he, like so many Rebels, including Ben Raines, was getting damn tired of fighting other peoples' wars for them.

"Yeah, Harris. It does. Sorry I popped off at you."

"I understand. Believe me, I do. Many times I've had to just grit my teeth and walk off before I shot some of the roll-over crybabies around here."

"Many sympathizers around?"

Harris spat on the littered, dirty sidewalk.

Mac and his partner got the message.

"What do you want me and my people to do?" Harris asked.

"Lay back and stay out of it. When we're finished, I imagine General Raines will put you in charge. Then you can deal with matters the way you see fit."

"With pleasure."

Mac and his partner waited on the outskirts of Redding, waited with Harris in the looted shell of the drugstore in the small shopping center . . . or what had once been one. Mac and his partner were just one of many two-person teams scattered in a loose circle around the airport. If any IPF people managed to escape the initial attack on the airport, they would be cut down by the Rebels encircling the area.

"You speak any Russian?" Mac asked Harris.

"Some. I'm no expert. But I picked up some while a prisoner of the IPF."

"How'd you get away from them?"

"Broke and ran one night. They shot me." He lifted his shirt; his stomach was pocked with bullet scars. "They thought they'd killed me. Left me and took off chasing the other guy who broke out with me. I managed to crawl into a ditch before I passed out. My people found me before morning. I just made it. Charlie didn't. He died pretty damned hard, so I was later told. Never again will I allow my freedom to be taken from me. Never!" the word was spoken hard.

"And I'll kill any person who tries."

Mac smiled through the gathering gloom at his partner. Harris would do to ride the river with.

"Any weak links in your group?"

"None. But there was . . . for a long time. I kept wonderin' why the IPF knew every move we were gonna make. We'd change hideouts; they'd be right there. Lost a lot of people durin' that time. Better than twenty-five percent of my group bought it. That's how I got captured. After I got on my feet, I started some hard checkin'. I found out who it was and killed him. We've had no more leaks. But it was a damned hard thing for me to do."

It was a story the Rebels were accustomed to hearing. "Friend of yours, huh?"

Harris looked at him. "Yeah. He was my brother."

Ten

Like silent ghosts in tiger-stripe and lizard camo, the Rebels moved along the buildings of the Redding airport. Those IPF personnel who happened to be on foot patrol, or just unfortunate enough to be outside while the Rebels were moving into position, met silent, abrupt death with black wire or darkened blades. Their bodies were dragged out of sight and dumped.

Swiftly and softly, the Rebels took their positions, all of them just a bit nervous about this raid. For the general was personally leading this attack.

"Damned fool!" Sylvia whispered to him, as they crouched inside the tower, on the tarmac. "You've got men and women thirty years younger that you and Ike personally trained to do this sort of work. What are you trying to prove?"

Ben's smile flashed in the night. He leaned close and whispered, "Are you trying to tell me I'm over the hill, kid?"

Sylvia flushed and blushed. She knew damn well Ben was far from being over the hill. In more ways than one. Then her eyes widened in shock as Ben leaned closer still and blew softly in her ear.

"Ben! Quit! Shit!" she whispered. "You're insane!"

Ben kissed her cheek and chuckled softly. "Are you trying to tell me this is not the place for romance, kid?"

Sylvia could but shake her head and sigh. All her life she had heard stories about how totally unpredictable General Ben Raines was.

She could damn well believe it now.

Ben looked up at the tower. "Into the jaws of death, Into the mouth of hell, Rode the six hundred."

"What'd you say, Ben?"

"Tennyson. You ready?"

She looked at him. "For *what*?"

He chuckled. "My daughter, Tina, is fond of quoting something she says she read in one of my books. Kill a commie for mommie. I swear I don't remember *ever* writing anything like that. But it's a good phrase for this night."

Ben and Sylvia looked up as footsteps sounded on the stairwell above where they crouched inside the tower building. A man had stepped out of the tower area to have a smoke. His lighter flashed in the darkness, for a moment illuminating his face. His face was cruel-looking. He wore the insignia of a major on his collar points. He turned his back to the stairs and stood looking out a small window.

Ben handed Sylvia his Thompson and drew his long-bladed knife, the edge honed to razor-sharpness. Ben had shaved with it more than once.

He slowly climbed the stairs toward the Russian. On his hip, for this mission replacing his .45 caliber Colt Army automatic, he carried a Colt Woodsman automatic. If he missed any of his targets in the tower, his repair people might be able to fix what a .22 slug caused. But with a hollow point .45 slug? . . .

And he was not going to give the Russian any chance to struggle during the conventional hand-over-the-mouth, knife-across-the-throat business.

Ben swung the heavy knife, decapitating the man. Blood splattered on the walls and floor as the man's head struck the floor with a sticky thud. Ben grabbed the body and slowly lowered it to the floor.

He motioned for Sylvia to stay put. Ben removed a gas mask from its container and slipped it over his face, checking it. It worked. Ben had never liked the damn things. He slipped a combination irritant gas and smoke grenade from his web belt and glanced down at Sylvia. He nodded at her. She returned the nod and lifted her walkie-talkie, speaking just one word: *Go!*"

Ben pulled the pin, released the spoon, and jerked open the door, tossing the grenade inside with his left hand. His right hand was full of Colt Woodsman. He shot one IPF man in the chest and another in the face, then stepped inside, closing the door behind him.

The room was filled with smoke and the shouted alarms of the IPF personnel. One blindly bumped into Ben and Ben stuck the muzzle of the Colt into the woman's throat and pulled the trigger.

There had been four people in the tower when Ben had stepped inside. Two had been shot before the gas and smoke erupted, he had just shot the third—now where was the fourth?

Ben heard choking cries from across the room. He inched his way toward the source. The man was trying to operate the radio, but he was blinded by the irritant, tears streaming down his face. Ben spun him around and shot him between the eyes.

The tower was secure.

Ben shot each of the four in the tower in the head, making certain they were going to stay down, then began opening all the windows. He stepped out onto the stairwell and removed his mask, closing the door behind him. He stood in the thickening blood from the Russian major and grinned at Sylvia.

She glared up at him. "You worry the hell out of me, you know that? You . . . you . . . *asshole*!"

Ben laughed at her.

A few of the IPF personnel got away from the wrath of Raines's Rebels, fleeing into the night. Safe, but only for a very short time.

No matter which way they ran, they ran into more Rebels, lying in ambush.

Mac, after listening to Sylvia, and only then, turned to Harris and said, "Take out the rest of the IPF in town."

"Why didn't you tell me this before?"

"Because I didn't trust you," Mac's reply was blunt.

"Believe me," Harris said, "I know the feeling."

It had taken them years to reach America, for America had not been their destination of choice. Just the thought of America still left a bitter, ugly taste in their mouths. They had traveled first to France, or what was left of it, and then to Spain,

104

there again, what was left of it. They had lingered for a couple of years in each place, gathering their own, recruiting others, accepting them into the Faith, then moving on, always moving on.

And always gaining strength.

They had moved to the island of Corsica, finding it and overwhelming the small garrison of French Foreign Legion troops still there. They had tortured and mutilated and raped and killed, leaving behind only a lonely, blood-stained reminder of a place that had virtually escaped the horror of the final war that very nearly wiped out earth.

From Corsica they had traveled to South America, finding some areas hot from radiation, others reverting back to barbarism. They had found recruits in every place they visited. And ships.

They had traveled around the Horn and back, looking, always looking, but never really satisfied with what they found.

Then they looked toward the United States. They set sail for Florida. But Miami was a mess. They had no desire to dock there.

They sailed north and reached the Georgia coast. They anchored off Wassaw Island and sent teams into Savannah to look the situation over.

They found the city almost deserted.

A week after they landed, the city was totally deserted.

Any Americans found there were killed. Outright, if they were lucky. The unlucky ones were tortured and raped. And then killed.

"We shall travel no more," the leader of the thirty-thousand-plus-strong force said. "I find it darkly amusing that we have come full circle and now find ourselves here in the most hated land in the world."

His fellow officers agreed.

The Islamic Peoples Army, the IPA, was made up of the survivors of every terrorist group known to exist before the world blew up. The PLO, Baader-Meinhof, Rengo Sekigun (Japanese Red Army), YPR, Black September, Al Fatah, PFLP, Dev Gench, TPLA, the Liberation Front, the Socialist Patients-Collective, the DGI, the Red Cell, German Action Group, and others.

As maggots tend to gather on the unattended dead, terrorist groups have a way of gathering like lice on the unwashed.

The commander of the IPA was a Colonel Khamsin. His idol was Muammar Kaddafi.

The gunfire had long died away; every member of the IPF stationed in the Redding area had been accounted for. No prisoners had been taken.

Harris and his people were now in control of the city.

And not all of the citizens liked it.

A fat, obviously well-fed and well-cared-for man was shoved in front of Ben. "John Stoggen," Harris informed him. "Big buddies with the local IPF major."

"Would you like to see your buddy now?" Ben asked him.

"Yes," John said. His voice trembled. He stank of fear.

"All right," Ben said. "Excuse me for a moment.

I'll be right back."

Ben returned in a moment, carrying something in his left hand. He held the dripping head of the major up to John. "Here's your buddy, now, Stoggen. Say hello."

John Stoggen fainted on the tarmac.

Ben tossed the head to one side.

Harris swallowed hard. He had heard that General Ben Raines was one hard-assed man. Now he knew for certain. "Stoggen was responsible for the deaths of a lot of good people, General. Men and women. And a couple of young people, as well."

"Do what you want to with him," Ben said. "I've spoken with several people about you, Harris. They seem to think you're a good man. I'm putting you in charge. We'll outfit you with our tiger-stripe or lizard cammies. I'll meet with your people in the morning."

"Yes, sir." Harris saluted and left.

"General," a Rebel approached Ben. "We've just been in contact with Base Camp One. They want to know if you've ever heard of a Colonel Khamsin?"

"Khamsin? No. Why?"

"Well, sir, it's kind of confusing and not, as yet, confirmed, but a small group of people came to Base One a couple of days ago. They're from south Georgia. They claim that a large force landed in Savannah about a month ago. They're commanded by this Colonel Khamsin."

"How large a force?"

"About forty to fifty thousand men."

Ben stood stunned for a moment. "Forty or fifty *thousand*?"

"Yes, sir."

"They must be mistaken. Do you have any idea how many ships it would take to transport that many men and supplies?"

"No, sir."

"I don't believe there are that many ships still seaworthy, anywhere. Khamsin," Ben said.

"Yes, sir. The people said it means a hot wind."

"Wonderful," Ben said drily. "Back in 1941, it was a divine wind. Now sixty years later we have a hot wind to contend with."

"Divine wind, sir?"

"Pearl Harbor, son."

"I . . . don't know that I ever heard of that place, sir."

Ben smiled. "Well, believe it or not, I wasn't born then either, son. But I do know a little something about history."

"Yes, sir."

"Get Base One on the scrambler. Tell them I said to send out some recon teams; try to find out what in the hell is going on down in Georgia."

"Yes, sir." He saluted and left.

Ben looked for his XO. "Let's get this airport cleaned up and the bodies disposed of . . ."

A shot cut the darkness.

Ben had a hunch that John Stoggen had collaborated his last.

". . . Get Cecil on the horn and have him get our pilots back here to ferry these planes out. Let's start inventorying supplies and moving it out for shipment back and caching in this part of the country."

"Yes, sir."

Sylvia came to stand by Ben's side. "A hot wind,

Ben?"

"That's what the man said."

"Forty or fifty *thousand* troops, Ben?"

"That's what the man said."

"Ben, we can't fight that many troops."

"Something tells me we're going to have to do it, kid."

Eleven

Once again, Raines's Rebels had lucked out, in more ways than one. They had uncovered several tons of supplies: food, clothing, guns and ammo, walkie-talkies, and planes.

The Rebels outfitted Harris and his people, then waited for the pilots from the old Tri-States.

While they waited, Ben radioed back to Cecil, asking if Dr. Chase had attempted any contact with General Striganov.

"Not yet, Ben."

"Tell him to forget it. We're on a roll out here and I don't want to tip our hand."

"Ten-four. What about this Colonel Khamsin business, Ben?"

"Bring me up to date."

"I just spoke with Base Camp One not half an hour ago. They're convinced those people are telling the truth about the IPA."

"About the what, Cec?"

"The Islamic Peoples Army. It was the children

with them that convinced our people they're telling the truth. Seems the kids all say that several times a day, these . . . whatever the hell they are, stop whatever they're doing, spread some sort of mat, and squat down, as the kids put it, and pray. All in the same direction."

Ben's sigh was audible over the miles. "I think, Cec, we've got big trouble."

"I think you're right, buddy. Even if the IPA's force is only a quarter of what is claimed, we're in trouble."

"It never ends, does it, Ben?"

"It certainly appears that way. Talk to you later. Hold down the fort."

Ben signed off. He turned to Harris. "Maintain this charade for as long as possible, Harris. I don't think we can continue playing radio interference for very much longer. Striganov is probably suspicious by now, and I'm sure Hartline is. But if we can keep this up for another twenty-four hours, we'll have shaved the odds down and gained a lot of ground. The more outposts we can seize, the more Striganov is going to have to split his forces to regain them."

"But won't that also cut down the size of your personnel?" Harris asked.

Ben smiled. "Perhaps," he said, and would say no more about it.

Ben had no inclination to discuss his battle plans with anyone—not even his own people. Yet.

The northernmost IPF outpost in California, located at Yreka, just a few miles south of the Oregon border, lay quiet under the springtime sun. It was a small outpost, but a vital one. It was also a lonely post for the soldiers stationed there. Before the bombings, now more than a decade past, the town's population was about six thousand. Now it was down to about two hundred men, women, and children.

The IPF lieutenant in charge of the Yreka station had monitored all the requests of General Striganov's radio operator; and listened to the garbled responses from some stations. It was puzzling, but, to his mind, nothing to get alarmed about. It probably was that radioactive belt that had hovered over the earth for years.

He stepped outside the building for a smoke and a breath of air.

The silence got his attention. He looked around him.

There were usually some townspeople about, begging for food or asking to see some friend or relative that had been seized by the IPF.

Or some local woman willing to sell herself for better treatment.

Sometimes a man or boy willing to do the same.

That always amused the lieutenant. He held Americans in contempt. The mighty Eagle. Now clawless, its people groveling about, willing to suck a cock for a can of beans or spread her legs for a package of cigarettes.

Or part of the cheeks of male or female ass for a good butt-fucking.

He wondered where the people were on this bright, beautiful morning.

He would never know the answer to that.

He heard a *twang* and lifted his head just as the fiberglass, field-pointed bolt, fired from a crossbow, hit his chest. He knew a few seconds of very intense pain as the point hit his heart, shattering it. He dropped to the ground, only seconds away from dying.

An attack, he thought. Against *us*? Here? Impossible, he thought. Not from these cowardly Americans.

Then he died.

The Eagle had risen, silently screaming its rage.

Lizard-camoed Rebels rushed the outpost, leaping over the body of the arrogant lieutenant. The point man reached the door and slipped inside, darting to his left; other Rebels quickly entered the blockhouse; they carried .22 automatics, the pistols silenced.

Two Rebels stepped into the radio room. They lifted the silenced .22s and shot the two people in the room in the back of the head. They closed the door and pulled the bodies out of the chairs, taking their place behind the wall of equipment.

Other Rebels were going about their deadly work, silently and efficiently.

The Rebels assigned to the small barracks-room found a half dozen IPF personnel sleeping in their bunks.

The Russians never awakened from their sleep.

In less than two minutes the blockhouse was secure and in Rebel hands.

The section leader opened the door to the radio room. "Can you change to our frequency and scramble?"

"Yes," he was told. "Just as soon as I change out some parts. Take me about five minutes."

"As soon as you do, inform Eagle One we are secure here."

The radio operator nodded his understanding.

Some two hundred and fifty miles south of Yreka, in Woodland, Rebels from Ike's contingent slipped quietly and unseen around the IPF compound. The small band of Rebels was heavily outnumbered and Ike had told them to forget about salvaging any of the radio equipment; just knock out the installation and let the chips fall where they may.

Or in this case, the bodies of the IPF personnel inside the compound.

At a signal from the section leader, a Rebel lifted a 66mm rocket launcher, sighted it in, and put the rocket through the window of the radio room. The room exploded in a cloud of mortar, brick, wood, blood, and pieces of human bodies.

Raines's Rebels gave no quarter to the IPF forces inside the compound. If Ben and his Rebels were to build something constructive out of the ashes he would play the fiddle and call the tunes. He had turned his theory into fact back in the Tri-States. He had proven that a society can exist without criminals or crime. For if you don't have one, you won't have the other.

And Ben's philosophy was instilled into the hearts and minds of his Rebels.

Ike's contingent hit the IPF hard, taking no prisoners. In less than half an hour, the battle was over; all that remained was the dust and smoke that lingered like a bitter reminder over the compound.

"Radio Eagle One that Woodland is ours," the section leader said.

The Rebels now controlled nine of the IPF's outposts, stretching from Yreka down to the Napa Valley.

Then Ben abruptly called a halt to it, confusing all his teams and team leaders, including Ike.

It was late afternoon when Ike finally got through to Ben.

"Cease and hold, Ben?" he questioned.

"Yes. I want to discuss it, but not over the air. There is always a chance our transmissions could be descrambled. I've already spoken with Dan. You both have access to small planes and people to fly them." He gave Ike map coordinates. "Meet me there in the morning. We'll go over the plans. I'll see you then."

Ben signed off.

Ike scratched his head and looked at his XO.

"What's up, Ike?"

"With Ben, you just never know. But whatever it is, the Russian and Hartline ain't gonna like it, you can bet on that."

"Another outpost cannot be reached, General," Hedda reported to Striganov.

"You mean the signals are garbled?"

"No, sir. Silent."

Georgi turned slowly in his chair. He sighed deeply; a man in frustration. "Raines," he said. "He's making his move. I was wrong and Hartline was right. But where is the son of a bitch?"

"Hartline?" Hedda asked, confused.

"No! Goddammit, woman. *Raines.*"

Hedda wisely chose to remain silent.

"He's pulling something. But what? — other than the obvious. Raines is a wolf. He's circling, not yet showing me his plan. Just as sure as I commit personnel to one place, the guerrilla bastard is going to pop up in another. I know how his mind works."

Wrong. He did not know how Ben's mind worked. He just thought he did. Arrogant people always think they're much smarter than they really are.

"Yes, sir," Hedda said. She would never admit it to the general, but she was very frightened of Ben Raines and his Rebels. They were savages. Brutal Vikings. Ben Raines and his Rebels paid no attention to the rules of warfare. They were all, to a person, thugs.

"Contact Hartline," Striganov ordered. "Have him fly down here first thing in the morning. We have to start planning our strategy. We cannot allow Raines to get the upper hand, in *anything.*"

"Yes, sir. Will that be all, sir?"

"Yes."

When Hedda had closed the door behind her, General Georgi Striganov's face tightened as he jerked out a map of his IPF-controlled territory and quickly scanned it. With a colored pen, he carefully *X*'ed each outpost that had a garbled signal, and the one that had gone silent.

He stared at the map. He could make no sense of any of it.

There were two hundred and fifty miles between the northern outpost and the southern outpost. Raines just didn't have that many men.

Or did he?

Striganov leaned back in his chair, his mind busy. Perhaps Raines had recruited more people . . . *Yes!* That had to be it. Just as he had recruited — or rather, Hartline — those warlords, Ben Raines had probably done the same.

But that would not be like Ben Raines. Raines hated even the thought of warlords.

But would he use them as a last resort?

Yes, Striganov thought, he probably would. The end would justify the means.

The Russian carefully noted each position he had marked on the map. Raines would be the strongest south of Highway 20, he felt. At least four of his outposts, probably five, had been knocked out there. So it reasoned that Raines would be the weakest at Yreka . . .

No!

Big Lake. Raines would have teams spread out north and south along Interstate 5. Big Lake would be stretching it thin for Raines, out of his supply route.

Big Lake would be the first outpost the IPF would retake. But first he and Hartline would monitor the transmissions coming from the outposts. Raines would make a mistake; he would slip up. Striganov was sure of that.

And then the IPF would pounce.

He smiled. It was a good plan.

She took her assigned place in the short column

Twelve

"Sneaky, Ben," Ike said. "Real sneaky. But it's risky, buddy."

"I know. But I've already sent for Cecil and his battalion. There is an airstrip here"—he punched the map—"just a few miles from Big Lake. The strip is big enough to handle twin-engined cargo planes. Cecil's bunch will slip into position along the southeast side. Dan, your bunch will take the north side, forming the top of the triangle. My people will be in position on the west side, forming the west angle of the scalene. When the IPF people enter, then I'll close the box. If we do this right, we can really cut the odds down."

"I like it," Dan said. "It's dirty and mean." He looked at Ike and grinned.

"You would," Ike said with a grunt and a grin. "But then, so do I."

"Get your people into position and out of sight. For a fact, Striganov is going to make some fly-bys in recon aircraft."

121

"And start transmitting between the outposts we've captured?" Ike asked.

"Right. But warn your operators not to make it too obvious. Just chitchat. Lots of Rebels between 101 and Interstate five to the south. Lots of people at the border. We're waiting for fresh troops to arrive. But it's lonely as hell at Big Lake. Keep it simple and plain. Let drop once or twice that we've got two platoons at Big Lake. I don't really know Striganov's mind—no one knows another's mind—but if I were in his boots, I'd send at least a full battalion into the Big Lake area, just to be on the safe side. What do you people think?"

"Just to add a bit of spice to the tea," Dan said, "I would suggest a conversation or two about some green troops mixed in with the regulars at Big Lake. Since it's so isolated, and the danger of attack so slim, that would be a good place for new troops."

"Yes," Ben said. "Good idea. But not too obvious with it."

"Right, sir!" the Englishman said cheerfully.

"I like it," Ike said.

"Move out," Ben ordered.

"I don't like it worth a shit!" Sam Hartline said.

"State your objections," Striganov said.

"You can't trust that goddamned Ben Raines! I'm tellin' you, Georgi, he's pulling some crap on us. It's not like him to put up with all this bragging his people are doing on the air. It's like . . . well, he's trying to goad us into doing something stupid."

"Oh, I agree with that. But you've listened to all the

tapes we've made. Someone put a stop to any mention of those green troops at Big Lake. Raines, I'd wager."

Hartline sat back down and calmed himself, mentally, silently, going over Striganov's plan. It had merit, he was forced to admit that.

But Hartline felt he knew Ben Raines far better than Striganov did. He should, he thought, hiding a smile, for the two men were alike in a lot, well, *some* ways.

"What are you thinking, Sam?"

"A mixed bag of thoughts, Georgi. I'll admit that I like most of your plan. All right, then, we'll have a go at it."

"I'll order recon teams in and we'll do a fly-by. Tomorrow morning all right?"

"Fine."

The Rebels had worked furiously all day and well into the night. Teams had begun arriving at the Big Lake site only a few hours after the meeting of Ben, Ike, and Dan had broken up. Cecil and his reserve battalion had landed and were digging in along the eastern borders of Big Lake.

Machine gun emplacements, mortar pits, and bunkers were almost finished. Booby traps were being laid out; Claymores were going into place. Artillery was anchored and camouflaged.

And then they waited.

Ro and Wade had received their orders. It was up to them and their young charges to see that no member of the attacking IPF forces made it past the triangle's northern angle alive. At the Big Lake site, Ben watched the young boys and girls of the woods-children as they received their orders. If there was any fear in them, they did not allow it to show on their faces. They stood impassively.

And it almost broke Ben's heart.

Ike was standing by Ben's side; he picked up on his friend's silent feelings.

"I don't like it any more than you do, buddy," he said. "But if they didn't receive an assignment, they'd go off on their own and maybe get mauled."

"You and me, Ike, we've seen a lot together. But I'll be damned if I've ever seen anything to compare with this sight."

"Kids have fought in every war since the beginning of time, Ben." He sighed, a sign of frustration.

Dan joined them. "Those children should be in school. This should be the happiest times of their lives."

Ben glanced at him, smiling. "Do you want to be the one to order them out of here?"

Dan grunted, remembering when he had first encountered the woods-children. He had offered one little sweet-looking girl of about nine or ten a candy bar. The child had bitten his hand to the bone, kicked him in the shins, grabbed his AK-47, and took off into the timber, leaving Dan hopping around on one foot, cussing.

"Thank you, but *no!*" he said flatly.

Ben and Ike managed to contain their laughter, both of them knowing what Dan was thinking. Dan had lost his cool. Ben's eyes found a little girl, standing by herself, apart from the other children.

124

Her carbine was almost as tall as she was. But he had absolutely no doubt that she could, and had, used it. And used it expertly, too.

He left Ike and Dan and walked to the child. As he approached, he could see the fear build in her eyes.

Goddammit! he silently cursed. Why are these children afraid of *me*?

But he knew.

And knew that he must, at all costs, put a halt to the myths that were growing daily about him.

But how?

He knelt in front of her. "I'm Ben Raines."

"Yes, General, I know," the girl said, her voice small in the great living cathedral that was the wilderness.

"Call me Ben."

She shook her head. "That is not permitted."

"Nonsense! If I permit it, who can challenge it?" Wrong way to go, Ben, he cautioned. But it was too late; he had said it.

She shook her head, not replying.

"What is your name, girl?"

"Lora."

"All right, Lora. How old are you?"

"I . . . think I have eleven years."

Jesus God! Ben thought. Eleven years old and a warrior. "Your parents?"

She shook her head.

"Brothers, sisters?"

"I . . . think I had some. But they're dead, I'm sure."

"Lora, how would you like a job?"

"A job? But I have a job."

"What?"

"Fighting for you."

"Yes, well . . ." Ben cleared his throat and shifted his weight. Damn bad knee was beginning to ache. "I have another job for you. I'd like for you to be my aide."

"I don't know what that means."

"Well, it would be a very important job. I wouldn't ask just anyone to do it. You would assist me; be with me—most of the time," he added. "Would you like that?"

"Yes, General."

"Call me Ben."

She shook her head.

"Well, we'll . . . work on that part of it." He stood up. Immediately his knee felt better. He held out his hand and Lora slipped her small, and very dirty, hand into it.

Ben and Lora walked to Dan and Ike. "This is Lora." Ben said. "She's going to be my aide."

"Sure she can handle it?" Ike said straight-faced, looking at Ben. "That's a high-falutin' job."

"Oh, quite," Dan said. "Very responsible position for one so young."

"I can do it," Lora said, looking at Dan.

Dan looked at the child. She sure looked familiar. Great Scott! Dan thought. This is the child that *assaulted me*!

Ike was looking off into the distance, scarcely able to keep his laughter locked up.

"Don't I know you?" Dan asked, kneeling down.

"You might," Lora said.

"Yes," Dan said. "I do believe we have met before."

"You still got that candy bar?" Lora asked.

"No," Dan said, ice in his voice. "I ate it."

"Good," the girl replied. "Bad for your teeth anyway."

Dan stood up, drawing himself to his full height. "Impudent girl!"

"Blow it out your ear," Lora told him.

Dan walked away, muttering.

Ike walked away to a tree, leaning against it, laughing so hard he could not see.

Sylvia walked up and looked first at Lora, then at Ben. "Who's your friend, Ben?"

"My new aide. Lora, this is Sylvia."

All the Rebels had been forced to harden their hearts toward the sights of the aftermath of total global war. Dan's defense was a self-imposed coldness; but he ached just as much as the next person.

"She, ah, needs a bath," Ben said. "Would you see to that, Sylvia?"

"Sure." Sylvia put an arm around the child's slender shoulders. "You'll get used to Ben, Lora. His bark is worse than his bite."

Lora had no idea what she was talking about.

"Speaking of *bites*!" Ike yelled, then burst into fits of laughter.

Dan wheeled about. "How would you like a good thrashing, you . . . *dirigible*!"

Cecil walked up, catching the last part of it.

"What in the world is going on, Ben?" Sylvia asked.

"Oh, Dan just recalled a rather biting memory." Then Ben started laughing.

Sylvia walked away, shaking her head, leading Lora

off to a bath and a change of clothing. "Men!" she said. "They are the strangest things."

Lora sneaked a peek back at Ben Raines. Funny, she thought, he doesn't look like a god.

But then, what do gods look like?

Thirteen

Striganov and Hartline did a quick fly-by of the Big Lake area. It looked just as Striganov expected. Unchanged. But his soldier's eyes could see a few things out of place. New gun emplacements; a truck that did not belong to his IPF teams.

"Home," he told the pilot. "We've seen enough."

"Green troops or not," Hartline said. "It's going to take a full battalion to dig them out of there."

"I want this to be a total defeat for Ben Raines," Striganov said. "I want this to be humiliating for this so-called god among men."

"He's a god, all right." Hartline looked down at the land. "He's a goddamned nuisance. But, in a strange way, I'll be sorry to see him killed."

"He has been a fine adversary," Striganov agreed. "But there will be others."

Some of the Russian's bubbling confidence was beginning to rub off onto Hartline.

"I feel better about this upcoming operation, Georgi," Hartline said with a smile. "Kick-ass-and-take-names time."

"Crudely put but certainly fitting the situation. Sam, have you been receiving any . . . well, rather odd transmissions from the east lately?"

Hartline was silent for a moment, staring out the window of the expensive twin-engined aircraft. He turned to Striganov. "Come to think of it, yes. My operators keep saying they're picking up some foreign-language transmissions they think are originating from South Carolina or Georgia. But they can't make any sense out of them."

"Have you heard any of them?"

"Yes. It's Islamic. I don't speak it."

"What about this 'hot wind' that will blow over the land? What do you make of that?"

"I don't know. I haven't heard that one. The only thing I've heard about is some guy who calls himself Colonel Khamsin . . . or something like that."

"Yes. Well. A *khamsin* is a hot wind. It originates in the Sahara and blows in the spring."

"How interesting," Hartline said, totally uninterested.

"You might become more interested when you learn the troop strength of this Colonel Khamsin."

"Oh?"

"Something in the neighborhood of thirty to fifty thousand."

That got the mercenary's attention very quickly. He stared at the Russian. "Did I hear you right?"

"Two divisions. Yes."

"Jesus God! Raines has maybe, at the most, five thousand Rebels, and that's stretching it. And he's

130

been kicking our ass every time we meet."

"Don't remind me. Besides, all that is about to change. I think Raines is rapidly becoming a secondary matter. I want joint teams of IPF recon and men from your command sent east. As soon as possible. I want this Colonel Khamsin checked out. They will have to go in by vehicle. Since Raines seems to have effectively grounded what remains of our air force."

"You've reached that conclusion, too?"

"Yes. I tried this morning to reach our people at Redding and Red Bluff. More unintelligible garble." He sighed. "Well, we fell for it for a time. And now we're paying for our folly. Dearly. I don't know how many people we've lost. But it will not happen again. We move against the Big Lake Rebels in two days, Sam. Get your people ready and in place."

Ben felt the Russian had fallen for it. He was ninety-five percent sure of it. But he knew he was taking a very large gamble. A gamble that would cost the Rebels in blood should it fail.

Therefore, it must not fail.

He looked up from his studying of maps as Sylvia and Lora entered his squad tent. At first he didn't recognize the young girl.

She was clean, her hair freshly washed and shining. The Rebels had found clothes to fit her, from her feet up. She no longer looked like a ragamuffin. Sylvia grinned at Ben.

"Here's your newest aide, General."

Ben smiled at the woman and the girl. "Good

afternoon, ladies."

Lora grinned, proud of herself. "I look like one of them kids in the pitcher-books!"

"Oh?" Ben said. "What, ah, picture book is that, Lora?"

"I left it in my pack. But I found it back in . . . wherever it was we got on them planes. Found it in a building. It was all right for me to have it, wasn't it?"

"Of course." Ben had noticed the child still carried her carbine. "Where'd you get that rifle, Lora?"

"Took off a guy about a year back. He didn't have no more use for it."

"Oh?"

"Yes, sir. I killed him."

When she was ten years old. Jesus Christ, Ben thought. Jesus and God alone only know what this child has gone through. "Was the man, ah, bothering you, Lora?"

"Tryin' to rape me."

It was obvious she did not wish to discuss it, so Ben didn't push it. "Have either of you had lunch?"

Sylvia shook her head. "We haven't had time. Lora, ah, well, it took some time to get her cleaned up. She, ah, had fleas. Among other tiny vermin. If you know what I mean."

Ben knew. Lice. He resisted an impulse to scratch. It was a problem with all the woods-children.

It was not that they shunned baths, for they didn't. But to a person they preferred the ground to a bed. The open starry sky to a building or tent. And back at the base camp, they all had dogs. Which they slept with.

Ben grinned as Sylvia scratched first one arm and then the other.

"I'm glad you think it's so funny, General," she said sourly.

"I've been there, Lieutenant," he told her. "We all have. Remember the fleas and rats from not that long ago?"

She shuddered as she recalled that particular horror. "Only too well."

"Well, on that happy note, let's have some lunch."

The IPA was pushing their lines of control out of the Savannah area. And they were savage and murderous in their advance. Those men and women and children they did not kill were taken prisoner, to be used as slaves on the farms they planned to put back into production. And since women had become a valuable commodity, world-wide, women under forty were spared, taken prisoner, and carefully guarded. Almost all the very young were spared. They would be schooled in the Islamic way and after a time accepted into the IPA's society.

The Islamic Peoples Army now was in firm control of everything between Interstates 20 and 26, from Columbia back to the coast. Their advance had stopped at the Georgia line—for the time being.

There had been pockets of resistance, but those were few and very ineffective against the overwhelming numbers of the IPA. Only a few Americans had escaped, and those headed straight for Ben Raines's Base Camp One in north Georgia, bringing with them whatever they could hurriedly grab and carry on the run. And they brought horror stories. Stories of rape and torture and murder.

Terrorism in the twenty-first century.

Something else that Ben and his Rebels would someday very soon have to deal with.

But for now, Colonel Khamsin and his IPA seemed content with the land they had seized. They would spend some time indoctrinating the people they spared, and get the land back in shape for production. When that was done, then they would move out to claim more land in the name of Allah.

"Everybody ready?" Ben radioed to his commanders.

Everyone was in position and ready to go.

The Rebels were dug in tight, their positions deep and expertly camouflaged. Machine gun emplacements were angled to afford the best possible field of fire against approaching troops. And the bunkers had rabbit holes which would allow the Rebels to slip out and away.

They waited.

The first recon teams from Striganov and Hartline moved close to the western perimeter of Big Lake, approaching on either side of an old, once-state-maintained road. They moved cautiously, very alert for mines and booby traps, for the team leaders had been warned about Ben Raines and his Rebels. They had been warned to expect anything; for Ben Raines did not adhere to conventional rules of warfare. Ben

Raines was mean and dirty and vicious; a man thoroughly trained in the art of guerrilla warfare. They were armed to expect anything.

They found nothing.

And the recon teams of Hartline and the Russian could not understand this development. It confused them. What was happening here? Where were all the dirty tricks they had been warned to expect? And where in the name of Lenin were the Rebels?

The team leaders radioed back to the staging areas of their commanders, asking, What was going on? What to do?

Advance cautiously, came the order.

The recon teams moved out. And out. They encountered nothing human. Birds were singing and squirrels were chattering and barking happily in the timber. And that was a sure sign no Rebels were about. The recon teams began to relax a bit.

But human eyes watched them, watched them from bunkers and deep brush and heavy timber. The Rebels remained motionless, breathing shallow, eyes unblinking. They waited.

From the north the recon teams came, encountering the same thing as the teams who came in from the west. Nothing. And as their comrades had done, they radioed back to the staging area for instructions, not understanding the nothingness of the deep timber.

Striganov smiled as he turned to Sam Hartline. "Ben Raines has become what I knew he would, Sam."

"Oh?"

"Overconfident. I knew it would happen. The man

has had things go his way for too long. His people have become lack; discipline has softened. They think we're still falling for the garbled transmissions."

Hartline agreed with the Russian, but damned if he'd give Striganov the satisfaction of knowing it. "I'm ordering my people in."

"It's time," Striganov agreed. He nodded at an aide. "No prisoners. Kill them all. Wipe them from the face of the earth."

The orders were given and the combined forces of Sam Hartline and the Russian moved out. One force from the north, one force from the west.

But Ben had suspected a trick, and he ordered his people to hold their fire and keep their positions, their heads down. Remain silent and unseen.

Lora stood wtih Sylvia in Ben's bunker, watching the man.

"What's the hang-up, Ben?" Sylvia asked. "What are we waiting for?"

Ben listened to his headset for a moment, not immediately answering. "I thought as much," he spoke into his mike. "Let them come on."

He turned to Sylvia, conscious of Lora's unblinking eyes on him. "Striganov and Hartline have committed only about twenty-five percent of their troops. They're holding the others back." He smiled a warrior's smile; the smile of a hunting tiger about to taste the hot blood of prey. "We'll let them come; play their game. They'll learn a hard lesson about me. And I think a very decisive one in our favor."

"You knew the enemy was going to do this?" Lora asked.

"I suspected it," Ben replied, looking down at the child.

"You knew," she said flatly.

"All right; have it your way, then. I knew."

"How?"

Ben softened his hunter's smile as he looked at the child. "I'm an old soldier, Lora. There are things one learns over the years."

She nodded her head. He knew, she thought. He looked through all the silence and knew. She would tell the others about this.

Ben's headset crackled. "The underground people have halted their advance, General. How in the hell did they *know* to wait?"

"I don't know," Ben spoke into his mike. "They sensed it, probably. How many of them have you spotted?"

"Fifty, maybe. If I've seen fifty, there are probably five hundred more I can't see."

"I agree. Stay with it. Ike?"

"Here."

"Cecil?"

"Here."

"Dan?"

"Here, sir."

All were on scramble, on a high-band frequency. "Let those few companies come on; let them get deep. When they meet no resistance, the others will be forced to follow. Striganov and Sam know better than to permit too much distance between their forces. Or I'm betting they do, at least. Hold what you've got."

The commander of the point company of IPF men

radioed to Hartline's point company, advancing from the north. "I have heard no gunfire."

"Hell, there isn't anything to shoot *at*!" Hartline's company commander radioed back, knowing both Sam and the Russian were monitoring the transmissions. "So far as I can tell, all of Raines's men are in the compound area. What in the fuck are we waiting for?"

Sam turned to Georgi. "We can't let much more distance between companies."

"I know. I believe your point man is correct. Raines has made a fatal mistake by bunching up his men. Commit your troops." He turned to his radio operator. "Go! Go! Go!"

And the rear companies surged forward.

"Let them come," Ben said, after receiving the message from his forward observers. "Let them get deep and link up with the forward company. Steady now, people. Keep it steady and cool. Just hold what you've got."

"My people are getting edgy, Ben!" Ike radioed.

"Tell them I'm calm and confident, Ike. To all company commanders and section leaders, this is Raines. I'll personally shoot the first person who opens fire without my direct orders to do so. Is that understood?"

Perfectly. And they all knew Ben Raines meant every word.

The Rebels waited. The woods-children waited. The underground people waited.

"West angle clear and free," a forward observer radioed to Ben.

"North angle free and clear," Ben was informed. "Close it off," Ben ordered. "Plug it up."

"IPF and Hartline's men about a mile from the compound," Ben was informed.

"Destroy them," Ben ordered.

And Lora looked at Ben, love in her eyes.

Fourteen

Electrically controlled Claymores were activated, filling the air with explosions that maimed and killed. Mortar rounds were dropped down the tubes, *thunking* into life, popping up and out, fluttering their way to death-creating explosions. Artillery began pounding the IPF and Hartline's men. 152mm, 155mm, and 8-inch howitzers began spewing out their lethal rounds. They were joined by 81mm mortars. Parts of once-living human bodies were flung high into the smoke and noise-shattered air of the living wilderness.

Fifty-caliber machine guns began hammering out death for those who escaped the initial onslaught of mines, mortars, and heavy artillery. For those men and women of the IPF and Hartline's mercenaries who staggered through the torn earth and smoky, hellish air where they had been trapped, the woods-children and the underground people were waiting in the bush and deep timber, with knives and axes and bows and arrows and guns.

Caught by the totally unexpected, the IPF and mercenaries ran, not so much in fear, as in confusion and panic. They ran to escape the exploding and yammering fury and ran right into booby traps. Swing traps with sharpened stakes, tripped by wire or cord, slammed into bodies, chest-high, the stakes driving through, bloody tips protruding out the back. Knees and ankles were broken when running feet stepped into punji pits. The pits were filled with sharpened stakes, the stakes jamming through boots or shoes, or puncturing the flesh of calf, leaving the victim pinned, unable to move. Those trapped remained there . . . until they were found and shot.

The cool earth of the wilderness, shaded by tall trees and flowering shrubs, was now littered with the dead and the dying and badly wounded. Screams of those in more pain than they could endure ripped the charged air; pleas for mercy were abruptly ended by pistol or rifle shot.

The rules of this battle and any upcoming battle were being laid down by the Rebels. They would give no quarter to the enemy, and they expected none.

"Cease firing all artillery," Ben ordered, from his deep bunker.

The big guns fell silent.

"All mortar crews down," Ben ordered.

The last of the projectiles fluttered to earth and exploded. The mortars fell silent.

"Search and destroy," Ben ordered.

The hunters became the hunted as Rebels left their holes and bunkers and locked in combat with the mercenaries and the IPF.

It was a tribute to Ben's planning that not one enemy made it out of the Big Lake area. Ben had so carefully placed his people that any who tried to escape found themselves facing not one, but three, lines of Rebels to cross, each circle of Rebels forming a smaller loop from the outside of the perimeter in.

And not one enemy made it to within a mile of Ben's bunker.

Long before the mopping-up was concluded, Ben stepped out of his bunker for a visual. Smoke still clung close to the ground and a few fires had been started by the exploding rounds.

"Get people working on putting those fires out," Ben ordered. "Watkins was a smoke-jumper, wasn't he?"

"Yes, sir," an aide said. "Up in what used to be Wyoming."

"Contact him and put him in charge. Who is he with?"

"Second Battalion."

"Get moving."

"Yes, sir." The young man disappeared into the bunker, to contact the ex-firefighter.

Ben walked down the slope to level ground, causing Sylvia and his aides no small amount of nervousness, even though most had seen Ben walk calmly into the heat of battle many times before, seemingly unconcerned.

Ben stood for a moment, his old Thompson submachine gun in his right hand. The sounds of gunfire could still be heard around the smoking battlefield. A scream of anguish cut the air, ending with a gunshot for punctuation.

Ben began walking toward the nearest battle area. A dozen Rebels, in lizard camo, ran to join them, forming a protective box around him.

143

"Don't you have anything better to do?" Ben asked a young sergeant.

"No, sir," he replied.

Ben let it slide. He knew these Rebels had probably been ordered to him before the battle, either by Ike or Dan or Cecil. To order them away would only get them in trouble with one of the three.

He walked into the body-littered, smoking battle area, stopping often to look at the uniforms of the dead and dying. A mixture of IPF and Hartline's mercenaries. Something was wrong, but Ben could not immediately dredge it up to visual mental light.

He walked on, stepping around or over the gorier messes made by parts of human bodies: still-steaming twisted ropes of intestines; a severed human head, the eyes wide open in pain-filled shock; a boot, with the foot still encased within the leather; a hand, just a hand, still gripping an AK-47; a torn-open torso.

He walked on, still trying to figure out what was wrong—if anything.

But he knew something was.

Then it came to him. He turned to a Rebel with a radio. "Contact the other commanders. Ask them if they've seen any of the warlord's men mixed in with these regulars. Our intelligence stated their dress was oftentimes bizzare. They don't wear any type of standard uniform."

None of the others had seen anything other than regular troops.

"What does it mean, Ben?" Cecil radioed.

"It means, I think, that while we won this battle, one of our recently taken outposts, I'd guess Yreka, was hit by the warlords."

144

"We only left a squad there, Ben," Ike radioed, the sounds of gunfire mingled in with his words.

"Striganov pulled a fast one," Dan said. Someone screamed in pain in the background of his words.

"Not the Russian; he's too conceited," Ben said. "This was Sam Hartline's doing. Bet on it."

"Then our people at Yreka are in for a very bad time of it," Dan opined.

"To say the least," Ben signed off.

Sonny Boy walked up and down the thin line of Rebels he and his men had taken at the Yreka outpost. Sonny Boy and his men looked like a scriptwriter's nightmare of a twenty-first century motorcycle gang. They dressed in whatever suited their personality.

Bizarre would be too tame a word.

Their headgear ranged from Nazi helmets to berets. Some wore combat boots, others cowboy boots. Some had chains looped and wound around their chests and waists. Some wore only vests with no shirt. Others were dressed in leather from ankle to neck.

To a man, they were dirty, lice-infested, ugly, and vicious. Hartline had promised them a free hand to deal with the enemy in any way they saw fit, "The enemy" being anyone opposed to General Georgi Striganov.

But they had been getting bored. Life in the Northwest was getting too tame.

Until now.

This particular bunch of outlaws rode motorcycles

145

exclusively. This was Sonny Boy's bunch.

Skinhead's bunch rode motorcycles, drove souped-up dune buggies and chopper bikes.

Grizzly's bunch rode motorcycles and drove souped-up pickup trucks.

Popeye's gang rode motorcycles.

About five hundred strong in all, they were, to a person, a very odious crew. In more ways than one.

Sonny Boy walked up and down in front of the captured Rebels. When he grinned his mouth was filled with rotten and blackened teeth. His breath would fell an ox.

He stopped in front of a woman Rebel. "Lookie here, boys. This here is prime pussy."

The woman spat in his face.

Sonny Boy reached out, grabbed a breast, and twisted harshly.

She screamed as pain bent her almost double. Sonny Boy brought his open palm around and slapped the woman, knocking her sprawling. Reaching down, he jerked the field pants from her and shredded her panties. He jerked her to her feet and threw her to his men. Several caught her, their hands roaming her body.

"Take turns with 'er," Sonny Boy said. "I wonder if it's possible for a woman to be fucked to death?"

In less than a minute, Reba began screaming as the rape began.

Sonny grinned as he stared at the only other woman in the Rebel team. "My, my, ain't you the pretty one. You gonna be my woman, bitch."

The woman stared at him, her face impassive.

"Think you're tough, don't you?" Sonny Boy

146

asked.

She shrugged.

Sonny Boy's men laughed, their laughter bringing a flush to his face. "You'll be beggin' me to quit 'fore it's all over, bitch," he said.

She stared at him in silence.

"You got a name, bitch?"

"Sally."

"Ain't that pretty? You be nice to me, now Sally, and I'll be nice to you. You fuck up with me, and I'll stick a grenade up your ass, you understand? And don't nod your goddamn head, *speak!*"

"I understand."

"Good. Hope for you yet." He waved toward his people. "Take them men prisoners. Hartline wants to torture them; see if he can get anything out of them."

Reba screamed as two men took her at once, front and back.

Striganov was silent, deep in savage thoughts, as he rode back to his command post by the raging sea.

He should have known better, he kept thinking. He should have known better than to try and second-guess Ben Raines. For every time he did . . . he failed.

And Georgi Striganov did not like to fail.

But what galled him more than Ben Raines destroying two full battalions of his people . . . was Sam Hartline sending those cretins in to seize the outpost at Yreka.

Sam had suspected Ben Raines was going to pull something. But if so, why hadn't he voiced stronger objections?

Unless? . . .

No, that was unthinkable!

Or was it?

Striganov tried to clear his head of those thoughts. But they persisted.

Was Sam trying to pull something? If so, what could it be? For he lost men in the battle with Raines, too. Although not nearly as many as Georgi did.

Georgi would have to give this some thought. A lot of thought. But he could not believe Sam Hartline would be stupid enough to try some sort of coup. They needed each other to continue the fight against the common enemy: Ben Raines.

"Outpost at Yreka on the horn, General," Ben was informed.

"It's pretty bad. They're raping Reba."

"They call us?"

"Yes, sir."

Ben walked to the communication truck. The battleground was nearly void of living beings, the Rebels pulling out, leaving the dead silent, for the earth to claim.

Ben glanced at his watch. Hartline would have had time to get there by car.

"Get them on the horn," Ben ordered.

"Hello, Ben," the cheerful voice of Sam Hartline cracked through the speaker.

"Hartline," Ben replied, without the cheerfulness.

"You won one, Raines," Hartline said. "Going to come get your woman warrior?"

"Doubtful," Ben said honestly.

"You're a hard man, Ben. 'Bout as hard as me. Hell, maybe you're harder. God knows I've tried to kill you often enough."

Ben could hear faint screaming in the background. But it was not a woman's screaming.

"That's one of your Rebels, Ben," Hartline told him. "One of my boys is burning his feet off. I don't think he likes it very much."

Ben cursed; got it out of his system before he keyed the mike. Keeping his voice level, he said, "What do you want, Hartline?"

"Why, just a friendly chat with an old enemy, Ben. That's all."

The screaming of the burning Rebel became louder. Then Ben heard Reba screaming.

"I opened a window just in case you wanted to get a better . . . ah, picture, shall we say, of what is happening here."

"I could have done without it, Hartline."

"Oh, I wouldn't want you to miss a thing, Ben. Oh, by the way, the woman you had in the cabin, Rani Jordan? I suppose you know by now that she's dead."

"I know."

"I tortured her to death, Ben. Of course I fucked her, too. Several times. In several different ways."

Ben said nothing.

"A lot of my, ah, newer colleagues had a whack at her, too. They're anxious to meet you, Ben."

"Oh, we'll meet, Hartline. Bet on that," Ben assured him.

"Oh my, Ben! I wish you could see this. It's very entertaining. Two of my men are double-teaming Reba. Poor girl doesn't appear to be enjoying it. I wonder why?"

"Where is Sally?"

"Sonny Boy claimed her for his woman. He's such a delightful man, Ben."

"One of your warlords, Sam?"

"That's a big ten-four."

"I'm looking forward to meeting them all, Sam."

Hartline chuckled. "I know what you're doing, Ben. Oh, I'll tell you their names. Sonny Boy, Grizzly, Skinhead, Popeye. Nice boys, all."

Just before Ben signed off, he said, "I'm going to kill you, Hartline. That is a promise."

Fifteen

"You know what's going to happen now, don't you, Georgi?" Sam asked the Russian.

They were enjoying a late dinner in the Russian's lovely home near Pepperwood, just off Highway 101. The Russian insisted on living as luxuriously as possible, considering the conditions around them. Not two miles away, people were just barely clinging to life.

When Striganov and his IPF first landed on American soil, after years in Iceland, Georgi had treated the Aryan race quite differently.*

But all that had proved too expensive in terms of food and clothing and medical treatment.

Now anyone who did not willingly embrace the Russian's lopsided philosophy was left to fend for themselves, as best they could.

"No. You tell me, Sam," Striganov said.

"Ben Raines is going to pull out all the stops now. He's going to hit us from all sides. He's going to use

*Anarchy in the Ashes

151

every tactic he knows, and believe me, he knows them all."

"Stand up and slug it out across battlefields?" the Russian asked, a hopeful note to his voice.

"You know better." Sam waved away the offer of dessert. But his eyes took in the trim little ass of Jane as she moved around the table to serve the Russian.

"You may eat now, Jane," Georgi told the girl. "Then take your bath. I'll be along shortly."

"Yes, sir," Jane said.

"Cute little cunt," Sam said, watching the young girl leave the room.

"She is coming along quite well. She responded to me the other night."

"You don't say?" He shook his head. Who gave a fuck whether the woman enjoyed it or not? The important thing was the man getting his nuts off.

"Were there any survivors?" Georgi asked.

"No. At least not that I know of. He kicked the shit out of us, Georgi."

"We lost the battle, not the war. Did you get any information out of those Rebels you seized at Yreka?"

"Naw. Burned one's feet off. He was still cussing me when I got hot and shoved a bayonet up his butt." Sam sighed. "I never saw a man or woman I couldn't break. But these goddamned Rebels are a breed apart."

"I wish you had told me you were going into Yreka, Sam."

"Spur-of-the-minute thing." He looked at the Russian. "Do you object?"

"Oh, no. I was curious for a time, though."

Sam laughed. "Georgi, if I ever decide to pull anything. I'll just shoot you first and be done with it."

"That's so comforting to know, Sam."

"Give me the final tally," Ben said.

"Nine dead," Ike told him. "Twenty-one wounded. Two seriously. Pilots have already flown the badly wounded back to Dr. Chase. We buried the dead where they fell."

"The lads performed quite well, General," Dan said. He looked up, feeling Tina and Sylvia's eyes on him. "And the lassies as well, of course." Dan looked over at Lora. She stuck her tongue out at him. He made a face at her. She gave him the finger.

Muttering under his breath, Dan rose from the table and poured himself another cup of tea.

"That isn't very nice, Lora," Sylvia gently admonished the child. She spoke around a smile.

Ike had to hide his face behind a big hand.

"Yes, ma'am," Lora said.

"Any word from our recon teams heading to South Carolina?" Ben asked.

"They're well on their way, Ben," Cecil said. "But I don't like the sounds of what's shaping up down there."

"Nor do I." Dan sat back down. "I think when we finish with the Russian and Sam Hartline—and I intend to finish it, once and for all—we are really going to have a fight on our hands."

"And badly outnumbered," Tina said.

"Let's talk about our present situation," Ben

153

brought them back to the present. They would deal with the future when it arrived.

"Are we going to retake the outpost at Yreka?" Sylvia asked. She had been present when Ben had spoken with Sam Hartline. She had heard the painful screaming of Reba. She wondered if Reba was dead by now. She felt it would be the best thing for her.

"Probably," Ben said. "But don't think that we'll ever see Reba or Sally alive again. The odds are hard against that happening."

No one present expected to see the women again. Not alive.

"What bothers me the most is that we have no good intelligence on these warlords . . ."

"Ask the kids," Lora spoke up.

"What do you mean?" Ben asked, looking at the girl.

"The kids who live in whatever area the warlords operate out of. Adults like young girls. Grownups like the warlords and them who ride with them, I mean. The kids can tell you all about them."

"We'll send Ro or Wade in," Ike suggested.

"No," Lora quickly spoke. "Send girls in. Some girls out of Ro or Wade's group. Boys will tell more to girls than to other boys. I'll go in."

Sylvia put an arm around Lora's shoulders. "No, I don't think so, Lora. You have to stay here and help us. Right, Ben?"

"Right. Who would you suggest, Lora?"

"I'll go pick them now." Before anyone would ask any further questions, or object, the child was gone, taking her carbine with her.

Dan shook his head. "Kids fighting wars. General,

are you seriously considering sending young girls into enemy territory? To face the possibility of capture and rape and . . . other forms of perversion?"

Ben sighed. "I don't know, Dan. You listened to Wade and Ro's verbal report this afternoon, did you not?"

"Yes," the Englishman said softly.

All present had. They silently recalled the words from the young men.

"We kilt ten times ten of the enemy, General. Some we shot with bullets, some we kilt with arrows. Most of them we just cut their throats."

A girl of about twelve stood off to one side, slowly honing a big-bladed knife back to razor sharpness. Blood from the enemy had splattered her clothing. She seemed oblivious to it.

A boy of perhaps thirteen, maybe younger—with the woods-children it was hard to tell ages; they were almost all undernourished—stood by the girl, sharpening his knife. Like the girl, his clothing was stained with blood.

"I done three myself," the girl said proudly. "Come up from behind them. Barry, here, got two." She looked at the boy by her side.

Dan broke the silence around the table. "Yes," he said with a sigh. "I see what you mean, General. But not Lora. I . . . ah, rather like the child. I would not like to see harm come to her."

All knew Dan was fond of Lora. But the ex-SAS man had little firsthand knowledge of dealing with kids. And kids knew his gruff manner was only a bluff.

"No," Ben said—and he knew he was being unfairly prejudiced with the statement — "certainly not Lora."

Lora returned, bringing with her three girls. The girls appeared to be very uncomfortable in the presence of Ben Raines. Ben asked them to be seated and then looked hard at them.

"Did Lora tell you anything about why you're here?" he asked.

"Yes, sir," one replied. "We're ready to go."

"What are your names?"

Judy, Kim, Sandra.

"Your ages?" Ben asked.

Judy was twelve, Kim and Sandra thirteen.

"Have you killed before?"

All had taken life.

Ben leaned back in his chair. He did not like this, not one bit. He had not liked the idea of committing the woods-children to any type of action; but knew no way to keep them out. They had come to him originally to fight, and that they were going to do. Whether General Ben Raines liked it, or not.

"Have you spoken with Ro or Wade about this, girls?"

They had. But they took orders from General Raines. They would go wherever the general chose to send them.

"*I* don't choose to send you on this mission," Ben told them. "I don't like it at all. Not one bit. If you go, it will be solely voluntary on your part. I personally wish you would all refuse."

"Why?" Kim asked.

"For heaven's sake!" Dan said, considerable heat in his voice. "Because you're all *children*, that's why.

156

You should all be back in Georgia, attending school, going to parties, dancing, getting all . . . ga-ga over the boys. Not running around in the woods slicing throats."

The trio of girls sat in silence, looking at Dan.

Lora came to Dan's side and put a small, and clean, hand on his big shoulder. "Mister Dan, we don't know nothin' about no dancin'. Ain't none of us ever been to no party in our life. And there ain't nothin' about boys to go ga-ga over. Whatever that means. All we know is fightin' to stay alive. We know what plants in the woods to eat, and which ones not to eat. We can catch fish with our hands and build traps to catch rabbits. We can hunt and make shoes and jackets out of the skins of animals. We know how to catch snakes and skin and eat them. The woods is our home, and when it ain't rainin', the sky is our roof. We know things about gettin' by that none of you grownups do. We ain't afraid, none of us. What is there to be afraid of? Can't no man do nothin' to us that ain't been done before. Front or back."

Dan looked at Kim and Judy and Sandra. They met his gaze with hard, wise, knowing eyes.

Dear God, the Englishman thought. Did You know what the aftermath of this evil would bring? Surely, You did. But by all that is Holy, I will never understand why You permitted it. Here I sit, in the wilderness that was once America, listening to three children speaking of getting pronged with less emotion than if they were discussing how best to dress up dolls.

Dan leaned over and, quite unlike him, kissed Lora on her cheek. "All right, child. I don't understand,

157

but I will accept your words." He looked at the girls. "Go with God, children."

Ike stood up and cleared his throat. When he spoke, his words were pushed out with a husky timbre. "I'll get them equipped with radios." He quickly left the room.

Then the girls shocked everyone in the room, except Lora, when Judy said, "If we get in a tight, don't send no people in after us, sir. You treat us just like you would any other Rebel."

"I'll bear that in mind," Ben said. "But you keep in touch with us by radio. Ike will show you how to operate the equipment you'll be going in with. I want you in and out fast. Do you understand?" They understood.

"No heroics, girls. Stay down and out of sight as much as possible. Do you hear me?" Dan asked.

They nodded their understanding.

"Go get some sleep," Ben told them. "You'll be moving out before dawn."

The girls left.

Ben waited until he was sure they were out of earshot before he exploded. "*Shit!* Goddammit, what have I done?"

Sylvia came to his side and put a slender hand on his shoulder. "You're doing what you have to do in order to defeat an evil, Ben. You have to look at it like that. None of us like it, but it has to be."

"They'll be back," Lora spoke with the confidence of the young. "The underground people will help them on their way and while they are inside the warlords' territory."

"Speaking of the underground people . . .?" Ben

158

said.

"They vanished as quickly as they came," Tina said. "I never even got a glimpse of any of them. But they sure did do some damage to the IPF troops."

"Bows and arrow and knives and axes?" Ben asked.

"Yes," Dan said.

"I want to meet with them," Ben said. "I've got to convince them to surface and rejoin the human race; that their way is wrong."

"They will not listen to that kind of talk," Lora said. "They worship you, but not your ways. They are content to live the way they do."

Sometimes, Ben noted, the girl spoke as though she possessed much more education than Ben knew she did. He wondered about that.

"I would still like to meet with some of them."

"Perhaps someday," Lora said.

"You know where they live, don't you, Lora?" Ben asked.

"If you don't ask me that, sir, I won't have to tell you a lie."

Ben nodded and did not repeat his question. An underground society, he mused. A society of men and women and children who, in slightly more than a decade, have reverted to the caves. They shun modern ways and modern weapons. Yet they have survived; indeed, grown.

Is this where we, as a nation, are heading?

No! he thought. Not as long as there is breath left in me to fight. We cannot exist as a nation by going backward.

Tina seemed to know what he was thinking. "Dad?"

159

He cut his eyes to her.

"Let them live as they see fit."

"I have no intention of bothering them, Tina. They are our allies; I wouldn't harm any of them. I simply want to talk with them and try to understand why they did what they did."

"As Lora said. Maybe someday."

But Ben doubted that day would ever arrive.

Sixteen

While Georgi Striganov and Sam Hartline sat back in their still-safe areas and licked their wounds and mentally massaged their bruised egos, Ben Raines was issuing orders and sending out teams to wreak havoc within the IPF-controlled territory.

Ike's people returned to the area just north of Vallejo, spread out, and began slowly inching their way north, liberating towns and freeing the residents from the yoke of General Striganov's IPF.

The woods-children, mixed in with Gray's Scouts, remained around the Big Lake area; they would begin working their way slowly westward.

Ben's command would head south to the Lake Almanor area and then cut west, slowly fighting their way westward.

Cecil's command would no longer be held in reserve, for Ben knew that after the Big Lake massacre, the Russian and Sam Hartline would pull out all the stops in their efforts to halt the advancing Rebels. Cecil's Rebels would free any captive towns east of Interstate 5 and west of Highway 395, with Interstate 80 their southern stopping point.

The recon teams sent out to South Carolina were working their way southeast, but the going was slow, and they were meeting some resistance from Sam Hartline's eastern-based warlords—trash and thugs and outlaws the mercenary had recruited months before, knowing that Raines and his Rebels would be moving westward after him.

The recon teams radioed this new development back to Ben.

"Why didn't they hit us on the way west?" Sylvia asked.

"Probably because they were ordered not to," Ben told her.

"Then the Russian planned this out very carefully, didn't he?"

"Not Striganov. Striganov is a very vain, arrogant man, with very little imagination. He's a good field commander, as long as it's restricted to book-type war: the movement and placement of great armies. No, this is Sam Hartline's work. Like me, Hartline is a mercenary; a man thoroughly trained in the art of guerrilla warfare, deception, counterinsurgency— that type of warfare. Sam realized we'd be coming after him, so he planned ahead, and didn't call his middle troops off even when he thought he'd killed me some months back. And that in itself gives me some very personal insight about Sam Hartline."

Sylvia looked at him, waiting.

"The man is afraid of me. And that's both good and bad. If he didn't have any fear in him, toward me, he might do something careless and reckless. But now he's going to be very cautious. We stung them very badly the other day up at Big Lake. The Rebels put some serious hurt on them. And both Striganov and Hartline will be cautious from this point on. That's bad for us, for from now on, we'll be engaging in pure guerrilla warfare: hit hard and run like hell. But from this point on, they'll be waiting and ready for us. And that's not good news for the Rebels."

"Ben . . ." She leaned forward, closely facing him. "What are we going to do with the . . . people Striganov has experimented on? What happens to them when we free them?"

Again, Ben sighed. That was a question he'd asked himself many times. From the scant intelligence he had on the Russian's experiment stations, located all up and down the California coast, and extending into Oregon, they were each a chamber of horrors. Just as bad, maybe even worse, than anything Hitler and his goons had envisioned in their mad minds and then implemented back in the 1940s.

Ben had no idea what he and his Rebels would encounter when they opened the gates and doors and cells of the IPF's experiment stations.

But he knew one thing: he was not looking forward to it.

"We've done it!" Dr. Vasily Lvov told General Striganov, excitement in his voice. "The cross-bred babies have an ample degree of intelligence to perform as workers. I've tested them, and know it for a *fact*."

For a time, the bitterness of being mauled by Ben Raines's Rebels left Georgi. He rose from his chair and waved Lvov toward the door. "Let's go see them."

They were hideously ugly. But Striganov already knew that, having seen pictures of the cross-bred babies. What both shocked and amazed him were how big they were and how fast they were growing. They were going to be huge.

Georgi knew little about science, but he did know that humans and animals simply could not produce a baby together. Something to do with chromosomes, he thought, if he remembered his college days correctly. But he had never been interested in those classes.

Now he wished he had paid more attention.

"How?" he asked Lvov.

"By altering the reproductive system by the use of desoxyribonucleic acids—"

"The *what*?"

"DNA," Lvov the scientist replied, very patiently. The general was a great leader of men, but a total nincompoop in a laboratory. He drew a deep breath and began explaining the procedure.

Georgi waved him silent. "Enough. You're giving me a headache. My God, these infants are *huge*. How much bigger will they get?"

"That, I cannot say, General. But I suspect they will grow to mammoth sizes. Their weight proportionate to their height. I want to put one to death and study its brain," Lvov said calmly.

"Fine. Whatever it takes to further the breed. What is the gestation period?"

Idiot! the scientist silently fumed. Count on your fingers. Use your toes if you have to. "Four months and fifteen days."

"Why exactly half the time it takes a human

female, Vasily?"

"I don't know," Lvov admitted. "We're working on that."

"Because they're half human?" Georgi said.

"It's a . . . bit more complicated than that, General." Vasily Lvov hated it when the general asked a question he could not answer.

"That's probably it," Georgi said. "Half human."

Lvov rolled his eyes but elected to keep his mouth shut. He almost said: You stick to guns, I'll stay with science. Wisely, he kept that unspoken thought to himself.

"Yes, General. That's probably it."

Georgi looked at him. "Of course it is." He looked at the hideously ugly infant. "Born with a mouthful of teeth, too. Very good work, Vasily. How about the mothers?"

"Unfortunately, we were forced to take the babies by Caesarean. There was no way the mothers could birth normally. Some did not survive the birthing."

Georgi waved that aside. "The women are expendable. It's the infants that matter. Do you need more women?"

"Always. I have . . . other experiments in mind."

"And they are?"

"To improve the breed, General. I'd like to have some black women, General."

Georgi stared at him for a moment. "We're trying to eliminate the black race, Vasily."

"And so we shall," Vasily said smoothly. "But how about a worker race that is totally controllable? The perfect slaves. How does that sound?"

"How could a basically inferior breed be perfect?"

165

Again, Vasily Lvov launched into a stream of scientific jargon that flew right over Striganov's head. Again, Georgi waved him silent. "Enough. I shall see to it you get your Negro women. Is there anything else?"

"Not that I can think of, General."

Striganov nodded and left the medicinal-smelling building. And as soon as he did, Ben Raines popped back into his mind. If General Georgi Striganov had an obsession, it was Ben Raines.

At the beginning, he did not hate Ben Raines. As a matter of fact, he had rather liked the man. He was intelligent, well-read, enjoyed the finer things of life, and was a good soldier.

But all that had soon changed as Ben Raines and his Rebels seemed to block every effort the Russian could come up with toward perfecting the master race.

Even a few weeks ago, Striganov did not hate Ben Raines.

But now he hated the man.

Despised him.

Ben Raines had to be stopped.

Striganov leaned against the outside of the building. But, goddammit — *how*?

Colonel Khamsin turned his cold, dark eyes toward the man who now stood before him. "Speak!"

"Well, like I done tole the other feller I come up on . . ."

"I am not that other . . . *feller*," Khamsin said, his English flawless, without a trace of any accent. "You

166

will tell me exactly what you told him."

"Okay," the man said. "Can I sit down?"

"No."

"I'm tared."

"What you are, I believe, is an idiot. Your life means nothing to me, American. Have you ever seen a human being skinned alive?"

The man swallowed hard. "No, sir."

"Would you like to experience it? Personally?"

"God, no!"

"Then speak!"

"I know how to get to Ben Raines."

Khamsin leaned back in his chair. He stared hard at the ragged American standing before him. Fiftyish, he guessed. He sighed. Khamsin really did not have much interest in Ben Raines—not at this time. Ben Raines, from what he had been able to gather, was a malcontent and a troublemaker. A man who had a small force of people, perhaps five or six thousand strong, who ran about like a modern-day Robin Hood, preaching all sorts of strange dogma.

Ben Raines was obviously a fool.

But, Khamsin thought, perhaps he should listen to what this whining wimp standing before him had to say. It might someday be useful.

So he listened as the man droned on and on. Khamsin finally cut him off with a curt slash of his hand.

"Enough of your prattling. I thank you for your information. Go get something to eat and stay close. I might wish to speak with you again."

As the man left, one of Khamsin's closest aides entered the office. What he had to say caught Khamsin's attention and held it.

"We have underestimated this General Ben Raines, Colonel. Badly underestimated him."

"Elaborate, please."

"Ben Raines was once President of the United States. For a brief period of time. Before the disease-carrying rodents came and very nearly wiped out the population."

Khamsin nodded. *That* Ben Raines. His people had been at sea during that time of death. And at that time, Khamsin had not been terribly interested in settling in the Americas. The climate was terrible.

"More, please."

"Right now, Ben Raines is fighting in the west, fighting a General Striganov and some mercenary named Sam Hartline."

"I am familiar with Hartline. We used him about fifteen years ago. In Lebanon. He's a good soldier, but his brains sometimes are located in his cock. Put him around a woman and he forgets everything except what is between his legs and what is between her legs. Go on."

"Ben Raines and his Rebels have lost a few battles, Colonel. But they have never lost a war."

Khamsin's eyes locked with those of his young aide. "Never?"

"Never."

"Continue."

"Many people believe the man is a god."

Ben looked at the blood that stained his hands. He let his eyes drop to the warm body of the dead IPF soldier with the sliced throat. He wiped his blade clean on the IPF man's battle shirt and sheathed it. Lifting his right arm, Ben waved his team forward. They rushed silently past the now-cooling body of a forward sentry.

Soon, the small towns surrounding Lake Almanor would be free of the yoke of the Russian, Striganov.

Ben and his Rebels began with the easternmost town of Westwood.

"About a dozen heavily armed and bunkered-in IPF people there," a recon team reported back.

"Don't risk your asses with heroics," Ben ordered. "Blow them out of there."

Mortar teams were rushed into position, the tubes checked, the bubbles leveled, and what was to pass for aiming stakes sighted in. The small complex of the IPF erupted in smoke as the 81mm rounds fluttered true.

Any IPF personnel who escaped the initial attack were shot down as they tried to flee.

Raines's Rebels moved on to Clear Creek and blasted the equally small contingent of IPF people out of their holes.

"The survivors want to surrender, General," he was informed.

Ben merely looked at the young man.

He got the message.

No prisoners.

Ben had preached it and thought he had it drilled into the heads of all his people: When in war, whether one is fighting a cause, a faction, a nation . . . it must be made clear from the outset, before the hostilities begin, to the common soldier and to the leaders, this

169

is how it will be: I will kill your mother and father, your sister and brother, your dogs and cats and horses and cattle and sheep and pigs. I will poison your water, burn your houses to the ground. I will kill your kids and your wife; I shall show no mercy to anyone or anything aligned with you. I shall inflict so much personal grief and pain and suffering and outrage, that, to a person, you will have but two choices: surrender or die.

"They are trying to surrender, Ben," Sylvia said, standing by his side.

"But they wanted to fight a moment ago, kid. And that is not the way I play the game." He gave the orders. "Destroy them."

He turned to Sylvia and waved the young man away. "Don't ever question an order of mine again, Sylvia. Not ever."

She flushed but said nothing.

The Rebels moved on to Canyondam and found the largest contingent of IPF people thus far. They were spread out over several acres, in a heavily bunkered and fortified complex.

Ben studied the situation through long lenses.

Lora stood by his side, looking at him, watching every move he made. Sylvia and some of the other Rebels had found the smallest camo uniform around and cut that down even smaller to fit her. But they could not find any combat boots to fit her tiny feet. She wore tennis shoes.

Ben lowered his binoculars. "For some reason, as yet unknown, this complex is very important to the IPF. Judging from the antennas it could be a relay station. Whatever it is, I'm not going to lose people taking it. Bring up a tank. We'll take a break while we're waiting."

While they waited for the tank to rumble its way from the northern part of the lake, the Rebels rested as they ringed the complex and waited.

Two M60A1 main battle tanks rumbled up. The lead tank's commander stuck his head out of the cupola. "Yes, sir?"

"Take it down," Ben ordered, pointing. "Then gun it with white phosphorus."

"Yes, sir!"

The tanks lurched around and pulled back a few hundred meters.

Ben ordered his people down.

The 105mm guns began belching out their lethal projectiles. They corrected aim and settled down to methodically destroy the complex. Ben ordered a halt to the shelling and ordered in WP rounds.

The complex was soon burning; those who survived the initial shelling were now on fire, and screaming to their burning death.

The Rebels that ringed the complex sat or squatted or stood with impassive faces. This was nothing new to most of them. They had heard it all before, many times.

The screaming soon died away.

"Mop it up," Ben ordered.

But as he suspected, there was nothing to mop up.

The Rebels moved around the lake to Almanor. There, they found a hastily deserted IPF complex, the food on the tables still warm.

As before, the Rebels were gathering more weapons and ammo and other equipment than they could stagger with. But looking at the citizens who remained in these small towns, Ben decided not to trust them, and therefore, not to arm them.

"They're pitiful, Ben," Sylvia said.

"They're losers," Ben said harshly. "These people we've found so far are, I suspect, the very types who pissed and moaned and sobbed about criminals' rights a decade or so ago. They blubbered and snorted about all the bad ol' guns in the hands of citizens, and were oh-so-happy when the assholes in Congress finally disarmed Americans. Now look at them. Slaves to the IPF, and probably, before Striganov came, slaves to any warlord who happened along. I would die before I became a slave to any person. You may feel sorry for them if you wish. I feel nothing but contempt and disgust."

He looked at Lora. "How do you feel about them, girl?"

"I don't trust them," she said. "I've been in the hands of men just like them. They are no better than the enemy we are fighting."

"Out of the mouths of babes," Ben said, and walked away, Lora by his side, her carbine shoulder-slung.

Seventeen

Ben and his contingent rested and spent the night at the northwestern tip of the lake that night, near the deserted town of Chester. The IPF had been in Chester, but abandoned it quickly as the Rebels began their latest moves. Here, as in the other town, the Rebels found huge amounts of supplies.

And a small band of citizens that Ben didn't like and didn't trust.

Ben called the leader of the surviving group to his command post for that night.

"Name?" Ben said shortly.

"Reed. Harry Reed. I sure am glad to see you and your people, General. You're here to stay; to protect us?"

"No."

Ben's curt reply startled the man. "I beg your pardon, General?"

"Why don't you people protect yourselves?"

"Why . . . we don't have the training for that. We . . ."

Ben tuned the man out, letting him rattle on. Same old song, different jukebox. Reasons, explanations, rationalizations. Put them all together and they boiled down to the same thing: Excuses.

"Shut up!" Ben told him.

The man ceased his prattling, stopping in midsentence, standing before Ben, his mouth hanging open.

The older Ben got, the less patience he had with those who would not help themselves. And it *was* "would not." Not "could not." Ben had and would continue putting his life on the line for the elderly and the very young and the helpless. Just as he had done back in . . . '88, he thought, with those elderly people.*

But he had nothing but contempt for people like Harry Reed.

"How many people in this area?" Ben asked.

" 'Bout a hundred and fifty, or so."

"You mean you don't know how many?"

"Naw, sir."

"How many children?"

"Bunches."

Bunches. Marvelous. "Before the IPF arrived — bearing in mind they only got here about a year ago — did you have school for the young?"

"Never got around to it. Always something else to worry about." Harry was finding his balls and beginning to stand up to Ben — verbally and in his stance.

For when he had tried to sit down, when first entering the house, Ben had told him to get up and remain standing.

"Do you have gardens . . . vegetable gardens?"

"Some folks do. I never had much luck with them, myself."

*Out of the Ashes

"What do you do with your time?"

"Scrounge around."

"Before the IPF arrived?"

"Same thing. Why you asking me all these questions? I ain't your enemy."

"I don't know whether you are, or not. I am trying to determine if you're worth my attention."

"Say what?"

"Harry, give me a couple of reasons why I *should* help you."

"We're human bein's."

"Is that a reason or an excuse, Harry?"

Harry's eyes became hard as they locked with Ben's eyes. "I don't think I like you very much, Ben Raines."

"I don't think I'll lose much sleep over it, Harry."

"You was a writer before you became what you are now, right, Ben Raines?"

"That is correct."

"And before that?"

"Some people called me a mercenary. I was not. What I was, was a soldier of fortune."

"Is there a difference?"

"Yes." Ben had no desire to discuss that great difference. People who didn't know the difference between the two were very naive.

"And before that?"

"I was a paratrooper, a Ranger, a Green Beret, then a member of the Hell-Hounds."

"I never was even a Boy Scout."

"That's your problem."

"Sir?"

"We're about the same age, Harry. Give or take a

few years. We both grew up in the days of the draft and the volunteer military. If you didn't elect to serve, don't blame me for it. If you chose not to learn weapons—as a civilian—that's your problem, not mine. How did you feel about guns back when the U.S. was flourishing . . . back when you and others like you had somebody else to do your fighting for you?"

"You . . . !" Harry bit off the unspoken scathing.

"Go ahead and say it, Harry. I'm not going to shoot you for it."

"Fuck you, Raines!"

Ben laughed at him.

Harry picked up a straight-backed chair, slammed the legs to the floor, and sat down, glaring at Ben, daring him to say something about his being seated.

Instead, Ben said, "Answer my question, Harry."

"I despised guns, Raines."

"I bet you didn't like cops either, did you, Harry?"

"I didn't have much use for them."

"But you'd call one if you got in trouble, wouldn't you, Harry?"

"I did on several occasions. What's the point of all this, Raines?"

"You, Harry. How long have you lived in this area?"

"I came here just after the bombings. I was in business in Davis."

"And you just scrounged around for food and clothing? No gardens, no schools for the kids, no organization, no forming of any type of defense? Is that right, Harry?"

"Yeah."

"And now you people want me and my Rebels to pick your asses out of the ashes of war, dust you off, feed you and fight your battles for you, right, Harry?"

"I've heard for years what a horse's ass you really are, Raines. I guess the rumors were true."

"They may be, Harry. I may well be a horse's butt. But I haven't been sitting around feeling sorry for myself."

"So what are you going to do with us, Raines?"

"Nothing," Ben said softly. "Except take every kid I can find and all the helpless and elderly and transport them back to our base camp. The rest of you people can go straight to hell."

"You're just going to *leave* us?"

"Yeah."

"But you're supposed to be some sort of savior! You're supposed to be . . . to be going around the country, helping people!"

"Who want to help themselves," Ben corrected. "And I don't recall running for this so-called position of mine, Harry. I never asked for this job."

Harry stared at Ben for a long moment, his expression unbelieving. "Will you arm us, at least?"

"With a *gun*, Harry?" Ben said, his words laced with sarcasm.

The red crept up Harry's neck, coloring his face.

"What are you going to do with a gun, Harry? Shoot yourself in the foot?"

Lora walked into the room, a pistol belted around her waist. She leaned her carbine against a wall and sat down in a chair.

Harry looked at her, then at Ben. He opened his

mouth to speak, then closed it.

"Yeah, Harry," Ben said. "She's carrying guns."

"Will you arm us?"

"I'll leave some of the IPF's weapons and ammo for you, Harry. But when push comes to shove, you people will never use them. The next time some crazy warlord and his men roll through, you'll all run and hide. You'll let your women get raped and you men will drop your pants and bend over. I would help you, Harry. But there are too many obstacles in the way. You don't like authority, Harry. People like you question every order given you by people who are trying to help. You want lots of things, Harry. But you don't want to work for them. I saw that the instant I drove into town. The place is filthy. You don't look like you've had a bath in a month."

"There isn't any goddamned *soap*!" Harry flared.

"Then make some."

"*Make* it? How?"

Ben rubbed his temples with his fingertips. "Can you read, Harry?"

"Of course I can read! I was a very successful businessman back in Davis."

"There is a library in town, Harry. I drove past what is left of it. It looks like it hasn't been used in years."

Harry's face was flushed a deep red.

"When did you last read a book, Harry?"

Harry looked like he was ready to explode. He stuttered and sputtered and managed to say nothing.

Ben momentarily forgot Lora was in the room. "You're a dumb motherfucker, Harry."

Lora laughed.

178

"Harry, you can make soap by boiling plain ol' ordinary kitchen fat with wood lye; you can get that from leaching ashes of hard wood. You go *scrounge* around and find coconut oil, or linseed oil, soybean oil, or other vegetable oil. Add that, it'll take the sting out of it. Then take a bath, Harry. You stink!"

Harry was crying as he rose from his chair and stumbled to the door. He turned around and said, "You ain't got no right to treat me like this, Ben Raines. The Good Book says the meek will inherit the earth."

"Six feet of it, Harry." Ben winked at him. "Hang in there, Harry."

Eighteen

Ike's Rebels were now in firm control of everything south of Highway 20 down to the Bay area of San Francisco. And Ike was just as tough as Ben in his treatment of those who would not help themselves. He had no pity for them.

He was highly compassionate toward the very young and the very old; but anything in-between who groveled and allowed themselves to be enslaved, he brushed aside with contempt.

In Santa Rosa, a once thriving city, Ike found that cults had sprung up, worshipping everything from salt and pepper shakers to billy goats—and anything and everything in-between.

But out of every bad situation, there is usually some good—if one looks for it.

Ike and his Rebels looked.

Just a few miles northeast of the city, Scouts reported a large colony of people, living in well-kept houses, with neat fields, huge gardens, and herds of cattle and sheep and hogs.

And a lot of guns.

"Say again," Ike spoke into his mike.

"Guns, sir. Lots of guns. And the people look like they know how to use them."

"How many people?" Ike asked.

"Countin' the kids, close to a thousand, I'd guess."

"We're on our way. See if you can make friendly contact with them."

"Yes, sir."

The community stretched for several miles, with lots of space between houses, so the residents would not feel hemmed-in. The lawns were neat and well-kept, spring flowers just beginning to bloom.

But what really caught Ike's eyes were the four missile silos he'd seen spread out over the four miles or so. A grin began crinkling his face. Now he knew how and why these people were left alone.

But old soldier that he was, or sailor, as the case was, he also knew these people were, in all probability, running one hell of a bluff.

But he'd play it their way for a time; see what developed.

As his column rolled past the homes, with Ike's Jeep in the lead, the people had stepped out of their homes, watching. Watching with no apparent fear. All were heavily armed, and very capable looking.

"Pull in right up there," Ike ordered his driver. "Looks like some sort of community center."

Ike stepped out of the Jeep and slung his weapon, leaning against the Jeep, watching as a well-built man walked toward him. The man appeared to be just about the same age as Ike, fiftyish, and in good physical shape, with close-cropped hair and big, work-hardened hands. Ike guessed him about six feet tall.

"I'm Ike McGowen," Ike said. "Commander of this contingent of General Ben Raines's Rebels."

The man grinned. "You people finally decided to check out the west coast, huh. Good. Glad to see you. I'm John Dunning. The people sort of put me in charge around here. From what radio messages we have intercepted, you people are kicking the hell out of the IPF and those mercenaries. Welcome to our little community, Ike."

John and Ike shook hands.

"Tell your people to park and relax. And get ready for a good home-cooked meal. You're safe here," John said.

"Yes," Ike said drily. "I saw the . . . ah, silos."

John caught the twinkle in Ike's eyes. His own eyes twinkled. "You doubt we would use them, Ike?"

"Oh, you'd probably use them . . . if you had any activated missiles in there to use."

"Well, let's put this way, Ike. We have a lot of electronics people who came here from Silicon Valley after the bombings. They can be quite convincing; *were* quite convincing when the IPF came in here. If you get my drift."

"I get it, John. But you're playing a dangerous game. What if Striganov calls your bluff?"

"Then we fight with what we have, Ike," the man's reply was simply stated.

"One more thing, John. How do you know I am who I say I am?"

"Because our people have been tracking you and

Ben and Dan and Cecil since you first came to California. Well, not exactly *our* people. But people who are aligned with us against the Russian and the mercenary."

"The underground people?"

"Yes."

Ike sighed. "But how in the hell do you meet with them? They refuse to meet with us."

"That is a problem," John admitted. "But we've overcome that by working out a series of drops. We leave messages for them, they leave messages for us."

"What is their problem, John? Why do they live the way they do?"

John shrugged heavy shoulders, packed with muscle. "Call them dropouts, I suppose. They just reject things modern. They feel that the ancient ways were the best. They have tiny, well-hidden gardens in the timber. They trap, hunt, fish, and live underground. And before you ask, I don't know their numbers. I would guess in the hundreds."

"That many?"

"Yes. And they are either good friends, or vicious, terrible enemies. Luckily for us, we started out befriending some of them. They always returned the favor in some small way. Then some of our children became friends with some of their children. It just grew from there."

John opened the door to the large community building. Ike stepped in. He could smell the aroma of fresh-cooked food. Men and women were busy setting plates and silver on long tables.

"Looks like we were expected, John."

John smiled. "Yes. We'll talk as we eat. I feel the

time has come for us join up with General Raines."

"Oh, little girlie!" the man panted, hunching between Kim's wide-spread legs. "That's the tightest I've had in a long time."

The half-dozen men from the warlord Popeye's group had grabbed Kim as she scouted ahead of her friends just inside Oregon.

Bird bent his head and began licking Kim's nipples. She accepted the assault on her with stoicism. She had already spotted her friends moving up, silently, through the timber by the roadside.

"Move around some, Bird," an outlaw said. "Let her get on top so's I can screw her butt."

Hurry up, gang! Kim thought. Please hurry.

Bird shifted, getting on the bottom, his gross nakedness on the grass, the girl on top. He pulled her head down to his slobbery lips and licked at her mouth.

Kim almost puked in his face from the stink of his horrible breath.

She felt the cheeks of her buttocks being spread apart. She looked up as a third man dropped his dirty trousers to his ankles and stepped out of them. He stroked his hardness and glared at her through mean little piggy eyes.

"If you bite me, you'll die hard," he said. "*Real* hard. You understand?"

Kim nodded her head and then screamed as the outlaw behind her penetrated her tightness. *Where were her friends?*

"Hey!" through the foggy mist of pain that filled

185

her she heard an outlaw say. "Where in the shit is Tiger?"

"Prob'ly sitting out the woods jackin' off!" another man laughed.

Then somewhere in the bright light of pain, Kim heard a man scream.

"Jesus God!" the man howled.

"What the hell's that?" the outlaw behind her panted.

If there was a reply, he never heard it. Something smashed into the side of his head, dropping him into unconsciousness, knocking him backward.

At the same time the outlaw standing in front of the girl caught the butt of an AK-47 on the side of his head. He fell to the ground like a dropped sack of potatoes.

The outlaw called Bird looked up from the ground from beneath Kim—smack into the muzzle of an AK-47. Lifting his eyes, he looked into the face of Judy.

Kim rolled away from him and began gathering up her torn clothing, getting dressed as best she could with what she had left.

"You kids got yourselves into a peck of trouble," Bird said. "Y'all know that?"

Judy reversed the AK and smashed the butt into the man's mouth, shattering what remained of his front teeth, top and bottom. Bird squalled and rolled on the ground, holding both hands to his bleeding mouth.

"Get some rope," Kim said. "These the only ones left alive?"

"Yeah," Sandra said. "We killed the others. You better clean yourself up," she said, looking at Kim.

"You don't wanna come up pregnant."

"I can't get in no family way," Kim told her. "I was raped when I about seven or eight. Tore me up bad. Old Dr. Chase done told me I can't never have no kids. But I do wanna wash."

"Stream over yonder," Judy said, jerking her head to the south. "We'll get 'em ready for you."

"What the hell you gonna do?" Bird moaned the question, his mouth bleeding.

"You'll find out," Sandra told him, the words hard out of her young mouth.

The girls poked and pushed and prodded Bird to a tree. There, they tied him securely, his back hard against the bark of the tree.

"What's them ol' boys' names?" Sandra asked, pointing to the outlaws on the ground.

"That'n over yonder is called Big Dave. The other one is called Daddy."

Big Dave and Daddy were spread-eagled on the ground, their ankles and wrists tied to stakes driven deep into the earth. When they awakened, they immediately knew they were in for a very bad time.

They were to soon discover just how bad a time.

Kim stood between Bird and the two men staked out on the ground. She had a knife in her hand. She had started a small fire burning in the clearing. One of the outlaw's knives lay among the coals, the blade turning cherry-red.

Judy opened a map and held it out for the men to see.

Sandra said, "Tell us the location of every warlord Sam Hartline has. How many men in each spot. Name names."

"Fuck you, girlie!" Big Daddy said with a laugh.

Sandra looked at him. She smiled. But her smile was totally without mirth. She looked at Kim. "Cut it off," she said softly.

Big Daddy began screaming and before Kim was finished he'd passed out from the pain. When it was over, the girl picked up the knife from the fire, holding it by the stag handle, and seared the wound between his legs, closing it.

Sandra glanced at Bird. "You'll tell us everything you know, won't you?"

"God, yes! If you promise not to do that to me!"

"Oh, I promise I won't do that to you," the girl said. She turned to Big Dave. "How about you, mister?"

"Anything you say, girl," Big Dave said, fear causing slobber to leak from his mouth. "I'll tell you anything you want to know."

"Move Bird," Sandra told the others. "Separate the men so they cannot hear the questions or answers. Then we'll compare what they say."

Bird was untied and moved a hundred yards from the staked-down Dave. The locations of the warlords were compared, found that they matched, and were marked on the map.

Daddy was still unconscious on the ground. The odor of seared flesh clung close.

"All the answers match," Kim said.

"And so do the numbers of men," Judy said.

"And Daddy is still out," Sandra said. "Shoot the other two. We'll turn Daddy loose. He won't know they have talked."

"But he'll never rape another girl," Kim said, grim satisfaction in her voice.

And deep in the now-uncontrolled and wildly growing

188

timber, hidden among the shrubs and bushes, those underground people who had been tracking the young women nodded their heads in agreement with what had been done.

It had been a just sentence. They would have done the same. Rape was not tolerated among their society. Crime was virtually nonexistent among their members. It simply was not tolerated.

The underground people had taken another chapter from the book of Ben Raines, emulating what he had done in the old Tri-States.

He had wiped out crime simply by not tolerating it.

The underground people squatted and lay silently in the deep timber, watching the young people. They were curious now as to what they planned to do.

The girls had the information they had been sent to find. Now what were they going to do?

"Do we go on?" Judy asked.

"Let's vote on it. That's the way I'm told it used to be," Kim said.

"When was that?" Judy asked.

"Before."

"Ah," she said.

They voted, agreeing to continue; they might pick up more information useful to the general.

The girls picked up their weapons and packs and moved out.

Into the unknown and the ashes of what used to be. Before.

Nineteen

"The man's plan might have some merit," Khamsin's aides told him.

"Perhaps," Colonel Khamsin said. "It is for a fact that Ben Raines must be removed. With him out of the way, we will have no opposition; nothing standing in our way of total takeover."

"Do you suppose the man is telling the truth?"

"Yes," Khamsin said after a moment of thought. "I think he is. I believe him. But"—he held up a warning finger—"we must move slowly and with much caution. We must think this out very carefully."

"Perhaps it would be best to wait," another aide suggested.

"Why?" Khamsin asked.

"Let the fight go uninterrupted in the west. Let Raines and the Russian thin their ranks during the war. That would help us."

"Yes," Khamsin agreed. "But we need to have people out there, watching. Have you sent out patrols as I requested?" That was directed to a young woman.

"Yes, sir. They reported back that they are halfway

to their objective."

"Very good. Keep the man in camp. Give him new clothing and food and lodgings. Give him a woman for entertainment. Watch him at all times. Be friendly, but firm. Let's move on to more pressing matters. How are the farms looking?"

"Excellent, Colonel."

"The people working them?"

"We've had . . . ah, some trouble with a few of them."

"And? . . ."

"We shot them."

"And now?"

"The rest seem to have accepted their fate and are falling into line quite well."

"Resistance groups?"

"A few. We're eliminating them one by one."

"See that you get them all. Quickly. Do not let them spread," Khamsin ordered. "Rebellion must be crushed brutally and swiftly."

"Yes, sir."

"Dismissed."

But Khamsin, along with the other terrorists who made up his army, forgot one little item: This was America. Battered, bruised, on her knees, but not yet down for the count. Americans have always been stubborn types, slow to anger, but when angered, many Americans have a tendency to shove back when shoved; to reach for a gun when all else fails—or sometimes before anything else is tried.

More resistance groups than the Islamic Peoples Army thought were forming. They were forming along the borders of Georgia and Florida and North Carolina.

Under the direct command of teams of Rebels from North Georgia. From Ben Raines's Base Camp One. They were getting training in guerrilla warfare and the use of automatic weapons.

And their ranks were growing; slowly, but steadily.

They were not yet strong enough to make any major moves against the IPA. But soon, they hoped. Soon.

Striganov stood before a wall map of territory controlled—or once controlled—by his people.

Damn! he silently cursed.

How does one stop the silent wind? he thought.

Then he shook his head. Stupid! he berated himself. Silly and childish to compare Ben Raines with the wind. The man is a mere mortal.

A chill touched him lightly.

Or is he?

This time the Russian was successful in pushing that thought from him. He more closely studied the map.

He began replacing tiny red flags with blue ones, denoting territory lost to Raines and his Rebels.

Great God! That many?

"Yes," he muttered.

Everything south of Highway 20 was now in Rebel hands. And informants near Santa Rosa reported that one Rebel commander just brazenly drove his column right through the city and up to that settlement of malcontents outside the city.

No doubt that arrogant John Dunning and his

people would be linking up with the Rebels.

More problems.

Striganov had felt from the outset that those silos held nothing but rusting, inoperable missiles. But he would not take the one-in-a-million chance that they contained the real thing. The Russian would not risk more radiation in the air. He felt John Dunning was bluffing.

But? . . .

The alternative was unthinkable.

With a sigh, he turned away from the map and sat back down behind his desk.

He rubbed his temples with the tips of his fingers. Where in the hell was Ben Raines now?

"They've pulled out, General," a recon patrol reported back to Ben. "Chico, Paradise, and Oroville IPF outposts are abandoned."

"Did they leave anything behind?" Ben radioed.

"Looks like they left behind a lot, General. They seemed to be in quite a hurry to clear out."

"The civilians?"

A short pause. "Pretty well beat down, General."

"I'm on my way." Ben handed the mike back to the radio operator and checked his maps. About an hour's drive down to Chico. "Let's go," he ordered.

Chico had once been a progressive little city of about thirty thousand. Now, to Ben's eyes, it appeared that no more than three to four hundred people survived.

And they were a sad-looking lot.

"Jesus!" Ben muttered, his eyes taking in the dirty,

ragged, and woebegone-looking bands of men and women. They stood in silence, staring at the Rebels through eyes sunk deep into their heads.

Sylvia and Lora sat in the back of the Jeep, Ben on the passenger side, front seat, his Thompson in his lap, muzzle pointed to the outside.

"What is it with these people out here, General?" his driver asked. "The survivors in the midwest and the south act . . . well, *different*."

"How do you mean, Chuck?" Ben knew what he meant, but he wanted the young man to put his thoughts into words.

"Well, you take those folks we found in Missouri and Tennessee and Georgia and Arkansas. They were fightin' the IPF with everything they had available. Many of them chose death over slavery. It's just . . . different out here."

"But yet Ike reports a large colony of people south of here who stood up to the Russian," Ben reminded the young man.

"Yes, sir. But how many of those kind have *we* seen?"

"It's about fifty-fifty, Chuck."

"That don't tell me the why of it, though."

"It's all in how you're raised, Chuck. States—back when we had states that resisted the government's attempts to disarm the citizens. They fought, sometimes violently, the move toward gun control. But others advocated the disarming of citizens. I remember reading about a man here in California who killed a rattlesnake in his front yard. Killed it with a gun. The courts ordered him arrested and fined him."

"Are you serious, General?"

195

"Sure am. I came down pretty hard on Harry Reed the other day. Maybe I shocked him enough for him to survive, but I doubt it. Harry was brainwashed. Since he was old enough to watch TV or read a newspaper, he was bombarded with people saying things like it's society's fault that we have criminals, that guns are evil and the death penalty is wrong."

"General," Chuck said. "Good people don't steal things. Assholes steal things."

"You and I know that," Ben said. "How old were you when the bombs came, Chuck?"

"Eleven, I think, sir."

"And you've blocked out most of the horror, right, Chuck?"

"Yes, sir."

Ben nodded. Many of those he'd spoken with had done the same. Ben didn't blame them. Sometimes he wished he could.

"Pull over there to our patrol," Ben said, pointing at a Jeep parked curbside, a group of men and women gathered around it.

"Probably beggin' for food," Chuck muttered. "Goddamn, are they helpless?"

"No," Ben said.

"Then they're fools."

"Foolish, at the very least," Ben agreed in part.

Ben sat in his Jeep and looked at the people, standing silently, looking at him. They knew who he was, and Ben could sense the mixture of fear and resentment emanating from them, directed toward him.

Why him and not me? drifted the silent vibes.

"Well, the big bad wolf is gone," Ben shattered the

196

silence. "Now what are you going to do?"

A man broke from the crowd and walked up to Ben. "Are your people going to stay and help us?"

Ben checked his temper and bit back a smart-assed reply.

"No," he said with a sigh. "That's doubtful at this time."

"Then what are we going to do?" the man asked.

"How about helping yourselves?" Ben offered.

"Give us the means and we will," the man said.

Hope for them yet, Ben thought. "What's your name?"

"George Williams. You're Ben Raines?"

"Yeah. What do you want?"

"Guns," George said, a firmness in his voice.

Ben waved one of the recon team over to his Jeep. When he spoke, it was as if George was not present. "These people know anything about guns, Jimmy?"

"From what they told me, General, no."

Ben arched an eyebrow. He looked at George. "Yeah, George. You can have your guns and ammo."

"But you and your people are not going to stay and help us, are you?"

"Not at this time, no."

"General, can I tell you something?"

"Sure. It's still a free country. What's left of it."

"General, we both hold vastly different political views. As you have a right to yours, I have a right to mine."

"That's right, George."

Ben thought of another George, the civilian he'd met briefly back in Red Bluff and left in charge. That George had been tough and capable looking, not willing to be enslaved by any person. Ben had left him in charge.

He looked at the recon man. "Don't waste too much time on them."

"Yes, sir."

He told Jimmy, "Let's get out of here."

Twenty

"Now both them girlies is dead," an outlaw reported to Sonny Boy. He cocked his dirty head to one side and stared at the warlord. "I thought you was gonna keep that woman Rebel for yourself?"

"Too damn much trouble," the warlord grunted his reply. "Ever' time I wanted to stuck it up her ass I had to pract'ally whup her half to death. It wasn't worth it. I'm gettin' bored, Snake. All this doin' nothing is makin' me edgy. You?"

"Yeah. How come Hartline don't just cut us loose and let us go kick the ass off of Raines and them Rebels?"

Sonny Boy shook his head. "I don't know. All that shit we've heard about Raines and them people of his'n don't add up to what I've seen about them. I think Raines is runnin' a bluff. That's what I think."

"You think we could take 'em, Sonny Boy?" Snake asked.

"Hell, yes! Snake, you go get the rest of the boys on the horn. We gonna have us a sit-down. And I don't give a shit whether Hartline likes it or not."

But before Snake could turn away, a shout came

from the gang's radio operator. "Popeye's on the horn, Sonny Boy! Wants to talk to you. Says it's important."

"Comin'!" What the hell? he thought.

Sonny Boy listened through the headset, his face first paling, then turning red, as anger overrode shock. "Yeah," he said. "We can't have no more of that shit. You right. Look, you call Skinhead and I'll call Grizzly. We'll have us a meet tomorrow at noon." His eyes lifted to a dirty map tacked to the wall. "We'll meet at old Fort Klamath. Yeah. I'm with you, Popeye. Looks like it's gonna be up to us to kick the ass off Raines and his people. Right. Is Daddy gonna make it?"

He listened for a moment longer, then signed off.

"What's up, Boss?" an outlaw called Grease asked. He scratched at his lice-infested crotch.

"Some of Popeye's boys was out on the prowl two, three days ago. They come up on some little pussy. Twelve, thirteen years old. They got her down when some more little cunts showed up. Seems like these little girlies done killed them boys that wasn't bangin' the kid. They killed Bird and Big Dave, and then cut the pecker off of Daddy. Closed the wound with a hot blade and left him."

"Jesus!" Grease said.

"Get me Grizzly on the horn. We're all gonna have a sit-down tomorrow at noon. I'll take the lieutenants with me. Rest of you guys hang tough."

"You reckon them that done it to Popeye's boys is out of Ben Raines's people?" an outlaw asked.

"Hell, yes. And I'm tired of fuckin' around with Raines and his bunch. We're gonna settle this thing

200

once and for all. Kick his ass back east of the Muddy."

"We can do it, too!" an outlaw called Tony said.

"Damn right!" Snake said.

"I sure would like to find them girlies that done it," Sonny Boy said dreamily. "I like to listen to little girlies holler. We could have us some fun with them."

One member of Striganov's IPF was definitely not having any fun with Sandra, Judy, and Kim. His fun days were over. His heart still pumped blood, but the blood was gushing out of the knife-inflicted wound in his throat. His friends were spread-eagled on the cracking concrete of the old highway, their weapons stacked to one side.

The recon patrol had been returning to their Oregon base when they came up on a half-dozen boys and girls trying to make it out of IPF-controlled territory. The recon members had had their fun with the girls, and were sodomizing the youngest boy when the trio of woods-children suddenly charged out of the timber by the side of the road.

Twelve-year-old Judy looked at the ragged bunch of children. Her young-old eyes flicked from one to the other. No weapons except for an empty knife sheath on one boy's belt. "Where's you kids goin?" she asked.

"Runnin'." A boy said. He appeared to be the oldest. Maybe fourteen years old.

"Runnin' *where*?"

"Just gettin' out," a girl said. She was trying to cover her nakedness with the torn rags of clothing ripped from her by the IPF men.

"How come y'all ain't got no guns?" Kim asked.

"There ain't no guns to be had," the girl said. "We looked, too."

"You didn't look very good," Sandra said. "You got to know where to look."

The girl started crying.

Judy walked to her and slapped her across the face, rocking her head. "Shut up," Judy said. "That don't do no good. You oughta know that by now. If you ain't tough, you better get tough. If you don't, you're gonna die out here. You wanna cry, do it at night, where nobody can see or hear you. That's the way it's gotta be."

The children looked at the gun-toting twelve-year-old with shock in their eyes. They had, to a person, never seen anything like this tough little girl.

"I don't know what the hell to do with you, ya'll," Judy said. "We can't take you with us; but you don't act like you can survive by yourselves."

"We can survive!" a girl said hotly.

"I don't know how," Judy said, looking at her, standing there crying. "You ain't got no weapons. And to me, that means you ain't got no smarts."

Kim and Sandra let Judy carry the verbal ball.

"You trust adults," Judy said. "That's a bad mistake. If they ain't wearin' tiger-stripe or lizard cammies, you can't trust 'em. You can trust the underground people, but the odds are, they've seen you but you ain't seen them."

"Who?"

"Never mind." One of the IPF recon team chose that time to leap to his feet and attempt to run. Judy shot him in the back, severing his spine. The man fell to the broken concrete and lay still.

Judy turned her eyes back to the kids. "You got names?"

Larry was the youngest boy. Eight years old.

Mary was the girl she'd been speaking to. Twelve years old. The girl's shirt was torn open. No buttons.

"Your first time?" Judy asked.

Mary shook her head.

"Then you oughta know you ain't gonna die from it. But you're stupid tryin' to fight them. You fight them, and they'll hurt you real bad or kill you. Give it to them then wait it out 'til you get a chance to run."

Lisa was twelve. Already her breasts were as full as a grown woman's. She was shapely with a grown woman's face and body.

"You in trouble right off," Judy told her. "Wear loose shirts so's the men can't see how big you are. And get jeans that's too big for you. Cut that long hair off. Try to make yourself ugly. If you don't, you gonna get jumped everytime you turn around."

Lisa started crying.

Rich was the oldest. Fourteen. But small for his age. He was scared, and looked it.

"You just left some city or town, didn't you?" Judy asked him.

Rich nodded.

"I figured it. You don't know nothin' about stayin' alive, do you?"

"My parents just got taken away from me. By the IPF. I don't know where they were taken. They hid me in the basement."

"You'll never see them again," Judy said bluntly.

"So forget them. I can't even hardly remember mine. and if you tune up and start blubberin', I'm gonna knock the crap outta you."

Rich tightened his face, holding back tears.

"You gotta get tough, boy," Judy told him. "Or die. I bet your parents protected you, didn't they?"

"Yes."

"They didn't do you no favors, boy. But you hang around with us, you'll grow up fast."

Ann was thirteen; looked younger than that.

Carol was twelve. Pretty and very innocent looking, with blond hair and big blue eyes.

Judy walked over to Kim and Sandra.

"What are we gonna do with them, girls?"

"They got crap for brains," Sandra said. "They could get us killed."

"Do you vote to leave them?" Judy asked.

"Naw," Sandra said. "I wouldn't feel right doin' that."

Judy looked at Kim.

Kim shrugged. "Hell, we can't leave them. But Lisa's gonna get us in trouble. I just know it. You all know how men feel about big-titted girls."

"Rich ain't got no guts," Judy said.

"Maybe he just ain't found them yet," Kim offered. "His momma and daddy kept him safe. Hell, it's his ass, girls. He'll either grow up or get dead."

Judy shook her head. "A big-titted kid and a boy with no guts. They've all been protected, all their lives. Okay, we all voted to go forward for Ben Raines. If we do that, we got to take them with us."

Sandra stepped out of the tight group and tossed a knife to Rich. The knife sparked on the concrete.

"Pick it up and cut his throat," Sandra nodded at the IPF man.

"Me?" Rich asked.

"I ain't talkin' to the goddamn road, boy," Sandra told him.

Rich backed away from the big-bladed knife. "I can't do it."

Lisa bent down, picked up the knife, and walked to the spread-eagled IPF man. She grabbed him by the hair and jerked his head back. Bending down, she sliced open his throat, then dropped the knife and threw up on the concrete.

The woods-children looked at each other. An unspoken message passed between them.

Lisa would do.

Watch Rich.

Kim lifted her AK and finished the remaining IPF members. She slung her AK and said, "Let's go."

Twenty-one

"There it is," Sonny Boy told the bizarre-looking gang leaders and their lieutenants and bodyguards gathered at Fort Klamath.

"What does Hartline have to say about it?" Grizzly asked, standing up and stretching. A huge man, six and a half feet tall, weighing almost three hundred pounds, some of it gone to fat, but much of it still muscle.

"He don't. I didn't talk to him about it."

"I'm 'bout tired of Hartline and that slick-lookin' Russian," Popeye said. "Both of 'em act like their shit don't stink. They just too damn high and mighty for my tastes."

Popeye was a freak; looked like a freak, and knew it. There was nothing, absolutely nothing, attractive about the man. His forehead was large and knotty, his eyes bugged out. He was skinny with a pot belly. Both arms had been broken and set badly; they were crooked. One eye was brown, the other blue; both were crossed.

Popeye had no redeeming qualities. None. They all shared that in common, but Popeye was the worst of the lot. He could kill man, woman, or child with absolutely no remorse. He could have sex with man, woman, or child, and enjoy it equally.

"Let's pull out," Skinhead suggested. "Hit the road and fuck with Ben Raines and them Rebels of his'n."

Skinhead was bald. After the bombings, all his hair fell out. He was short, stocky, ugly, and not only was he vicious looking . . . he was vicious. He was also stupid. His IQ might hit 85 if he was lucky.

"That your vote?" Sonny Boy asked.

"Yeah." Skinhead slobbered down the front of his dirty shirt. Skinhead slobbered a lot — especially during sex.

Sonny Boy looked at Grizzly. "You?"

Grizzly nodded his big head. "Yeah. I'm with Skinhead."

"Me, too," Popeye said.

"Hartline ain't gonna like it," Sonny Boy reminded them all.

"Fuck Hartline," Popeye said.

As a matter of fact, Hartline had no objection to the warlords pulling out. As a matter of fact, he thought it to be a fine idea. As a matter of fact, he was sick to death of the motorcyclists.

Filthy, ignorant lot.

"I think that's a grand idea, Sonny Boy," Hartline told the warlord. "I know it's been boring for you around here. I was about to suggest that you boys take to the field and make trouble for Ben Raines."

"You was?" Sonny Boy asked.

"Of course. You and your people are far too valuable to sit around just doing nothing."

And besides that, you all, to a man, stink like hogs and I'm going to have to de-louse my office after you leave.

"Yeah? Well, you right," Sonny Boy said.

"If I might make a suggestion?" Sam said with a smile.

"Whatever flips your dress up, man."

Sam resisted an impulse to shoot the bastard right between the eyes.

"Don't try to meet the Rebels head-on. As good as you are, they're too strong; you'll be heavily outnumbered. I would suggest ambush. Hit and run. And by all means, take as many of the Rebel women as possible. Do with them as you see fit."

" 'At 'airs a right good idea," Grizzly spoke up.

Skinhead nodded his head and slobbered his agreement.

Popeye's eyes bugged out and he grunted.

Hartline managed to hide his grimace of disgust.

Sonny Boy stood up and the others followed suit. "We'll be seein' you, Sam," he said.

"I'm so looking forward to it," the mercenary said with a sigh of relief that they were finally leaving.

"How 'bouts them ol' boys back east of here?" Grizzly asked.

"We'll hold them in reserve for the time being."

The warlords trooped out.

Sam called for an aide.

"Yes, sir?"

"Take those four chairs outside and burn them," he ordered. "Then find some bug-killer and spray my office." He scratched his head. Jesus, he had *fleas*!

At the end of the week, Ben ordered a halt to his rapidly advancing Rebels. They were meeting practically no resistance, and that worried Ben.

He called for a meeting of his field commanders.

They met in Redding, in what was left of a motel near the airport. Harris was there; the man Ben had left in charge at Redding. George from Red Bluff. John Dunning from Santa Rosa. And a Pete Ho from Ukiah. Dan had flown in from the northern part of the state. Ike and Cecil.

The meeting room had been cleaned up, and a large map of California was nailed to the wall. Ben stood up, a stick in his hand for a pointer.

"Look at the territory we've taken," he said, placing the stick on the map. "We control everything from Highway 20 south to the Bay area. Everything north of Highway 299 to the Oregon line. Practically everything east of Interstate 5. And none of us has met enough resistance to stop a flea. Why? Give me some input."

Dan studied the large map for a moment. "I think, General, we are being suckered. But for what and why, I haven't a clue."

"I got the same feelin'," Ike said. "My recon teams report that from the coast . . ." he rose and walked to the map—"from right about here"—he punched a blunt finger at Fort Bragg and traced it over to what had once been state and national forests and parks area, ". . . to here, there are heavy concentrations of IPF troops. Too goddamn many for us to punch through. Why? Why would the Russian mass his troops there?"

Cecil walked to the map, studying it for a moment. "I have reports that large numbers of troops are massing just south of Highway 299. From the coast to Weaverville." He looked at Ben. "I told you about that, Ben."

Ben nodded his head. "Yes. So Striganov doesn't want us to flank him. Either from the north or south. What options does that leave us?"

"Straight ahead," John Dunning said.

"That's right," Ben said. "Right into the wilderness areas. Take a look, people. From north to south between Highways 20 and 299. Trinity National Forest, Six Rivers National Forest, Yolla Bolly Wilderness area, Mendocino National Forest. That's where the Russian wants us. He's trying to play our game."

"General," Dan spoke. "There is no way he could effectively cover that much ground. He's got us outgunned, but he doesn't have that many troops. That's about five hundred miles deep, and at its widest point, about two hundred miles west to east. He can't have that many men."

"No, he doesn't," Ben agreed. "But he knows we couldn't possibly hack our way through the wilderness; that would take us forever. We'd have to use existing roads. That's where he's set up ambush sites."

"You have a plan?" Pete Ho asked.

"Oh, yes," Ben said with a smile. "We hold what we have taken thus far. We rest, we eat, we sleep, and we do nothing — nothing except stay very alert. Either

211

Hartline or Striganov will become impatient. One or the other will bust loose and do something."

A Rebel walked into the meeting room. "General, our listening post at Iron Gate Dam just received a message from the kids up in Oregon. The warlords have broken loose from Hartline and are heading out. Five, six hundred of them. Looks like, from the direction they've taken, they're going to head east, then cut south, come up behind us."

Ben glanced at Cecil. "It's your baby, Cec. Take off and good luck. If you need help, get on the horn."

Cec nodded, gathered up his aides, and quickly left the meeting room.

"How are the girls?" Ben asked.

"Seem to be fine. They report picking up a half-dozen more kids. I told Iron Gate to tell them to hold their position and wait for further orders."

Ben nodded. "Tell them to get back across the line into safe territory. No point in them staying up there."

"Yes, sir." The man hesitated.

"Something else?" Ben asked.

"Yes, sir. Iron Gate reported that the girls have mixed it up with two patrols. One patrol of outlaw bikers loyal to Hartline, and the other a regular IPF patrol. The girls left one biker alive—after they cut off his privates and cauterized the wound with a heated knife blade. They killed all the IPF bunch."

"Jesus!" Ben muttered.

Ike's smile was tight. "You remember the first rule of guerrilla warfare, Ben. Don't get taken prisoner by the women."

"Only too well," Ben said. He thanked the messenger and waited until the man had left, closing the door behind him. He turned to face the group of field commanders. "Any questions?"

"Do you suppose Cecil will need some help with those outlaw bikers?" John Dunning asked. "They can be terribly vicious."

The Rebels in the room smiled.

"Yes," Pete Ho said. "That bunch, the ones aligned with Sam Hartline, came through Ukiah above five months ago. Their leader, of that bunch, was some cretin named Popeye. At the time, my group of resistance fighters was up in the hills, knocking heads with the IPF. When we returned, victorious, I might add, the town had been looted, men and women killed, and several young girls taken prisoner. We never saw the kids again. I'll offer my people to assist General Jefferys."

Dan turned his head so the civilian freedom fighter could not see his grin.

Harris, out of Redding, said, "It was Grizzly's bunch of bikers who rolled through our town. They're much worse than any IPF people I ever saw. They kill and torture for no apparent reason. From what I am able to understand, General Jefferys only has a battalion of Rebels. I don't mean to second-guess you, General Raines, but I think he's going to need some help in dealing with these outlaw bikers."

Ike could not contain his laughter.

The civilians looked at the ex-Navy SEAL, not understanding the laughter; not knowing the why of it.

Ben waited until Ike's laughter faded. He faced the group. "People, listen to me. You are all now a part of the Rebel organization. So let me be terribly blunt. I want you all to understand the Rebel philosophy; let there be no misunderstandings concerning what we do and how we do it. We don't take prisoners, people. We *do not* take prisoners. Ever."

Ben let that sink in, his eyes flicking from one civilian to another.

"Never?" Pete Ho asked softly.

"Not any more," Ben told him.

"What do you do with those who offer to surrender, General?" George asked.

"Once the fighting starts, George, it's too late. The enemy can surrender en masse, or not at all. Those are the rules I've laid down. Striganov and Hartline know it. And the same rules apply to any Rebel. You'd all better know that going in."

"I don't know whether I could shoot any unarmed man," Harris said. "I mean, I've never done it."

Harris was suddenly very much aware of Dan Gray's extremely cold eyes on him. The unblinking gaze made the man very uncomfortable.

"Unless the people are standing stark naked in front of you," Ike said, "how do you know they're unarmed? Then there is this to consider: these people are your enemies. They have, to a person, committed acts so hideous as to be unspeakable. They have taken oaths to destroy the Rebel movement. Striganov wants a pure Aryan nation. Where does that leave you, Pete?"

The Chinese-American lifted his shoulders and spread his hands silently.

"Hartline wants war," Ben picked it back up. "And he'll switch sides faster than a snake can strike. Sam is

214

pure mercenary. He is not a soldier of fortune. The side that can offer him the most is the side he'll choose. These warlords and outlaw bikers are scum. They don't care if the country ever rises out of the ashes of destruction. I have more feelings for a roach then I do for them.

"You all wondered why Ike was laughing a moment ago. He was laughing because Cecil will deal with this filth and trash and scum in the same manner that we've dealt with them over the years—with extreme prejudice. No negotiating with them. No deals. No pity. No mercy. We just shoot them out of the saddle. On sight.

"The Rebel dream is to rebuild this nation. To have schools and hospitals and churches and libraries. To once more be able to produce. To build something for future generations. Outlaws and warlords and roaming gangs of thugs and punks and dickheads have no place in that society we dream of. None at all. We didn't tolerate them in the old Tri-States, and I will not tolerate them now."

Ben looked at the group of civilians; looked at them all. Gave each man a full ten seconds of unblinking stare.

"You are either one hundred percent for the Rebel movement, or you are one hundred percent against it. That's the way it has to be, for now, at least, and that's the way it's going to be. Give that some thought, people. For I will not tolerate traitors."

Ben walked out of the room.

Twenty-two

Ben stood alone outside the motel meeting room, his thoughts jumbled and disorganized. Then, one by one, he began separating them and assigning positions of numerical importance within his head.

Same old story, he thought, remembering the conversation back in the meeting room.

People still cling to the concepts of law and order as it existed back in the days when the nation was whole. They simply cannot, or will not, accept the glaring fact that the entire world, as far as we know, is in a state of anarchy: dog-eat-dog, the strong roll right over the weak, the lawless reign unchecked until they are shot dead.

Sometimes, even though he knew it was not true, Ben felt like a man alone.

The feelings expressed back in the meeting room could be boiled down to what Ben had called for years the Soldier Syndrome.

All the nice pretty people want a nice pretty society. But they won't fight for it. The Soldier Syndrome. You go fight my battles for me; and then, when you've done it . . . go away, 'cause we don't want your

217

kind around here.

You're not nice like us.

And no, we don't want to hear about the terrible, awful things you had to do to make us safe. Just make us safe, and then go away.

Those so-called "nice people" just cannot, still, after all that's happened, they still cannot understand that one simply does not attempt to pet a rabid animal.

One simply destroys it.

Ben turned as the door opened. Dan and Ike stepped out to join him.

"I think they'll stand, General," Dan said.

"But they don't like it," Ike added.

Ben nodded. "Sometimes I just want to give up. Just pull back, claim territory, rebuild to our liking, and to hell with the rest of the people."

"I know, Ben," Ike said. "I know."

"It would be a grand thing," Dan said. "A simple house, a garden, a lady, perhaps some children. I could work the land, have some cows for meat and milk. And together we could live peacefully. It would be a grand thing," he said wistfully.

"We had it in the Tri-States," Ike said. "And I'd be lyin' if I said I didn't miss it."

Ben looked at his close friends. "Do either of you ever think about the fact that we've been fighting other peoples' battles, off and on, for fifteen years? And it never seems to stop. Is this our destiny? Is this our hell? Is our philosophy so alien to others? Or is it so simple it's complex? What in the hell is it that people are clinging to?"

Both men knew Ben did not expect a reply, so

neither offered one.

"Shit!" Ben said.

Ike grinned and clasped his friend's shoulder. "Destiny, Ben? Hell? Maybe it is. But maybe it's just that we're all so goddamned hard-headed we won't give up on a dream. You ever think about that?"

Ben smiled and hitched at his web belt. "Well, boys, let's follow that dream."

Book Two

So we beat on, boats against the current, borne back ceaselessly into the past.
—F. Scott Fitzgerald

Twenty-three

The Rebels waited and rested. They cleaned equipment, spent hours pouring over maps of territory assigned them once they were inside IPF-controlled territory. They waited for word from Ben Raines to strike.

But there was only silence from Ben.

The men and women of the Rebels would see him at the most unexpected times and places. Always with Lora with him, sometimes with Sylvia. Sylvia no longer shared Ben's blankets. No one knew what had happened between them to cool the brief affair, and no one was going to ask the general. Lora, who stayed with two Rebel women at night, had nothing to say on the matter; the child could be as taciturn as Ben.

The outlaw warlords had yet to make their appearance. If any of them had the sense God allowed an idiot, they would have turned around and headed east, putting as much distance between themselves and Cecil Jefferys and his people as time would let them. For years the outlaws had called the tune as they rampaged about the ravaged and torn land, killing and raping and maiming and torturing at will.

There simply had been no organized force large enough to stop them.

Most of the survivors still clung—as Ben and his Rebels were constantly being reminded—to the concept of law and order that had died with the nation.

In other words, they were waiting for someone else to do it for them.

That someone had arrived, in force.

Now, all the outlaws had to do was tangle with that force. Just one time.

"Contact has been successfully made," Colonel Khamsin was informed.

"And? . . ." the colonel asked.

The aide shrugged expressively.

"Don't give me gestures!" Khamsin berated him. "Speak to me."

"The persons contacted were very interested. But they must have some time to think about it."

"How much time?"

"Our radio contact was brief, Colonel. That was not discussed."

"Very well. What else?"

"Our scouts' report confirmed any fears we may have had concerning Ben Raines and his Rebels. They are well-trained, highly disciplined, extremely well-armed, motivated, and quite large in numbers."

"How large?"

The aide sighed. Dealing with Khamsin was, at times, difficult. "The Rebels are spread out over a large area, Colonel. There are several thousand Rebels in the west. At least a battalion left in reserve up in what was once known as Georgia. About a company of Rebels helping to train resistance fighters on the borders that surround our territory. Four or five thousand Rebels in all. And that is not counting the underground people and various other civilian groups aligned with Ben Raines. We have no way of knowing how many those might be."

"What else did Hartline have to say?" Khamsin did not fully understand these underground people or what they represented. But he felt that anyone who lived in caves and tunnels could not amount to very much. So he dismissed them.

"He laughed a lot, so our scouts reported."

"That would be like Sam."

"Is the man a fool?"

"Hardly. Just very arrogant."

"Hartline said he could put Ben Raines in a box anytime he wanted to. He refused to elaborate on that."

"That also would be like Sam. And it also might mean he does not have *any* plan. With Sam Hartline, one must always be very careful. He can speak with glibness out of both sides of his mouth."

"The mercenary is demanding a great deal, Colonel."

"Now we get to it. Well, speak."

"A state."

"Hartline wants an entire *state*?"

"Yes, Colonel."

"What state?"

"He says he'll think about that and let you know. He said to tell you to . . ." The aide hesitated.

"To tell me what?"

"To keep your britches on. He'll get back to you."
The aide waited for Khamsin's explosion.

Khamsin leaned back in his chair and laughed.
"How very much like Sam. It is good to know he has
not changed over the years. He is still an unscrupulous bastard."

"Can he be trusted, Colonel?"

"No. But in this particular matter, he will do what
he says."

"How can you be sure?"

"Because there is no other force on earth, that I
know of, larger and stronger than ours. Sam Hartline
fell in with the Russian because he believed the
Russian had the manpower to defeat this Ben Raines.
Hartline obviously now believes that Raines will
defeat the Russian. Hartline *always* wants the winning side. As long as we remain victorious, Hartline
will keep his word."

"Hartline, it is reported, has a very powerful group
of mercenaries behind him."

"No doubt."

"We wait?"

"What else can we do?"

"We can kick the ass off that bunch of pussies,"
Skinhead said. He lowered his binoculars and looked
at the other warlords.

"Sure looks that way," Popeye said, his eyes bugging out. He flapped his crooked arms like a vulture.

Grizzly and Sonny Boy exchanged glances. "Maybe
not," Grizzly said.

"What'd you mean?" Popeye asked.

"Looks too easy," Sonny Boy told him.

"I think it's a setup," Grizzly stuck in his two cents' worth. Some native warning device alarmed within him.

"Shit!" Popeye said. "Sam said there was a nigger commandin' this bunch of Rebels. I can't believe you guys is scared of some goddamn sambo."

"That nigger down yonder was Vice-President of the United States," Sonny Boy reminded them all. "And he's Ben Raines's second-in-command. That makes him have some smarts."

"I don't like it," Grizzly said, once more looking through binoculars at the Rebel camp located in the small valley below the ridge. "And there's something else, too."

"What?" Popeye asked.

"How come Sam was so goddamn anxious to get rid of us? I never have trusted that slick bastard, noways. I'd like to know what he's got up his sleeve."

"I agree," Sonny Boy said. "We left in a big rush all hepped up and rarin' to go. Now we've all had some time to think about it." He glanced at Popeye. "Some of us have thought about it, that is. And I don't like what I've been thinkin.' "

"So what are we gonna do?" Skinhead slobbered the question.

"Back off," Grizzly said, his voice low.

"To where?"

"Let's head back an' link up with Plano and his boys. We'll compare notes about Sam Hartline."

"How many guys is Plano got?" Popeye asked.

"Three, four hundred. Buck's runnin' about two fifty or so. If we was to link up with them, that'd give us more'n a thousand men. Nobody could stop us then."

About five hundred meters away, two Rebels lay in the timber, watching the warlords through binoculars. They waited until the outlaws had pulled out. Picking up her walkie-talkie, the Rebel pressed the talk button.

"They're not buying it," she spoke softly. "They're pulling back."

"Keep them in sight and wait until our forward team reports back," she was told.

They waited in the timber for fifteen minutes. They listened as the forward team, located some five miles east of their position, radioed in.

"They're all leaving," the forward team reported. "Heading straight east. Must be five or six hundred bikers and chopper riders and dune buggies and pickup trucks. Never seen such a mess."

"They're leaving no one behind?"

"No. They appear to be riding with a destination in mind."

"They made us," Cecil said. "They smelled a trap and bugged out."

"Shit!" his XO summed up all their feelings.

Cecil laughed at his XO's disgusted one-word summation. "There'll be plenty of fighting in the near future," he said.

"I guess so, sir. But when is General Raines going to *do* something?"

"Only Ben knows that. And so far, he's not talking. But bet on this: he's worrying ideas around in his head like a dog with a bone."

"Goddammit!" Ben said, looking at his bare hook. "Stole my bait again."

Lora looked up as they sat on the bank of a small creek. She smiled at him. "It's easier to catch them with your hands."

"For you, maybe. But this is so relaxing. And fun."

Lora thought about that for a moment, watching as Ben put a fresh worm on the hook. "If it's so much fun, why do you cuss?"

Ben stuck his pole into the ground and lay back on the bank, laughing.

"Now you're having fun," Lora said. "Laying down. But not fishing."

Ben ruffled the child's hair. "You think too much, Lora. Be a kid for a while."

A Rebel stationed some distance behind Ben, in the brush, cleared his throat. A reminder to Ben that no matter where he went, he was never alone. A full squad of Rebels accompanied him whenever he stepped out of the house he was using for a command post.

Worse than being a damned king, Ben thought.

"I don't know how to be a kid, Ben," Lora said. After several weeks of Ben trying to get her to call him by his first name, she had finally agreed.

"Yeah, I know, Lora. Someday the fighting will be over. At least, this fighting. And when that's over, you young people are going back to Georgia. There, you'll learn to read and write and have fun. That sound okay to you?"

"Whatever you say, Ben."

Ben could tell she felt some degree of excitement about that, but would not let her feelings show. She'd been through too many disappointments in her young life.

"I promise you it will get better, Lora. I promise."

"Okay, Ben. Ben?"

"What?"

"There's a fish on your hook and your pole is out in the middle of the crick."

Ben jumped up, and in his haste slipped down the bank and fell into the creek, face first. A dozen Rebels came rushing from all directions, weapons at the ready.

Lora sat on the bank and clapped her hands, laughing at Ben's antics. "Now we're havin' fun, Ben!"

Twenty-four

"Whats he waiting on?" Georgi Striganov muttered, more to himself than to his officers gathered at his command post.

"Perhaps he's afraid of us?" a young IPF lieutenant suggested.

Striganov looked at the fresh-faced officer. There, he thought, stands a fool! But Striganov did not like to dress down fellow officers in the presence of brother officers, so he said nothing.

"The man is like an old lobo wolf," a senior officer said. "He can sense many things the younger wolves have yet to learn." He looked at the young lieutenant as he said the last.

The young lieutenant flushed.

Striganov hid his smile. No need to personally berate the young man; the major had done it for him, quite well.

"He's playing a waiting game, sir," the grizzled, battle-hardened major continued. "Cat and mouse, so to speak."

"But who is the cat and who is the mouse?" Striganov tossed the question out.

A question no one chose to answer.

"On another matter, sir," a captain said. "There is something odd going on in Oregon."

"Odd? With Hartline, you mean?"

"Yes, sir. Our people up there report that Hartline left his base camp for several days. When he returned, he was, well, different."

"Different? My God, give me something more to go on than different."

"Well, sir, he's spending a lot of time with his communications people, for one thing."

Striganov was immediately suspicious. Sam had not been in radio contact with him, he knew that. "Any idea who he might be contacting?"

"He's using ham radio equipment with special scramblers. Our people are busy trying to break it down now. But they have pinpointed the location of the returning transmissions. South Carolina."

Striganov turned in his chair, gazing at nothing. He had known it was bound to happen, someday. And that day had dawned.

Sam Hartline was selling out.

"Something wrong, General?" the major asked.

"Yes," Striganov replied, his back still to his men. "Sam Hartline is turning on us. It does not surprise me. Disappoints me, yes, but comes as no surprise."

"Do you wish to send in a K team, General?" the major asked.

"Not yet. Let's let Sam dig his own grave."

"A lot of radio between Oregon and South Carolina, General," Ben was informed.

"Can you make it out?"

"Bits and pieces. We know for certain Hartline is talking with the commander of the Islamic Peoples Army. Not talking to him directly, but the messages are directed to this Colonel Khamsin."

"So the Hot Wind is beginning to blow," Ben said. "Any further word from our recon teams?"

"Yes, sir. They're in place along the border of South Carolina. Teams from Base Camp One are working with resistance fighters. Recon reports everything is shaping up, but they're not very large in numbers. Not nearly strong enough to try anything head to head with the IPA."

"How about those outlaws and warlords that pulled out of here?"

"They're linked up with those outlaws Hartline put between us and the Mississippi. They're pretty careless about radio security. We can, so far, track every move they make. And . . . something else, sir. I think, our intelligence people think, Sam Hartline is going to turn on the Russian."

Ben nodded his head. "It would be like Sam to do something like that. Sam wants on the winning side. Always. What else?"

"Your name keeps cropping up in these radio transmissions, sir. And, sir . . . General Jefferys has ordered more security around you, at all times."

"Goddammit!" Ben exploded. "I've got a squad around me now. I can't move without bumping into someone."

The Rebel said nothing.

Ben cooled down a bit. "I'm not yelling at you, son. Just letting off a little steam in general."

"Yes, sir."

"James Riverson will be in charge of your security, sir," Ben was informed.

"James is getting entirely too goddamned old for this business," Ben bitched.

The young Rebel wondered how old Ben Raines was. Somewhere around fifty, he thought. He hoped when he was that old he would be as active as Ben.

"Sir? Ike radioed in. His people are getting restless."

"I'm sure," Ben said. "And he's getting too goddamn old for this mess, too."

Again, the Rebel said nothing. Ike McGowan was like a bull, commanding just about as much respect as Ben Raines.

Suddenly, Ben smiled. The young Rebel watched him closely.

"Let's go stick some needles into the IPF," Ben said. He slung on his battle harness and picked up his old Thompson. "Like right now, boy."

"All right," Ben told his hurriedly gathered commanders. "Striganov wants us to bring the fight to him. Fine. We'll do just that. A little at a time. He wants the whole sandwich — we'll give him crumbs."

Ike, Cecil, and Dan began smiling. They had known all along that Ben would not stand and slug it out with the Russian. The Russian had the superior numbers.

Ben was going back to his original plan: a dirty little guerrilla war.

"Ike," Ben said, "send your teams in from the

234

south. Dan, your people will come in from the north. I'll come in from the east. Cec, once again I'm asking you to stay in reserve."

Cecil nodded his understanding if not his liking.

Ben glanced at his watch. Noon. "We'll jump off in twenty-four hours. They'll be expecting us to strike either at night or at dawn. I'm betting they won't be expecting us at high noon, broad daylight. Carry short rations. We'll live off captured IPF supplies and the land. What you won't be carrying in rations, make it up with explosives and ammo. Until we establish some sort of front, we won't have any heavy support. So our first objective will be to clear the roads and get some heavy support in behind us. It's important we all strike at precisely the same time. Within seconds of each other. Good luck; God be with you all. Take off."

All had noticed that Sylvia was conspicuously absent at the briefing. And all wondered why.

But no one was going to ask.

When the room had emptied, James Riverson came to Ben's side. The huge Rebel towered over Ben. The two men had been friends for years, since back in '88, and there was no military formality between them.

"Risky, Ben," James said. "Leaving her behind with all the hard evidence we have against her."

"I think I'm probably doing the same thing Striganov is doing, James."

"Oh?"

Ben walked to a window and gazed outside. Summer was in full bloom in the wilderness. It was a gloriously beautiful day.

James waited, not verbally pushing Ben. He would

get to it when he was ready.

Ben gazed at the beauty of nature now uncontrolled by man's interference. He turned to look at James. "We're absolutely certain now that she has met with people from Colonel Khamsin's IPA?"

"Yes, sir. She was followed on two occasions."

"But we still don't know why she was meeting with them, do we?"

"No, Ben, we don't."

"All of a sudden she cooled toward me. And I don't know why. Why in God's name would she be meeting with representatives of something as odious as the IPA?"

"There again, Ben, I don't know. But I damn sure don't trust her."

"I share your feelings, James."

"What are you and the Russian doing, Ben?"

Ben's face hardened. "Letting a traitor dig their own grave."

Twenty-five

None of the commanders told their people, not yet, but they knew that once Ben started this push there would be no turning back for any of them.

Two things awaited them: victory or the grave.

Cecil returned to his battalion in the eastern part of the state. Ike returned to his people waiting just south of Clear Lake and began moving them out in small teams, toward the IPF's main battle lines. Dan headed back north and began breaking up his people into teams, sending them out toward the northernmost IPF lines. As Ike was doing, Dan's people would be moving into position on both sides of the IPF lines—whenever that was possible. That part of the operation was iffy, for if only one behind-the-lines team was discovered, the entire mission might well be jeopardized.

Ben had already begun sending teams west of Interstate 5, moving them toward the heavy timber and dense wilderness areas.

Ben found Lora and knelt down in front of her, taking her hands. "I'll be back. You look after things around this place, okay?"

"Okay, Ben."

"Keep your eyes on Sylvia, Lora. And don't trust her too far."

"She's a traitor, Ben," the girl said.

"I know."

"I thought she liked you, Ben. I mean . . . liked you a lot."

"So did I, Lora. When did you first suspect her?"

"When she started taking long walks in the woods, by herself. The underground people followed her; some of their kids told me about it."

"Why didn't you tell me?"

"Because you already knew."

Ben smiled. "What did she do in the timber, girl?"

"Met with dark people."

"Dark . . . like Cecil?"

"No. Not that dark. But darker than a good sun tan."

Members of the Islamic Peoples Army. But why? Why would she do it?

Ben had to find out the why.

"I wonder what they talked about?" Ben said, directing the question as much to himself as to the child.

"I don't know. They never could get that close. But . . ." She hesitated, then made up her mind. "The underground people know where the dark people are hiding. They can kill them whenever you want them dead."

And Ben realized then that for all his grand dreams of schooling for Lora and the others like her, and taking into consideration how much he liked her and she liked him, Lora would never give more than a part

238

of herself; the larger part would remain true to the silent code of the wilderness. Her future was as surely set in place as Ben's. Her formative years were behind her, her destiny outlined.

"You'd like to go back to your friends, wouldn't you, Lora?"

"A big part of me would," she said quickly.

"How about school and parties and having fun like other kids, Lora?"

"You don't miss what you never had, Ben."

"I want you all to learn to read and write, Lora. All of you."

"And if we do that for you, Ben?"

"Then the choice of what you want to do and how you want to live the rest of your lives will be up to you."

"It's that important to you?"

"Yes."

She nodded her head. "All right, Ben. We'll do it. For you."

And Ben knew where they would go, probably en masse, once the rudimentary teaching was concluded. Back to the timber.

He ruffled her hair and stood up.

"You're always going to have to have eyes and ears for you, Ben Raines," the child said. "That will be us."

"You take care, Lora."

"See you, Ben."

In his Jeep, Ben looked at his driver. "I would like to see what type of societies will flourish a hundred years from now. I certainly think it will be very interesting."

James Riverson walked up to Ben's Jeep and smiled at him. "The spokesperson for the woods-children pass along their wishes, Ben?"

"Sure did."

"I wondered when they'd tell you. And how. Their life may be hard, Ben, but it's one they've chosen."

"Maybe I can save a few of them by education."

"Maybe."

"But you wouldn't bet on that, would you, James?"

"No, I wouldn't, Ben. How much did Lora know about . . . the person we discussed?"

"A hell of a lot more than I did. Or any of our intelligence people."

"I thought she might. Don't worry about her, Ben. The person in question won't be able to trick Lora. That is one sharp cookie."

"One sharp cookie?" Ben laughed. "That expression dates you, James."

James joined in the laughter. "After we kick the ass off the Russian and kill Hartline, what then, Ben?"

"Then we stick the Hot Wind on ice."

"The bikers and outlaws and warlords?"

"We deal with them, too."

"Never stops, does it, Ben?"

"Well, ol' buddy, if you'll recall, we started this back in . . . '88 or '89. Hell, I can't remember what year it was."

"History will, Ben," the huge Rebel said gently. James Riverson was one of the gentlest and most easygoing men Ben had ever known. Until he got mad. Then he was awesome.

"I hope you're right about that, James. But if it is to be recorded, people are going to have to know how to *read* it."

"Our people will know how to read it, Ben. Our grandkids and their kids and so on up the line. You've seen to that."

Other Rebels had gathered around the Jeep, standing quietly, listening to the exchange between the general and the highest ranking sergeant in the Rebel army.

Ben had offered James officership many, many times in the past. He always refused it, feeling and knowing he could accomplish more as a command sergeant major.

"That isn't enough, James. Education is the key to wiping out savagery and barbarism and it's the only way to bring this nation back from the ashes. And I will destroy anyone or anything who tries to prevent me from accomplishing that." He winked at James. "Head 'em up and move 'em out, Sergeant Major."

"That dates *you*, Ben!" James said with a laugh.

He moved away, yelling orders.

"What'd the sergeant major mean by that, General?" Ben's driver asked.

"That was a line from a very popular TV show of years back," Ben explained. "I think Clint Eastwood used to star in it."

The driver blinked. "Who is Clint Eastwood?"

Ben and his people rode as far as they dared and then stepped down. From here on in, they would walk.

"Recon out," Ben ordered.

The recon teams began moving out.

Ben looked up at the sky. It would be full dark in another two hours. They could cover a lot of ground in that time. Ben took a sip of water from his canteen and squatted down, his team commanders gathered close-by.

"No point in going over it again," Ben said. "You all know where you're supposed to go and what to do when you get there. But I'll tell you now, this is one hell of a gamble. If the Russian has troops that I'm unaware of . . . well, we might find ourselves in a box with lid nailed down."

"Seems like everything we do is a gamble, General," a Rebel captain said. "I think we've all got to be pretty good odds-makers by now."

Ben stood up and pulled his Thompson off right-shoulder sling. "Let's go, gang."

As the recon teams had reported, there were no IPF troops between Interstate 5 and the edge of the great wilderness area. The Rebels force-marched until four o'clock in the morning. That put Ben's team less than two miles from the tiny town of Paskenta, on California state road A9. Ben called a halt, put out guards, and told the rest of his people to get some rest.

Five hours later, Ben's eyes popped open. It was rare for Ben to sleep more than four or five hours at any stretch. And he seldom took naps.

He bathed and shaved with cold water out of a camp bucket and began applying camouflage cream to his face. Black, green, and bark brown. Finished with his face, he painted the backs of his hands.

As he walked the silent camp, he noticed that those

Rebels who had slept their fill were busy with face paint. Getting ready.

Moving up to his forward outpost, Ben slipped into the ditch beside the Rebel manning it. "Seen anything?" Ben asked.

"Nothing lately, sir. But someone is on the roof of that building just to left of that old gas station."

Ben took his Steiner Commander binoculars from their case and sighted the building in. The 7x50 glasses brought it in close. He did not have to worry about sun glinting off the lenses for it was still morning and the sun was to their backs. Exactly as Ben had planned it.

"Damn!" Ben cussed.

"What, sir?"

"They've got an electronic listening device mounted up there. It looks like a good one, too. Those things can pick up sound from a mile away. Maybe even farther than that. Depends on the make. Shit!"

He once more studied the building through the long lenses.

"How's that ditch running up to the right of the building?"

The sentry's eyes twinkled and a smile cut his young face.

"Yeah," Ben said, smiling. "That's what I figured."

"They're just to the left of that clump of trees, General. They went in about two hours ago."

"Type of grenades?" Ben asked. He was not the least irritated that some of his people had taken the initiative. Raines's Rebels were taught that.

"Firefrag, sir."

Probably the most lethal hand grenade every produced. The firefrag is a combination of fragmentation and incendiary.

"Pray they don't get detected," Ben said. "Everybody has to jump off at precisely the same time." He looked at his watch. "Sweat-out time," he said.

Striganov was in a rage, storming around the office, shouting and insulting anyone who happened to have the misfortune to come near him.

His XO stood at formal at-ease in front of the general's desk, waiting out the tirade.

General Georgi Striganov finally wound down and sat down heavily in his padded leather desk chair. His face was flushed, his blood pressure up.

"How?" he said to his XO. "How does the son of a bitch know these things?"

"General Raines?" the XO asked.

"Who the fuck else am I talking about, you idiot!" Striganov screamed.

It was at that moment that the XO realized that what he had been fearing for some months was true. General Striganov was borderline insane. He had suspected, but now he felt his suspicions were true. The XO was a soldier, one hundred percent the Universal Soldier. But he preferred the type of soldiering that conformed to the Geneva Convention. Rules to follow. He did not like torture or other maltreatment of prisoners. Especially against fellow officers. That was unconscionable. And the perversions the general had so recently begun to enjoy. Sick. Sex with mere children. Sick. Sick. Sick.

But he had been with General Striganov for years.

And his thoughts of betrayal made him ill.

But something had to be done.

But what?

Perhaps a meeting with General Raines? . . .

". . . Goddammit, pay attention to me!" Striganov was screaming.

"Yes, General. I was thinking . . ."

"When I want you to think, I'll tell you."

"Yes, General."

"We are alone now. We can expect no help from Hartline. It's confirmed that he has gone over to the wog. We know there has been a pull-out of Raines's troops. So he's going to strike. Question is, where?"

"He'll use guerrilla tactics, sir!"

"Nonsense! He'll hit us hard at one point and try to break through. I know that. I know how Raines's mind works."

"Yes, sir." I have to confide in somebody, the XO thought. We have to stop the general before we lose everything we've fought too hard to attain.

But who?

Striganov rose and walked swiftly to a wall map of California. He punched a spot. "There! Right there is where that damnable Raines will strike."

Wrong, the XO thought. You're wrong. You're losing your grasp of reality, Georgi. And something has to be done. Quickly.

But Striganov was giving orders. "Move everything from the coast to Weaverville north to form a line from Crescent City to Yreka, west to east. Order artillery out, immediately. Then I want you to—"

"*No!*" the XO screamed. "No, goddamn you, no." He fumbled for his sidearm, pulling out the pistol.

"What?" Striganov said, turning, his face paling in shock. "How dare you!" he shouted.

The XO jacked back the hammer on the pistol. "Listen to me closely, Georgi. You're sick. You've got to have help. I respect and admire you, Comrade, but I've watched you deteriorate, mentally, over the months. Please, Georgi, let me help you."

"Put that gun down! Put it down and we'll say nothing about this outrage. But do it now."

"I can't!" the XO's voice was choked with scarcely controlled emotion. It was tearing his guts out to disobey the man he had served for so many years.

Striganov took a step toward his desk, his hand outstretched for the button panel.

"Don't do it!" the XO shouted.

"You won't shoot me," Striganov said.

"I will if I have to. Don't make me wound you, Georgi. Please. I'm begging you."

The office door suddenly banged open, startling both men.

General Georgi Striganov's executive officer pulled the trigger.

Twenty-six

"One more hour," Ben muttered. "I hate waiting."
He looked at his watch.

It was a minute later than the last time he'd glanced at it.

Twice he had detected movement on the rooftop through the long lenses. Those troops up there must be roasting beneath this hot sun, he thought. But that was good. They would not be as attentive with sweat running into their eyes.

He wondered how Ike was taking the waiting.

"Goddammit, I hate waiting!" Ike bitched.

Ike and his team were poised on the northernmost finger of Clear Lake, just outside a small town. An IPF outpost had been spotted and pinpointed. But unlike Ben's team, Ike had managed, due to the terrain, to get close enough for their small 60 mm mortars to be effective.

He glanced at his watch. "Come on, come on!" he muttered.

He wondered how Dan was taking it.

"Thank you," Dan said to his batman. "There is nothing like a good hot cup of tea to refresh one. Please join me, Carl."

"Thank you, sir. I believe I shall."

The two Englishmen sat on the ground and sipped their tea.

Dan's team was located between Big Bar and Helena, waiting for the time to plunge deep into the Trinity wilderness.

The former SAS man stretched out on the cool ground and closed his eyes. "Awaken me in thirty minutes, would you, Carl?"

"Certainly, sir."

The slug from the XO's gun caught Jane in the center of the forehead, busting out the back, splattering brains all over the wall. The girl hit the carpet, trembled once, then lay still.

"Oh, my God!" the XO shouted. "I didn't mean—"

He never got a chance to finish it. Striganov leveled his own pistol and shot the man dead.

The room filled with men and women.

"He went insane," Striganov said, holstering his weapon. "After all the years we spent together, he turned on me, tried to kill me. Poor Jane." He shook his head.

The bodies were removed from the room.

Striganov repeated his original orders. "Full scale," he told the officers. "We stand and slug it out with

Ben Raines. As men of honor should do. Professionals. Move out."

"Sir!" Carl's voice brought Dan wide awake.

Dan glanced at his watch. "Carl, I've just closed my eyes."

"The entire northern line of IPF troops are moving forward, sir."

"Are you serious, Carl?"

Carl handed Dan his binoculars. "Look, sir."

Dan looked, then paled slightly as the lenses picked up the northern movement of a couple of thousand men in combat gear, half-tracks and tanks and motorized artillery moving behind them.

"Lady Di's bustle," Dan muttered. "Would you take a look at that."

Carl frowned at this disrespect toward royalty.

Dan waved his second-in-command over to his side. "Order all the lads and lassies to hunt a hole and to keep their heads down. Pick areas where the foot troops and the vehicles are not likely to go. Move!"

Dan smiled at Carl. "Come on, Carl. We've got to get to a radio."

Momentarily safe in timber on a small rise, Dan raised Ben's radio operator. "Get General Raines right now!" he said.

Ben listened, disbelief clouding his features. But he knew Dan too well. If the Englishman said IPF troops were advancing en masse, they were. "How many, Dan?"

"At least three battalions, sir. With tanks and artillery with them."

Ben could hear the rumble of tanks and motorized artillery over the air, through the miles that separated them. "Jesus, Dan! They must be right on top of you."

"Close enough to permit me the indignity of smelling them," Dan said.

Ben grinned at the Englishman's calmness. "I don't know why Striganov is doing this, but the odds have suddenly swung in our favor. Dan, I've ordered the battalion north of you down. You swing in behind the IPF troops. Hit them hard, Dan."

"Yes, sir." Dan clicked off.

Ben radioed Ike, bringing him up to date. Ike laughed. "And a good time is gonna be had by all. Good luck, Ben."

"Same to you, buddy. Look at your watch, Ike."

"Twelve straight up, Ben."

"Go!"

Ike turned to his XO. "Drop the little birdies down the tubes."

Ben punched the talk button on his walkie-talkie. "Hit 'em hard!"

The rockets *thunked* out of the tubes.

Two hundred miles to the north, firefrag grenades were tossed onto the roof.

The attack was on.

"We are meeting no resistance," the commander of the IPF's northernmost troops radioed back to General Striganov. "We have not even *seen* the enemy."

"Fool!" Striganov screamed into the mike. "Of course the Rebels are there. Where else *could* they be?"

All in your crazied mind, the grizzled major thought, but did not vocalize. He had heard the XO had been killed by Georgi. That something terrible had happened. That the young girl, Jane, was dead. That the XO went insane and tried to kill Georgi. That Georgi had, all that morning, ranted and raved like a . . .

Like a . . .

Madman!

From his APC, the major made up his mind. "Halt advance!" he ordered through his headset.

The thinly spread column ground to a halt.

The foot soldiers dropped to the ground, thankful for the respite, however brief.

Less than a thousand yards away, a mortar team from Dan's command had leveled the bubble on the tube. His team had panted and sweated and cussed the 115-pound 81mm mortar through and over terrain that would have made a moose stagger.

Now the cammie-painted faces, streaked with dusty sweat, grinned. Now it would be worth it all.

"At the max we're gonna have time for three rounds before that Russian can react and move," the Rebel said. His team was the best in the Rebel army, able to get off one round every 3.05 seconds. "HE," he ordered, "followed by WP, then a frag round, then a WP. Do it."

It was luck, with more than a tad of skill. The first round landed ten feet from the APC. It lifted the armored personnel carrier off the ground and dumped it wrong side up. The second round landed on top of the APC, sending bits and pieces of seared and smoking metal and fried flesh all over the silence-shattered landscape.

There were three battalions of IPF troops spread over a ninety-mile stretch. Two full platoons of IPF infantry were close to the APC when the attack started. The IPF troops had no way of knowing how large a force was attacking them. Or how small a force.

Had they known that only a handful of Rebels stood between them and victory, they would have taken the initiative and easily overrun the Rebel's position.

Instead they panicked and ran.

The leading edge of the battalion of Raines's Rebels, moving swiftly from the north, had barreled down existing highways, the battalion split, one section coming down Highway 96, the other column rolling south on Highway 3. That column turned west at Weaverville and smashed through to Junction City, catching the IPF forces by surprise in a flanking movement.

They left the landscape littered with dead and dying members of the IPF.

The westernmost column of Rebels split up at Hoopa, taking a secondary highway and meeting the IPF troops just north of Highway 299.

Using sappers, they blew the bridge over the Redwood River and blocked Highway 299, trapping several platoons of IPF troops. The IPF troops could do nothing except retreat back to the south.

Leaving only a small force of heavily armed and well-dug-in Rebels north of the Redwood, the remainder of the motorized column headed east on 299.

With tanks spearheading, the Rebels blasted and smashed through the thin lines of already confused and demoralized IPF troops; those IPF troops now leaderless and in a panic.

The IPF troops, neither trained nor skilled in guerrilla warfare, found that whatever direction they turned, they faced some new hideousness from the Rebels.

Those bastards and bitches that made up Ben Raines's Rebel army just simply did not play the game of warfare fairly.

And what in God's name—God's name?—were children doing in war?

God's name?

That thought seared through the minds of many IPF troops as they ran in panic, searching for someone to tell them what to do.

But there was no one.

So the IPF ran and sweated and died.

Ike's team knocked out the small force of IPF personnel and stormed across the battle lines. All up and down Highway 20, from Fort Bragg on the coast to Nice, the Rebels surged across the line and into IPF territory.

Ike stepped around a corner and came face to face with a young Russian. Lifting his submachine gun, Ike sent the Russian into the arms of that shrouded bony gentlemen.

Swinging his weapon, on full auto, Ike cleared the street of all living things and waved his team forward, ejecting the empty clip and slapping home a full, fresh one.

He grabbed his radio operator and told him to get Ben on the horn.

"Ben! I'm going to skirt the heavy timber and ram up the coast on 101. Can you pull Cecil's bunch in?"

"Affirmative," Ben radioed back, the sounds of gunfire and explosives loud in Ike's ears through the headset. "Pull all your civilian fighters up from the valley and spread them along Highway 20. That'll close off the south end of the box. I'll have Cecil's gang spread along the edge of the wilderness, closing off the eastern escape hole. I'll put Dan in charge of everything up north and we'll start the squeeze. You copy this?"

"Ten-four, Ben. Out."

"I copy your transmission, General," Dan radioed in. "Carrying out orders."

"Ten-four, Dan."

"I'm moving now, Ben," Cecil radioed. "We'll plug it up from this end."

"Go!" Ben spoke into the mike. "Go, Go, Go!"

"Now I see why you wanted out," a mercenary said to Sam Hartline.

The men sat monitoring a radio. They could not understand any of the Rebel transmissions—they were all scrambled—but they could understand the frantic radio messages from IPF.

"Yeah," Sam said. "Striganov flipped out. I've been watching him over the months; especially the last few months. I could see it coming. Striganov is finished. Raines waited him out and he's going to win." He reached over and flipped off the radio. "Fuck him!" Sam said. "Khamsin may be a goddamned wog, but at least he's stable."

"But can he be trusted?"

"No," Sam said, then smiled. "But then, neither can I."

They all got a good laugh over that.

"How about the kid your patrol just captured? What's his name?"

"Rich is all I know. I think he's a fag."

"The girls got away?"

"Every one of them. One of my boys said one young chick had an ass and a set of tits you wouldn't believe. But looked to be just a kid."

"Shame," Hartline said. "Good-looking, young, tight pussy is getting hard to find. Bring the kid in."

Hartline watched as Rich was shoved into the room. He could go either way, Hartline thought. Just a little push and he's queer all the way.

"Has he been searched?"

"All the way, Sam."

"He's clean?"

"Right."

"You guys leave us alone. I wanna talk to Rich."

Sam and the boy were alone. Rich refused to meet Sam's knowing eyes."

"Get naked, boy," Sam told him.

Rich stripped and stood before Sam. He had a slight erection.

"I thought so," Sam said. He unzipped his trousers and exposed himself. "You ever seen a cock this big?"

Rich shook his head.

"Come here, boy. You give me some good head.

And then you and me are goin' to have a little chat. Aren't we, Rich?"

"Yes, sir."

"Come here, boy. Let's get to know each other."

Twenty-seven

Ben called a halt to it at five o'clock. His Rebels had the IPF on the run, and it was a near rout.

Ike and his people had advanced more than sixty miles up Highway 101. With the IPF on the run, Ben's forces had driven all the way through the wilderness area and linked up with Ike's troops at what remained of a town called Cummings, about thirty miles from the coast. Cecil and his troops had begun the dangerous job of mopping up behind Ben. Dan Gray and his troops had driven down and retaken towns all the way down to Highway 36. His people had taken two of Striganov's research centers.

"How do they look?" Ben had radioed.

"Disgusting. Sickening," he was told. "What do you want done with the IPF medical people we captured?"

Ben's first thought was to shoot them. Then he realized that they might best be kept alive. They were the ones who had done this to the humans they'd captured. He wanted to talk with them; see what kind of people would do—whatever it was they had done—to another human being.

"Keep them alive," he ordered. "I want to talk to them."

"Yes, sir."

"What do the . . . those experimented upon look like?"

"It's . . . they're babies, sir. The doctors told us they were perfecting a worker race. They aren't human, but they aren't animal, either. Sir, what are we going to do with them?"

"I don't know, son. I just don't know."

"Sir?" Dan's voice broke out of the speaker.

"Go ahead, Dan."

"The woods-children tell me the underground people will take the . . . ah, babies. Care for them. Raise them."

Ike sat looking at Ben and listening, sucking on a pipestem. When Ben looked at him, Ike lifted his shoulders in a "don't ask *me*" gesture.

"You're a lot of help," Ben good-naturedly bitched at him.

"Beg pardon, sir?" Dan spoke.

"Not you, Dan. Ike."

"Oh, yes, quite. Fatso."

Ike almost swallowed the pipestem.

Ben signed off quickly.

Vasily Lvov had ordered the loading of those patients—so-called—and the babies from the two medical centers close to Striganov's command post.

Then he went to see the general.

"It's over now, Georgi," the scientist said softly but bluntly.

"No," Striganov said. "I shall defeat Ben Raines."

"Sometime in the future, I am certain of that," Lvov said. "But not now. Georgi, we only have two full battalions left us."

Striganov looked at the doctor, inner pain visible in his pale eyes. "Two?"

"Two."

"But I had eight full battalions, Vasily. And two in reserve."

"Yes, I know. And it's very doubtful Raines's Rebels destroyed them all. But they are in a panic; a rout. When we get settled, they'll join us. Just like before. Remember, Georgi?"

Striganov sighed. Yes, he thought. Just like before, when Ben Raines and his Rebels slapped us down to our knees.

God*damn* the man!

God?

Then it came to General Georgi Striganov. My old friend was right. I am sick. Mentally sick. "Vasily?"

"Yes, General. I am here."

"Where will we go?"

"Canada."

"You've thought much on this." It was not phrased as a question.

"Yes, General. I have that."

"Vasily, is Ben Raines a god?"

"I . . . I don't know, Georgi. I rather doubt it. But I can't be sure. Do you believe in God, Georgi?"

"I . . . I think I might, Vasily. Some . . . form of higher power, at least."

259

"Truth time, Georgi?"

"Of course."

"I always have."

"I'm sick, Vasily."

"I know. But you're not very sick. You've been under tremendous pressure. But you're going to get well. We need you, Georgi. And I mean that. Not as a scientist; you don't know beans concerning that area. But as a leader, we need you."

Georgi managed a smile. "I suppose I have been a very large pain in the ass, haven't I, Vasily?"

The doctor returned the smile. "At times, Georgi. At times."

The two men enjoyed a rare moment of humor.

Vasily said, "I'm going to give you a shot, General. You will not remember the flight to Canada. It's very doubtful you will remember very much for several days. I'm going to keep you sedated. You're going to rest, you're going to eat, and you're not going to worry about anything. Do I have your permission, old friend?"

"Yes." He stood up and rolled up his sleeve. "I'm ready anytime you are."

Ben had been asleep for several hours when James shook his shoulder, waking him.

"Ben. Lots of planes taking off and leaving from the IPF HQ near the coast."

Ben quickly dressed and stepped outside, walking to the makeshift radio room in a deserted motel. He picked up the mic. Dan was on the other end.

"Where are they heading, Dan?"

"North-northeast, General. All of them taking and maintaining the same heading. My lads at the border report the course is true."

"And lassies," Ben said with a smile.

"Ah, yes, sir. Must'n forget the ladies. Your orders, sir?"

"Go back to bed and get some sleep. We're not going to do anything this night. Continue mopping up and advancing at first light. I've got a hunch Striganov is bugging out for Canada. Alberta or Saskatchewan. We'll find out soon enough, I'll bet. Thanks, Dan. And good night."

"Good night, General."

Ben stopped on his way back to his bed. He looked toward the north. "I wonder what that goddamned Hartline is up to?"

"Hello, baby," Sam spoke around his grin. "My, aren't you a little thing. What's your name?"

"Lisa."

"Pretty name for a pretty girl. We're going to have fun, baby. Just you and me."

She cut her eyes to Rich. There was a smirk on his face. "You told."

He shrugged.

"Oh, don't blame him, pretty baby. Rich just found something he liked better than pussy."

"The others got away," Lisa told Rich. "Kim figured it was you who tattled. They'll get you, Rich. They'll get you."

"You wanna watch this, Rich?" Sam asked the boy.

"I wouldn't miss it for the world," Rich said.

"It isn't Rich's fault," Ann said to the others. "He can't stand any type of pain. And he is what he is because of his parents. I grew up with Rich. We were neighbors."

"I'm not blaming him for what he is," Kim said. "We have boys and girls like that among our group back in the safe territory. They fight right alongside the rest of us. Some of them have gone to their death silently. So could Rich. My hunch is he never had any pain put on him. He's just weak all the way through. And I'll tell you something else he is."

The others waited.

Kim finished. "He's dead!"

Colonel Khamsin had difficulty sleeping that night. Finally, in the hours just before dawn, he kicked off his thin covering and got up. His recon teams to the west had reported a large-scale battle yesterday. And now many planes had been taking off from the Russian's location.

What did it mean? Was the Russian leaving? Had he been defeated? Or had Ben Raines been defeated?

It was so like Sam Hartline not to radio and inform him as to what was taking place.

When this was over and done, Khamsin felt the best thing he could do would be to kill Sam Hartline.

With that thought in mind, Colonel Khamsin returned to his bed and slept soundly.

Ben was not prepared for the sight that greeted him at the experiment station near Striganov's offices.

He walked outside and vomited his lunch on the ground.

"Jesus God!" Ben said. "What kind of creatures are those in there?"

"A near-perfect worker breed," one of the captured IPF doctors said.

Ben looked at him.

"And if you people had not come meddling along with your high and mighty—and ill-thought-out, I might add—ideals of races being equal, we would have succeeded in perfecting the breed."

Ben resisted an impulse to shoot the bastard where he stood.

"Why were these few left behind?" Ben asked.

"They probably didn't have room for them."

"Where did Striganov go?"

"I do not know, General Raines. But if I may make an educated guess? . . . Thank you. I would suggest Canada."

"Alberta, Saskatchewan?"

"Probably. It would be a fertile area where crops would grow. General Striganov has admitted on more than one occasion that this area was wrong; that he made a mistake coming here."

"Listen to me, whatever your name is . . ."

"My name is—"

"Shut your mouth!"

The Russian's mouth clamped shut. Tightly. He wasn't accustomed to being spoken to in such a crude manner. He was a scientist, not some grunting soldier. But he decided he'd best kept those thoughts to himself.

This Ben Raines was a savage-looking man. Such mean eyes!

"How many women left here are pregnant with these . . . things?"

"I'll have to examine them, sir."

"Fine. Good. You do that. And then you will abort them. Is that understood?"

"Yes, sir."

"And goddamn you, they'd better all survive. Do you understand *that*?"

"Sir! As a doctor and scientist, I cannot give any guarantees as to —"

Ben slapped him, first open-palmed, then a savage backhand. The man fell to the ground, moaning and holding his busted and bleeding mouth.

"Bear this in mind, then, *Doctor*. For the rest of your life, and that might be very short, you are going to look after these unfortunate men and women you slimy bastards and bitches used as guinea pigs. So don't screw up, Doctor. You can't afford it. Understood?"

"Yes, sir!"

"Move your ass!"

Hartline was oblivious to the girl's pain-filled cries and the bleeding where he had ripped her with his savage attack.

He rose from the floor where he had taken her in a maddened lust, and looked down at her.

"You'll see, baby," he said. "It'll get good to you after a time."

He threw back his head and laughed. "Tell me, Lisa, baby. You still think Ben Raines is a god?"

"Yes," she moaned.

Sam picked up his belt from the dresser and began beating her nakedness.

Seated in a chair, Rich watched in wet-lipped fascination. "Hit her again, Sam!" he yelled. "Hit her harder!"

Book Three

Life is eternal; and love is immortal; and death is only a horizon; and a horizon is nothing save the limit of our sight.

— Rossiter W. Raymond

Twenty-eight

Ben stood firm with his initial orders: no prisoners from among any IPF troops.

The order was really not necessary, for no IPF troops offered to surrender. Now Ben's Rebels had the unenviable task of mopping up after the swift victory.

And any combat vet can tell you that mopping up can be pure hell.

And nothing was heard from Sam Hartline. It was as if the mercenary did not really give a damn what happened south of the Oregon border.

But Ben wasn't buying that. He knew—felt, rather—than Hartline was up to something. Trouble was, Ben didn't know what.

Ben wasn't about to knock heads with Hartline . . . yet. Hartline's mercenary army was just about as large as Ben's force of Rebels. And they were well-rested and just as well-equipped as the Rebels.

So what were they waiting for? Why didn't they strike and strike hard?

Ben didn't know.

As Ben stood by the stone fence on the bluffs overlooking the Pacific Ocean, his thoughts kept turning away from impending war to the sight of the raging ocean. Huge waves battered the coastline, smashing with a seemingly organized fury. Ben wondered what had caused such climatic changes in the Pacific; and where did all this fury originate?

Standing by the stone fence, it was impossible to carry on any type of normal conversation. So when Ike approached him, Ben stepped away from nature's frenzy and walked with his friend to a spot where they could talk without having to scream at each other over the howling winds.

"That's a hell of a sight back there, isn't it, Ben?"

"Yes. And if it keeps up, that writer who predicted the fall of California is going to be correct. The coastline can't take many more years of this."

"The babies are gone, Ben," Ike said quietly.

"When?"

"Early this morning. Wade and Ro each came to a center and asked that all personnel leave. When the personnel returned, the babies were gone. What do you reckon the underground people will *do* with them?"

"Raise them, I suppose, Ike." And once again, the thought came to Ben that in a hundred years, the inhabitants of earth would surely be a sight to see. And he wondered if, at that time, it would be called the Ashes of Peace, or the Ashes of Silence?

He would like to view it.

"The areas clean, Ike?"

"Clean as a whistle. All the way from the Bay area to the Oregon line. If there are any pockets of IPF folks left, damned if we can find them."

"Probably in the heavy timber. Hell with them,"

Ben said. "Any word from the girls I sent into Hartline's territory?"

"The original three are okay. One of the kids they picked up got taken prisoner. By Hartline's men."

"A girl?"

"Yes. And a boy. The boy first. The girls think the boy betrayed them. They're not leaving until they get the girl back and see the boy dead."

Ben sighed. "How old was the girl taken?"

"Twelve, maybe thirteen. Cute kid, so Kim radioed back."

"You can bet that Hartline has used her badly."

"I'm sure."

"Ben?"

Ben cut his eyes.

"Cecil just sent word that Sylvia is in cahoots with some IPA people. It's firm."

"I suspected as much. It's the why of it that puzzles me."

"Me, too. But I have no idea."

"I'll deal with her very shortly. Lora?"

"Learnin' her ABC's. Some of Doc Chase's people took her in. Ben, you know she's gonna go back with her own kind, don't you?"

"Yes." But the word came hard; Ben had grown terribly fond of the child.

"I damn near forgot what I came over here to tell you, Ben. The civilian leaders are here. You wanted to talk to them, remember?"

"Yes. Come on, walk with me. We'll talk along the way."

Walking along, Ben said, "We lucked out again, Ike."

"I know. We'd have had a hell of a battle on our hands if the Russian hadn't of flipped out. Or whatever happened to him."

"We're not going to be so lucky with Hartline. I feel that in my guts."

"You ain't alone. That plus all those bikers and warlords between us and Base Camp One."

"We're going to stay right here until we can figure out what Hartline has on his mind. I want our people rested and ready to go." He smiled. "As soon as we can determine where we're going, that is."

Ben met with the civilian leaders in the warm open air of California summer. He was mildly surprised to see George Williams from Chico in attendance. The man looked fit, was dressed in decent clothing, and was standing a little taller than the last time Ben had seen him.

George shook hands with Ben, away from the others. "I guess you got to me, General Raines," George admitted. "I don't agree with all you say or stand for, but for a time, yours is the only way. I finally got that through my thick head."

"Good to have you with us, George."

Ben shook hands with the other George, from Red Bluff; Harris from Redding; Pete Ho from Ukiah; and John Dunning from Santa Rosa.

"We'll be leaving this area in a short time," Ben told the gathering. He watched their faces closely. No one seemed at all surprised by the announcement.

"By now you all know that General Striganov is gone. We have reason to believe he and what is left of his IPF went to Canada. It's doubtful that he'll return. But Sam Hartline is still very much around.

We're going to deal with Sam in due time. But let me warn you all of a new danger. Colonel Khamsin and his Islamic Peoples Army have landed in South Carolina. And I mean his *army*. He has thousands of men and women. You may think because you're all some three thousand miles away, you have nothing to fear.

"You're wrong."

Ben let that soak in.

"We have reason to believe Sam Hartline and his people have linked up with this Khamsin. My people will deal with Hartline. Most of you are not ready to join us as regulars. Not yet. But in time you'll be called upon to assist us. I'm not going to fight all your battles for you.

"I'm going to leave a small force of Rebels behind. They will train you. And people, you'd better goddamn well get ready for some hard training. What you'll be receiving is a combination of Ranger, SEAL, Marine Force Recon, and Green Beret training, with a touch of Special Air Service and French Foreign Legion training tossed in for good measure. When my people get through with you, you'll all be able to fight a grizzly with a stick . . . or you'll be dead. One or the other."

Pete Ho raised his hand. Ben nodded at him. "General, some of my people might not want to take part in this. What happens then?"

"Are you referring to able-bodied men and women, Pete?"

"Yes, sir."

"That won't cut it, Pete. We don't allow shirkers. One is either one hundred percent for the movement, or one hundred percent against it. It has to be that way. That answer your question?"

"And those who won't fight?" Pete persisted.

"You run them out," Ben said flatly.

"That's pretty hard, General."

"Hard times, Pete."

The warlords and outlaws had gathered in Colorado. Calling them a motley crew would be understating the matter. This gathering was the largest meeting of malcontents, trash, scum, and human filth to come together in years. One would be hard-pressed to find one redeeming quality in the entire force.

Their names were what one might expect from men of such low degree: Booger, Utah Jack, Pisser, Stud, Big Luke, Flash, Long Tongue . . . and so it went.

Some had roamed the country together for more than a decade, raping, robbing, killing, having their way wherever they chose and however they wanted it.

But they were always careful to abide by one hard and fast rule: Stay away from areas controlled by Ben Raines and his Rebels.

Now they felt they were strong enough to tackle Ben Raines and his Rebels—and come out on top.

"You trust Sam Hartline?" Plano asked Grizzly.

"No. Least not no hundred percent. He knows that we know he's usin' us. He also knows he can't do much of nothin' about it. We got to have him; he's got to have us."

"How 'bout these here A-rabs you was tellin' us about?" Buck asked.

"Colonel Khamsin. A Hot Wind."

"So's a fart," Booger said.

"Lemme put it another way," Grizzly said. "Khamsin impresses Sam Hartline."

That was enough to sober the outlaws. Sam Hartline might be a mercenary, but he was no dummy. If Khamsin had enough beef behind him to impress Hartline . . . well, that was good enough for the outlaws.

"And now we do what? . . ." Booger asked.

"We contact Hartline and wait for word. Way I figure it is Hartline will use us to mop up what's left of Raines's Rebels."

"Sounds good to me."

The rest of the outlaws gathered around laughed. "Just think," one said, straining his brain. "There must be four or five million pussies left in the States."

"So?" Skinhead asked.

"Without Ben Raines and his people standing in our way, hell, man! They're all ours!"

"Yeah!" they breathed.

"I like it!" Skinhead slobbered.

"I don't like it, Ben," Cecil said. "You're deliberately setting yourself up for a lot of trouble."

"Reading between the lines, Cec," Ben replied, smiling, "it would be a good plan if I weren't planning on leading it. Right?"

Cecil muttered something extremely vulgar under his breath.

"I must concur with General Jeffreys, sir," Dan said. "You are needed here. Not traipsing about the countryside, shooting outlaws."

"I got to go along with them, Ben," Ike said. "Let me take the unit out after the outlaws."

"I shall go!" Dan said.

"No, *I'll* go!" Cecil said.

"I'm leaving in the morning," Ben put an end to it.

Twenty-nine

Ben started sending his unit out in the darkness of night. As quietly as possible, running without lights. He had ordered his Rebels to bandage various parts of their bodies; to limp and stagger as if badly hurt. To be helped into the waiting trucks.

He knew Hartline had long-range recon teams watching the base camp through long lenses. And he knew Khamsin's people were close-by, watching. Maybe they would think the badly wounded were being trucked back to Base Camp One.

Maybe it would work long enough for Ben's unit to get close to the outlaws.

Maybe.

Ben and his personal team would be the last to pull out. Just moments before leaving, Ben walked to Sylvia's quarters.

She was sitting in a chair, as if expecting him.

The man and woman looked at each other in the sputtering light of a camp lantern.

"I cannot tolerate a traitor," Ben broke the silence.

"How long have you known?" she asked.

"I've suspected for some time."

"But you don't know or understand why I did it, do you, Ben?"

"No. I'd like to be able to say I'm not particularly interested. But I'd be lying."

"We had something good beginning, Ben."

"Using vernacular before you were born: You blew it, kid."

"It isn't too late, Ben."

"I could never trust you, Sylvia. Not ever again. You see, kid, I knew someone like you years ago. Back when the nation was whole. I fell hard for her. The only difference being, ours was a purely Platonic relationship. Do you know what that means?"

"Yes."

"As a matter of fact, you look a lot like her. You have many of her mannerisms. Perhaps that's why I felt something for you I haven't felt in a long, long time."

"You must have loved her a great deal, Ben."

Memories took Ben winging back over the years. She slipped into his mind, as she did from time to time. He had never spoken of her, not to anyone — ever. He had been about twenty years older than the girl — and even though she was in her twenties, she was still a girl. A girl in a woman's body.

And he loved her then, almost as strongly as he loved her now.

The tough ex-soldier and ex-soldier-of-fortune-turned-writer had fallen asshole over elbows in love.

If she had asked for the stars and the moon, Ben would have somehow gotten them for her.

Yet, so it seemed, to Ben, every time he turned around, she was crapping all over him.

Ben almost drank himself to death over a period of a few months . . . until he slowly began wising up and realizing what the young woman really was. Greedy, grasping, ungrateful, petty, petulant. A very pretty but shallow person.

And she had taken him like a schoolboy enduring the pain of first love.

And it still hurt.

Ben looked at Sylvia. "How much have you told Khamsin's people?"

"Troop strength. Placement. Plans for the future. Everything I knew."

"Why, Sylvia?"

"They have my father."

"How do you know it's him? I thought you told me he was dead?"

"He fits the description. It's him."

"Why didn't you just come to me and tell me?"

"I didn't think."

"That's right . . ." He almost called her by another name. She didn't think either. Only of now. Never of the future.

Ben felt he was reliving the past.

"You've probably gotten some Rebels killed, Sylvia. Have you thought about that?"

"I don't *care* about that. It's my father."

"If he fell in with Khamsin, then he must be a sorry bastard."

She did not reply. But Ben saw her right hand move ever so slowly toward her right boot. She carried a knife there.

"You know what happens to traitors, Sylvia," he said softly.

"I love you, Ben."

"You're a liar."

Just like . . . her.

"How do you know that? You can't be sure."

"I've been here before, kid. Unfortunately, I know your type very well."

"Asshole!" she hissed at him.

"We all have one."

"Aren't you afraid of dying, Ben Raines?" she asked him.

"Not particularly." He smiled. "But it always seems to come at such an inconvenient time. Doesn't it, kid?"

She came up fast, the double-edged dagger in her right hand.

Ben shot her right between her flashing green eyes. The .45 slug tore out the back of her head, lashing the wall behind her with fluid and gray matter and bits of bone. Sylvia slumped to the floor.

Ben walked out of the house just as Rebels came running.

Ike was the first to reach Ben. Ben cut sad eyes to his friend.

"Tell the underground people to destroy the IPA's forward recon team, Ike."

"Okay, Ben. Jesus, Ben! What happened in there?"

"A twenty-year-old one-sided love affair just ended, Ike."

"What?"

Ben walked away, the .45 in his hand. Ike noticed two things about his friend, as Ben walked into the velvet of night.

The man seemed to be a bit lonelier.

And Ben Raines was crying.

"What the hell's he up to, now?" Sam Hartline said, more to himself than to the other mercenaries gathered in Hartline's command post.

"Pullin' his wounded out, looks like."

"Maybe. But why didn't he fly them out? That's what he usually does."

No one had an answer to that.

"Anyone spotted Raines today?" Hartline asked.

"Our guys had to pull back. Things were gettin' too hot. The recon team from Khamsin bought it early this morning. Our guys got a little edgy and moved deeper into the timber."

Hartline nodded his handsome head. "Those weirdos that live in the caves?"

"Yeah."

Sam Hartline walked to a window and looked out. "Raines is up to something. I just don't know what. But what I don't want to do is butt heads with him just yet. We might be able to take him, but it would cost us. And Oregon just isn't worth it."

"You want me to contact Khamsin?" Sam was asked.

Hartline shook his head. "Not yet. Let's find out where that convoy went first. See if you can get ahold of those bikers. Ask them — no, *tell* them, to keep their heads up, stay alert. Raines is about to pull something. Sneaky son of a bitch."

"How's Rich?" a mercenary asked, a smile on his face.

Hartline laughed. "He has just about outlived his

usefulness. Any of you guys want him?"

No one did.

"I hate to just shoot the little bastard. He gives great head," Hartline said. "And he's like a whipped dog. He'll do anything you tell him to do." Hartline dismissed Rich with a curt wave of his hand. "I'll keep him around until I get tired of fuckin' with him." Sam laughed. "I been tryin' to get him to pork Lisa, but he won't do it."

Sam had left her alone for a couple of days, and some of the soreness had eased within her. Lisa had thought of and rejected a dozen plans of escape. Rich was always with her, watching, ready to tattle.

"You're a fool, Lisa!" Rich spat the words at her. "Why don't you be nice to Sam? He'd make it a lot easier on you if you'd just be nice to him."

"Like you're nice to him?" Lisa's words were scornful.

"I'll slap you!" Rich hissed.

"I'll kick your ass, too!" Lisa backed him down.

"He'll get tired of you, Lisa, if you don't start being nice to him. Then he'll give you to his men. You'd like that, wouldn't you, bitch?"

"No, I wouldn't, Rich." Her smile was not nice, filled with knowing. "But you would."

"God, I hate you!"

"Rich, if we worked together, we could get out of here."

"Why should I? I've got it made here. I have plenty to eat, nice clothes to wear, I can bathe every day in hot water and good-smelling soap. Sam likes me."

"Sure, Rich. Just as long as you suck him off, that is."

"I know you hate me."

"Rich, I don't hate you for what you are. That's your business. Your right. You can stay here or leave. That's up to you. I'm just asking you to help me get out. Will you?"

They both heard Hartline enter the fine house. Rich jumped up and ran out of the room.

"Sam! Sam!" Rich yelled. "Lisa's trying to get me to help her escape!"

Sam walked into the room and looked at Lisa. "You stupid bitch. You don't know what side your bread is buttered on, do you?"

Lisa sat on the floor, looking up at him.

Sam slowly removed his belt. "Strip, baby. I guess I'm going to have to break you like a goddamned horse."

Lisa made up her young mind. "I'll die first," she said.

"That's a distinct possibility, baby," Sam told her. "But if I can't break you, then I'll give you to my men. And if you think I'm kinky, you haven't seen anything yet."

Lisa jumped from the floor and tried to run out the door. Rich tripped her, sending her sprawling. She felt her jeans being ripped from her and Sam's laughter ringing in her head.

"I gave you a chance, pretty thing," Sam said. "I guess you were born to like it rough."

She was jerked to her knees and the leather began singing and popping against her flesh.

"We get to ambush a convoy of wounded Rebels," Plano said to Grizzly. "They'll be here in a couple of days. And they're headin' right for us."

"How many?"

"Hell, what difference does it make? For chrissakes, they're all shot up. Piece of cake."

"Any women with 'em?" Big Luke asked.

"Sure. And about a platoon of Rebels escortin' them. Let's start gettin' set."

"I'm gonna enjoy this," a biker said. "That goddamned Ben Raines has been a pain in the ass for years. I was down in Arkansas when him and them Rebels rolled in. Run me and my boys out. Didn't even give us a chance. I'm gonna really like this."

"Did they fall for it?" Ben asked James.

"Scouts report they did. They're getting into ambush position." He pointed to a spot on a map of Colorado. "Right there."

"How many?"

"About three hundred of them. The others have spread out north and south."

"They picked a pretty good spot for it," Ben conceded. "Have they mined the road?"

"Negative, Ben. They've got some dynamite and grenades, but no mines that our observers can detect."

"Straight bang-bang, shoot-'em-up ambush, huh? They must think we're idiots."

"I don't know what they think, Ben. I would imagine most of them are very stupid and very arrogant. And that's a bad combination."

"Lucky for us, though. All right, James. Send First Platoon to the north, Second Platoon to the south. How about those vehicles we found?"

"They'll run long enough to get the people there."

"That's all that matters. Tell our teams to skirt the outlaws north and south and get into position on the east end of the highway. Wait for our signal."

"Why are you doing this, Ben?" James asked. "Why the bikers first?"

"Saving the best for last, James. Hartline is going to be a tough nut to crack."

"You really want to kill him, don't you, Ben?"

Ben nodded. "Hartline doesn't know it. But he's a walking-around dead man."

Thirty

The outlaws had indeed chosen a fine place for an ambush. If the person they wished to ambush had not been Ben Raines, that is.

Ben was often referred to by his enemies as being a sneaky son of a bitch. The latter was totally incorrect. The former summed it up quite well.

The outlaws and warlords and their motley crews had gathered on both sides of the interstate, carefully hidden among the rocks and brush on each sloping side of the carved-through mountain. They lay in wait with automatic weapons and grenades.

They had only one small problem: Ben Raines wasn't about to drive through the ambush site.

Ben had halted the column less than two miles from the ambush site and ordered his people out to have lunch. Sitting by the side of the road, in the shade of the trucks.

"Of all the stupid, shitty times to stop and eat!" an outlaw leader named Flash said, looking at the halted convoy through binoculars. "Jesus Christ! Here we sit up here, sweating our balls off in the sun, and them fuckers is *eatin'*!"

"It ain't fair," another biker said. "We didn't bring no food with us."

"Well, that ain't my fault!" Flash said irritably. "How the hell did I know we was gonna be up here this long?"

None of them could hear or see the Rebels high above them, quietly getting into position. None of the outlaws could see or hear the Rebels who had circled around and were now getting into position on the east side of the interstate, about five hundred meters east of the ambush site.

The outlaws were now, unknowingly, in a deadly box. And the lid was just about to explode.

Literally.

Ordering his people to not so much as glance in an easterly direction, Ben sat by the side of the road and ate lunch. James Riverson sat beside him.

The walkie-talkie between the two men clicked twice, then clicked twice again.

"First Platoon is in place and everything is go," James said.

Ben nodded and chewed his food carefully.

The walkie-talkie clicked three times, then repeated the signal.

"Second Platoon ready," James said.

Ben finished his lunch and buried the trash in a hole dug with his knife blade. No Rebel dumped trash indiscriminately; the land was littered enough without adding to the mess.

"Start the fireworks," Ben said softly.

James lifted the walkie-talkie and said, "Go."

The tops of the cut-into mountain exploded as high explosives were detonated. Tons of rock were lifted up and dropped down on the ambushers, crushing the life out of those caught in the rocky onslaught.

Ben carefully rolled a cigarette — one of the few he allowed himself daily — and listened to the panicked screaming of the outlaws who survived the initial blast and rolling boulders as they ran from the reverse ambush, running for their bikes and dune buggies and choppers.

But the Rebels had been there first, and had done a little work on the vehicles.

The first chopper to be cranked exploded in a massive fireball, hurling chunks of hot metal and fried parts of human bodies high into the air. The exploding vehicles touched off other fuel tanks, and soon the depot was an almost-solid area of flame.

Outlaws ran from the raging inferno, their clothing and flesh on fire. They ran howling and shrieking, rolling on the rocky ground, attempting in vain to put out the fire that covered their unwashed bodies. They screamed their way into the darkness of death.

And Ben Raines sat by the side of the road and calmly smoked his hand-rolled cigarette.

His hard facial expression did not change as he slowly puffed.

Those outlaws who had elected not to run toward their cached vehicles escaped the hideous burning death of their buddies.

They were shot to death by Rebels lying in ambush, blocking all avenues of escape. They were shot from the front, the back, or the side.

The Rebels offered no quarter, and expected none.

One unwashed outlaw, the stink and stains of a recent rape and murder still on his clothing, threw up his hands and hollered, "I quit! I give up."

He was shot between the eyes.

Let me get out of here! another panicked outlaw thought, his breath ragged as he ran from planned murder and assault and rape. I'll be good! he thought. The same thought that thousands of others like him had thought back through the years.

And few had ever carried out once safe from whatever dilemma had faced them.

He rounded a bend in the rocky path and came face to face with a woman Rebel, a CAR-15 in her hands.

Good-lookin' cunt, he thought.

"I surrender, baby," the outlaw said.

She smiled at him and hope filled the outlaw. He wondered if she'd be any good in the sack? He wondered if she liked it up the ass?

Those were the last thoughts he ever had.

She lifted her CAR and shot the outlaw twice in the chest. She spat on the rocky ground and trotted off.

Ben sat on the ground and yawned. He had seen the outlaw carefully edging his way toward Ben's location. Ben had clicked his Thompson off safety and waited as the outlaw made his approach.

James was reading a worn paperback he'd found back in a nameless town the convoy had rumbled through.

The outlaw's boots grated on rock. James froze.

"Easy," Ben whispered. "I've been watching him for a couple of minutes."

"How's he armed?" James whispered.

"Pistol in his hand. How's the book?"

"Good. You want him?"

"Yeah. I'll let him get a little closer."

"Damn, Ben! I'm supposed to be guarding you, remember?"

"Read your book."

"Somehow I seem to have lost my concentration."

Ben chuckled softly. "Here he comes. He's about to make his play."

The outlaw inched closer. Ben's fingers tightened on the Thompson.

"Taking his sweet time," James muttered.

"And he hasn't got much of that left him," Ben replied.

James smiled.

The outlaw brought his pistol up and jacked back the hammer. Ben lifted the powerful old Thompson submachine gun, leveled it, and pulled the trigger, holding it back.

The .45 caliber slugs took the outlaw in the chest, raking him from left to right, making little bloody dust puffs as the slugs impacted. He was flung backward, arms outstretched, his pistol dropping from suddenly lifeless fingers.

Ben and James rose and looked around them, listening. The battle appeared to be over.

"Call in our people," Ben said. "Let's get the hell out of here."

High up in the still-dusty air of the slope, the outlaw Flash lay unnoticed and very, very still. And he wasn't about to move until these crazy bastards and bitches got long gone outta there.

Flash was so frightened he had both pissed and shit

291

his jeans. He wore no underwear.

Dust, dirt, and small rocks covered him. As long as he didn't move around, he'd be safe. High above him, he could see the buzzards circling. Flash suppressed a shudder. He hated buzzards. He had seen how the bastards tore at dead flesh, and he knew they always went for the eyes and kidneys first.

Flash just wanted to cry.

And Flash hadn't done that in more than twenty years. Not since he'd stood before that judge in juvenile court. After Flash had killed his sister.

Flash had put on quite an act that day. Flash had blubbered and snorted and wiped snot away with the handkerchief the judge had ordered given him. Stupid old bastard. Since he was a juvenile, Flash had spent three years in a country-club prison and then walked out, a free man.

Thanks to the almost-total asininity of juvenile laws . . . back then. Before.

Only thing Flash had ever regretted about the whole mess was that his sister had died before he could fuck her again.

Stupid cunt.

Flash heard the Rebel trucks crank up and begin moving out, backtracking around the now-blocked highway. But Flash wasn't about to move—not just yet. Ben Raines was such a sneaky son of a bitch he probably left people behind to shoot any outlaw who might have survived.

One of the few times in his life Flash was right.

Flash lay very still for more than thirty minutes after the battle. He counted seven shots that shattered the dusty stillness, and knew that seven of his buddies had bought it.

God*damn* these Rebels! Flash thought. They just don't, by God, play fair.

"Let's go!" Flash heard a man shout.

Flash heard two vehicles crank up and drive off. Still, he lay quietly for another hour. Only then did he move.

Three hours later, after jerking a pair of jeans off a dead outlaw and changing out of his own shitty jeans, Flash stumbled into the outlaw's base camp. He was worn out, almost hysterical with fear. He babbled out his story.

"*Everybody* is dead?" Plano shouted at the nearly exhausted Flash.

"Ever'body," Flash confirmed it.

"We gotta change out psyco . . . psycol . . . way of doin' things," Long Tongue said.

"I agree with whatever it was he said," Utah Jack looked at Long Tongue.

"Don't panic!" Booger shouted down the sudden babble of voices. "Now, goddammit, just ever'body hold it down for a minute."

The gaggle of human filth quieted down.

Another outlaw leader, nicknamed Pisser, said, "You got a plan, Booger, I'd sure like to hear it. 'Cause I'm about a minute away from pullin' my boys out and gettin' the hell away from that area."

Other leaders, including Utah Jack, Stud, Big Luke, agreed with Pisser. Loudly and profanely.

"Now, boys," Grizzly said, calming the group, or at the very least, quieting them. "Okay, we took a lickin'. No doubt about that. But since ol' Flash come staggerin' in, I been thinkin'. And I'm thinkin' our

293

big mistake is that we don't act like Ben Raines."

"What do you mean?" Plano asked.

"I·mean the mainest thing is, we got to think like Ben Raines. We can't just say 'okay' to the first plan we come up with. We got to really study a bunch of them."

"I think I know what you mean," Utah Jack said. "We're screwin' up by each of us actin' on our own. Is that part of it?"

"That's right!" Grizzly said. "The mainest thing is, we got to start actin' like soldiers!"

"Does I get to be a general?" Skinhead slobbered the question.

"No," Grizzly dashed his hopes. "But you do get to be an officer."

"I thought a general was an officer?" Skinhead drooled.

"It is," Plano said. "Now shut up."

"They's degrees of generals," Grizzly said. "But another mainest point is this: there can't be but one top general. One man givin' the orders."

"Who is that gonna be?" Popeye asked.

"We're gonna have to vote," Grizzly said. "But I got another idea to do first."

"Whut?" Sonny Boy asked.

"Let's get the hell outta this place!"

Thirty-one

Not one Rebel had been wounded in the ambush. No loss of life among the Rebels.

"That's the way I like it," Ben told James as they rode the deserted state highway in Colorado.

They were circling, trying to pick up the trail of the outlaws.

They were on Highway 9, now just a few miles outside of Kremmling. "Pull over here," Ben told James. "Let's wait for the scouts' report."

The convoy halted near the banks of the Colorado River, on the south side. Ben and James walked down to the river's edge.

The men stood there for a moment, silent, each with their own thoughts.

James broke the silence. "How are we going to handle Hartline, Ben?"

Ben shook his head. "I don't know," he admitted. "But I think we're going to have to slug it out with him."

"I don't have to remind you that he's got us outgunned."

Ben nodded his agreement. "Yes, and it's going to

be costly for us. I've thought of and discarded half a dozen plans. Including the use of planes."

"They wouldn't have a chance. Hartline's got plenty of SAMs."

"Sure does." Ben sighed. "Long-range intel says he's making no plans for a bug-out. I didn't think he would. What he's planning on is these outlaws knocking a hole in our ranks. That's why I'm not going to jack around with them. But this ambush was easy. I have a hunch they're going to get cautious; smarten up some."

"As much as they're capable of," James said, grinning.

"Colonel, our western patrol has gone silent," Khamsin was informed.

"How long have you been trying to reach them?"

"All day, sir."

Khamsin shrugged. "They have met Allah. They have done well. Have you tried to contact Hartline?"

"Yes, sir. He says his eastern-based warlords have ambushed Ben Raines, and probably inflicted heavy casualties on the Rebels."

"Probably? Sam doesn't know for certain?"

"Apparently not, sir."

"Sam is getting careless. We're going to have to be very careful in our dealings with Sam Hartline. From what our, ah, newest convert has told me, General Ben Raines and Sam Hartline are old enemies. That gives me some cause for alarm. What has the woman told you?"

"Nothing, sir."

"Are you certain she has anything to tell us?"

"Yes, sir. One of our patrols stole her out of the Rebels' base camp in Georgia. She is the wife of one of the Rebels now fighting in the west."

"Oh. Interesting. Truly his wife, blessed by Allah?"

The IPA member shrugged. "Who knows, sir. These remaining Americans are such a godless bunch."

"What is her name?"

"Nina. She is the wife, or mistress, whatever, of one Ike McGowen."

"Ike McGowen?" Colonel Khamsin's brow furrowed in thought. "That is one of Ben Raines's field commanders and closest friends."

"I believe so, sir."

"I *know* so. Have you tortured the woman?"

"Yes, sir."

"Cease it at once. See to her wounds and then bring her to me."

"We'll have to carry her, sir. She cannot walk. We have pulled out all her toenails."

"Then carry her. I know a way to split Ben Raines's western forces."

"Yes, sir. Right away, sir."

The outlaws had vanished, seemingly dropping off the face of the earth.

Ben called a halt to the search and ordered his people to dismount and make camp for the night. "Told you they'd smarten up," he said to James.

"They've tasted some of the hell and misery they've caused over the years," James said, quite unlike the big man. "And they don't like it."

"Very good, James. But don't worry, ol' buddy. We're going to give some more hell and misery."

"I never doubted that, Ben."

"Let's get some rest. We'll find them and start rooting them out in the morning."

"And you're sure that's where Lisa's being held?" Kim asked.

"I'm sure," the ragged little boy said. "I've been in there four, five times begging for food. I seen her twice."

"And the last time was? . . ." Judy asked.

"Yesterday. I flashed her a signal and she winked at me. She was walkin' kinda funny, though."

The girls exchanged knowing glances, shaking their heads in disgust.

The small boy picked up on the exchange. "You all don't have to talk around me. I been where she is. I know why she's walkin' that way."

Sandra put an arm around the boy's shoulders. So thin. "What's your name, Scooter?" she asked. "I mean, besides Scooter."

"I don't know no other name. I been called Scooter all my life."

"How many years do you have?"

"Nine or ten, I think. But I really don't know. I been travelin ever since I can remember."

"No blood kin?" Judy asked.

"Not that I know of," the ragged boy replied.

"Can you shoot that pistol you're carryin' ?" Kim asked, looking at the .22 caliber revolver belted

298

around Scooter's waist.

"I sure can. Some grownups tried to bugger me last month. I kilt two of 'em 'fore the others run off."

"You wanna stay with us?" Sandra asked.

"That'd be nice," Scooter said, looking up at the taller person. "We gonna get your friend away from Hartline?"

"Yes. And it's gonna be dangerous doing it."

The boy shrugged. "Livin' day to day is dangerous. That ain't nothin' new. Do I get to meet Ben Raines?"

"Probably. Soon as we get Lisa outta there." Kim looked at the compound below the heavily timbered knoll where they were hidden.

"I gotta tell you all something," Scooter said. "Hartline is ten times worse than the Russian. The Russian was bad enough. But Hartline will grab you and torture you just for fun. I heard some of his men talkin' one time. They said Sam Hartline is crazy. I believe it. I seen what he done to a friend of mine a few months back. Right before Ben Raines shot him up."

"A girl?" Judy asked softly.

"You know it," Scooter replied. "When he got done with her, he just throwed her out in the road." He pointed. "Right down there. Come dark, I dragged her back in the timber and tried to care for her. Me and the underground people. We couldn't do nothin' for her. She bled to death. She was about my age, but real little. Pretty. Hartline split her open. You know what I mean?"

The girls knew.

"If you want your friend to live," Scooter continued, "we gotta get her out of there. Hartline will do it

299

to her ever' way he can, then he'll give her to his men. I know some girls, and one boy, who went crazy after some time down there. You know what them men done to them after that?"

The girls waited.

"They used 'em for target practice. It was awful."

Judy was drawing the compound area on a dirty piece of paper. It was an amazingly accurate drawing, right down to the last detail.

"You got it?" Sandra asked.

"I got it."

"Let's get back to the others. We gotta plan this out real good."

Sam Hartline looked at the sobbing girl on the bed, the rumpled sheets stained with sweat and blood. He had beaten her practically unconscious but still she would not voluntarily submit to him.

He had to fight her every step of the way. Not that that was very difficult — it wasn't. It was just becoming annoying.

Sam Hartline could never — even back when the world was whole, understand why women thought so much of their pussy. Hell, it was there for screwing; what was the big deal?

He looked at the sobbing girl. "I've about had you, bitch," he snarled at Lisa. "Couple more days, if you don't shape up, I'm gonna toss you out that goddamn door and let my boys have you. Can't you understand that I *like* you?"

Lisa lifted her tear-stained face. "*Like* me? If you liked me, you wouldn't hurt me. Can't you be tender sometimes?"

Hartline's great booming laughter filled the room. "You *hurt* me!"

"What the hell's that got to do with the price of eggs, baby?" He stood naked before her. "Hell, if I hadn't liked fighting so much, I could have been a porn star. Made millions."

"What's a porn star?" she asked.

Hartline looked at her in disgust. "Aw, shit!" He turned and dressed, then slammed the door on his way out.

Lisa painfully rose from the bed and walked to the bathroom, running a tub of hot water. Easing her way into the soothing and calming liquid, she heard the door open and close. That would be Rich. He would sit on the commode seat and smirk at her.

But she could put up with Rich. She didn't hate him; she just felt sorry for him.

Ben slipped out of his blankets and looked at the horizon. Just breaking dawn. For the first time, he allowed his thoughts to return to Sylvia.

Of all the things in this world— or what was left of this world, he amended that—he could not abide a traitor.

He could tolerate many things, but never that.

Ben's radio people had heard from one recon team sent east to Khamsin's borders. Sylvia's betrayal had cost one team their lives.

One entire squad gone. Loyal lives snuffed out; people who were willing to lay down their lives for freedom.

301

Gone. Because of a traitor.

He pushed the woman from his thoughts. He would not think of her again.

He hoped.

James Riverson came to his side. "Recon reports finding a band of outlaws about ten miles from here, Ben."

"Get the people up, James. Let's go to work."

Thirty-two

The small band of outlaws knew what hit them, of course. There was little doubt in their minds about that. But they didn't have much time to think about it.

Ben hit them with a fury he had not experienced in years. And he knew what had brought it on. He had finally reached the limit of his understanding. He was weary of people who wanted something for nothing. Tired of ignorance and people who wore that unenlightenment as a badge of honor. He was fed up with those who demanded a life of terrorism and barbarism. Insisted upon it. Ben was reaching back to the days of the Tri-States; bringing it the forefront.

And he knew, now, the Tri-States' philosophy would rise again. He realized that his days of wandering, alone, throughout the ashes of what had been, were over. Here was where he was needed, and so here was where he would have to stay.

Leading the fight as long as there was breath left in his body.

A dirty, unshaven, wild-eyed outlaw made the mistake of trying to escape by overrunning Ben's position surrounding the camp.

Ben rose from his concealment and laid his Thompson on the ground. Ben felt the years leave him, a new youthfulness fill him. A man who for years had done hard exercise after he realized he could no longer take his body for granted, Ben smiled as the outlaw slid to a halt.

Ben smiled at the unarmed outlaw. He lifted his fists. He knew then how he was going to take out Sam Hartline.

With his bare hands.

"I'll kill you!" the outlaw panted.

"So come on, then," Ben challenged him.

The outlaw lunged at Ben, both fists swinging. Ben tripped him, sending the outlaw sprawling on the dirt. Ben kicked him in the side and the outlaw yelped in pain. Ben's training would have had him kick the outlaw in the head, shattering the skull and ending it, but Ben wanted this fight to last a while longer.

Ben stepped back, his hands open in the martial arts fashion. "Is that the best you can do?"

The outlaw roared off the ground, attempting to butt Ben in the stomach with his head and grab him in a bear hug. Ben sidestepped and kicked the outlaw on the knee with his boot. The outlaw, dressed in leather and chains, screamed in pain and fell to the earth, both hands holding his knee.

Ben kicked him in the mouth. The outlaw's head snapped back as he slumped to the ground, almost unconscious.

Ben walked to him and took out his canteen, emptying the contents on the outlaw's head. "Get up, you bastard!"

The outlaw grabbed Ben's leg and jerked, putting Ben on the ground. Ben rolled over and over, coming up some ten yards from the outlaw, who was still trying to get to his feet and shake the feathers out of his foggy, pain-racked brain.

Screaming his hate and rage, the outlaw charged Ben. Balling his hands into fists, Ben met him head-on and toe-to-toe. Ben staggered the heavyset man with a chopping right to the jaw then followed that with a short left hook—that glazed the outlaw's eyes. Ben hit the man in the center of his face with a vicious right that flattened the outlaw's nose and sent blood flying.

Ben laughed at the man.

Dimly Ben could hear James Riverson's voice. "Let them alone," the sergeant major ordered. "The general's gotta do it his way."

"Why?" a Rebel questioned.

"Because he's Ben Raines, that's why," was James's reply.

Ben hammered at the man's stomach with hard fists, punishing the man. Blood from the outlaw's mouth sprayed Ben.

"Gimme a break," the thug panted.

"All right," Ben said, then broke the outlaw's neck with a hard karate chop.

The outlaw fell to the ground, dying. He looked up at Ben through confused eyes. He seemed to want to say something. But before he could, death took him. And that surprised Ben, for he had seen lots of people live a long time with a broken neck. Then he saw the pink froth leak from the outlaw's mouth. Either he had ruptured the man's stomach—which wasn't unlikely—or he had shattered a rib and the rib had punctured a lung. Or nicked the heart.

Ben took several deep breaths. "Report," he said.

"The outlaw camp is wiped out. We suffered two wounded. No dead," James reported. "How do you feel, General?"

Somewhere down the line, Ben had lost his black beret. He took out a cammie bandana and wiped the sweat from his face, then tied the bandana around his head, leaving the ends dangling. "Good," Ben said.

James smiled. "Now you look like Rambo, Ben."

"Who the hell is Rambo?" a Rebel asked.

Ben and his Rebels made a wide circle, at one point moving deep into Wyoming after the outlaws. The Rebels found a half-dozen outlaw camps, destroying them, killing perhaps, in their two-week pursuit, an additional three hundred outlaws, not counting the several hundred killed in the botched ambush on the interstate.

They hammered straight across the center of what had once been known as Nevada. When they reached the base camp in Redding, Ben was met by a grim-faced Ike.

Ike brought Ben up to date. Quickly. "This god-damned Khamsin's grabbed Nina. Sent me a message, through Hartline. Hartline found it amusing."

"I just bet he did," Ben said. "Ike, can you push aside your emotions as the highly trained SEAL you are?"

Ike stiffened. "You know damn well I can, Ben."

"You'll be doing what you were trained to do, years

ago, Ike. Fighting a dirty little guerrilla war with the only supplies that you can carry with you."

"I know, Ben."

"And you know that Nina may be long dead?"

"I know."

"How many personnel you want?"

"Two platoons," Ike said quickly.

"You've thought this out carefully?"

"Many, many hours."

"All right, Ike. Call Base Camp One and get as many planes out here as you think you'll need to transport your people east. They'll leave immediately. Either way it goes, Ike, stay out there. Start helping train resistance fighters and put the needle into Khamsin. We'll never be strong enough to take him head to head, so we're going to have to hit and run. Might as well get used to it."

"Sam Hartline?"

"I'll take care of Sam Hartline. And I know just how I'll do it. I've given it much thought. I know how to pull the arrogant son of a bitch out of his fortress."

Ike cocked his head to one side. "How, Ben?"

"We're going to have a funeral, ol' buddy. With lots of weeping and wailing and moaning and slow walking and sad singing."

"A *funeral*? Whose?"

Ben smiled. "Mine."

Thirty-three

The transport planes roared in and settled down on the runways late the next day. The pilots slept for a few hours, then took off again in the dead of night, carrying Ike and his hand-picked teams.

Ben made himself comfortable inside his command post and stayed put. He ordered Dr. Chase and his people to start scurrying back and forth between the hospital and Ben's command post.

Cryptic messages began filling the air between the base camp and the outposts now manned by Rebels. From Yreka to the rocky raging coast of California the message went out: *THE EAGLE IS DOWN.*

In Oregon, Sam Hartline studied the messages as they came in. He was not sure what they meant; and until he was certain, he was going to stay put.

"It could mean only one thing," one of his field commanders pointed out. "Ben Raines is down."

"But from *what*?" Hartline questioned. "He and his people kicked the shit out of the outlaws. If he'd been wounded, we would have been informed, right?"

The commander shrugged. "Maybe, maybe not.

But Ben Raines is down, Sam. Bet on it."

"You wanna bet your life on it?" Sam challenged.

The commander hesitated. "Yeah, Sam. I do. The boys is gettin' restless. They got to have some action or they're gonna go stale."

Hartline expelled a long breath. "Yeah, I know. But you been with me a long time. You know how sneaky Raines can be. This could be a trap. We'll wait a few more days. I want every intercepted message on my desk within minutes after decoding it, understood?"

"Right, Sam."

Sam Hartline leaned back in his chair, his eyes on the ceiling.

If Ben Raines was down, hard hit, and Ike McGowen gone back east, all that commanded the Rebels was that nigger, Cecil Jefferys. And Sam had never seen a spook that was as smart as a white man.

He sat for a long time with his thoughts. None of them very pleasant for anybody, especially Ben Raines.

Sam punched a button on his desk. An aide stuck his head into the door. Sam never used women for anything in his army. Except to fuck. That's all they were good for.

"Yes, sir?"

"I want a fly-by," Sam said. "Four of them. Beginning at 0600 in the morning. Another at 0800, another at 1000, and the last one at 1600."

"Yes, sir."

"Where's Lisa?"

"Out back, sitting by the pool. Guards are posted at all four corners."

"Good. I'm gonna take a nap. Wake me in a hour."

"Yes, sir."

Sam went into a bedroom and closed the door.

Guards were around the pool, at staggered intervals. One of them sort of staggered as the knife blade entered between ribs, the long blade ramming into the heart. Young hands lowered the cooling carcass to a chair and set him in quietly. Young feet moved around the wall that encircled the pool, slipping to the next guard. Kim drove the blade of her dagger into the man's throat, the needle point pushing out the other side, dripping blood.

At the same instant, Judy's knife took out the third guard, and Sandra's dagger plunged deep into the back of the fourth man. Scooter and Mary and Larry helped lower the bodies to the concrete.

Lisa was already moving, on the run toward the friends she had thought she would never see again.

Rich chose that time to walk out to the pool area. The boy stood, his mouth open in shock.

Sandra's knife flashed end over end in the hot air of summer.

Rich uttered one word before the knife point hit him in the center of his chest.

"No!" the boy said.

He fell to the concrete

"I wasn't gonna kill him," Sandra said. "We talked it over. But it's too late now. Come on, Lisa, let's get the hell outta here."

Rich could hear them talking through a mist of pain.

"There's something you oughta know," Kim said to Lisa.

Rich listened.

"Ben Raines is dying."

billy-hell are you talking about?"

Thirty-four

"Well, the little bastard was loyal to me after all," Hartline said. "You just by God never know."

"So Ben Raines is really dying," a mercenary said. "Ain't that a kick in the. ass?"

"Yep," Hartline said. "But this time, we're going to be the ones who kick ass."

"It's about goddamn time."

Everyone, including Hartline, laughed at the truth in that remark. For years, Raines's Rebels had been kicking ass all over the battered nation. And a lot of the time, the asses kicked were Sam Hartline's mercenaries.

"Never have been able to understand Raines," Hartline was fond of saying. "The man was a mercenary in his time, just like me."

Ben Raines had never been a mercenary. He had been a soldier of fortune for a time, after his time in the Army. But never a mercenary. A mercenary will fight for any flag, any political ideology, regardless of the savagery of that particular regime.

A soldier of fortune will almost always fight with those waging war for democracy—many times for no pay, other than personal satisfaction.

There is a lot of difference between a mercenary and a soldier of fortune.

As much difference as between Sam Hartline and Ben Raines.

"What do you want done with Rich's body?" Sam was asked.

Sam laughed. "Dump the little shit in the ocean!"

The word spread like a raging, unchecked woods fire: Ben Raines is dying.

In less than a week, the rumor had spread all across the torn nation: Ben Raines is dying.

Only a few of Ben's most trusted Rebels knew the truth. The majority believed him to be near death.

Sam Hartline's fly-bys confirmed it. The spotters reported large groups of Rebels gathered around Ben's command post standing and sitting quietly. Waiting.

But still Hartline was not certain; not yet convinced in his own mind that it all wasn't some clever ruse on Ben's part. Sneaky son of a bitch!

"Wait," he told his people. "When the bastard is cold in the ground, that's when we'll move."

Then the word came, buzzing out of the radios: *THE EAGLE IS DEAD*.

Hartline sent a team into California, ordering them to get as close as possible and check it out. Report back.

They reported back, grim satisfaction in their report: Ben Raines is dead. The Rebel movement is in chaos. Ben Raines is being buried in the morning.

And Sam Hartline leaned back in his chair and howled his laughter.

"Get the boys ready," Hartline ordered. "We're gonna kick those Rebels clear into the sea."

On the South Carolina border, a young Rebel captain said, "We can't get much accurate intel out of there, Ike. This Khamsin, whoever he is and wherever he came from, is one hell of a top-flight soldier. But we have found out one thing that's firm."

Ike looked at him.

"He's got three divisions," the captain finished it.

"Shit!" Ike breathed. "I hope you're talkin' short divisions?"

"A little over thirty thousand personnel, Ike."

Ike shook his head. "I don't suppose there's much point in talkin' about artillery and tanks, right, Captain?"

"He's got it all, Ike."

"You know where this puts us, don't you?" Ike asked.

"Between a rock and a hard place, I reckon."

Ike nodded. "Well, me and Ben have been in tougher spots." But he couldn't recall a one.

"General Raines? . . . " the captain started to speak.

"Let it slide, son," Ike quieted him. "Just believe."

"Okay, sir."

Ike looked back at his teams. They were split up into twenty 6-person teams. "It's still up to y'all," Ike drawled. "I ain't orderin' nobody in that don't wanna go. Is that understood?"

The men and women of the Rebels squatted and stared in silence at him.

"Let's go," Ike said softly.

Cecil had called his section leaders, company commanders, and platoon sergeants together. Dan Gray stood beside the tall, well-built black man with the salt-and-pepper hair.

Dan knew what was going on in Cecil's mind, for the same thing had been buzzing in his mind since Ben had told them of his plan.

Ninety-nine percent of the Rebels believed Ben to be dead. Now, with hard intel that Sam Hartline and his army was on the move toward the Rebels strongholds, Ben was suddenly going to appear.

And that was only going to further the myth that Ben was larger than life. Not quite human.

A god.

"One of the risks of this plan," Ben had said, just hours before his "funeral."

Cecil stood on a raised platform and looked at the Rebels in the room.

"What do we do now, General?" a senior sergeant asked.

"We follow Ben Raines," Cecil said.

A low murmur spread around the room. Cecil let them talk for a moment before waving them silent.

"Rebels," he announced. "Let me try to explain. All that has happened over the past week was just a ruse. A plan of Ben's to pull Sam Hartline and his army into our territory. Ben is very much alive and well."

"No!" a Rebel shouted. "That's not true."

Ben walked out of a side room, his appearance bringing the room to a dead silence.

He climbed up beside Cecil and looked at the shock-numbed crowd. "As you can all clearly see," he said. "I am very much alive and doing quite well."

The Rebels stood and stared at him.

"I apologize for tricking you," Ben said. "I'm sorry to play with your emotions in this manner. But we had to pull Hartline and his people out of their stronghold. We've done that. They're on their way right now. Our forward recon teams report the mercenaries have neared the border and are barreling toward us." He looked at Cecil. "Join your battalion, Cec. Close it off behind us. Good luck."

The men shook hands and Cecil quickly left the room. A light plane would fly him to his battalion, located on both sides of Interstate 5, near Yreka.

Ben looked back at his Rebels, still staring at him in open-mouthed shock. "Wait until noon before breaking the news to your sections that I'm still alive. That will put Hartline and his people south of Cecil's position. They won't be able to turn back even should they hear the news.

"Now you listen to me, people. We've got a hard fight facing us. And it's just beginning. We have no choice in the matter. We have to fight, and we have to win. First against Hartline, then against Colonel Khamsin and his IPA. And we're going to take losses. Plenty of them. Hard losses. We're going to lose loved ones and close friends. But it's either that, or live as slaves. I refuse to bow down to any person. That's why we're Rebels.

"There isn't going to be much rest for us. It's going

to be one fight after another, for God only knows how many years. I'm not looking forward to it, and I know that none of you want to fight for the rest of your lives." Ben sighed. "Maybe someday we can all settle down and live in peace. I have to keep that hope alive. But I, and you, must keep this thought in mind at all times: We are all that stands between freedom and slavery. It's up to us. No one else. Get with your teams and prepare to fight. Move out!"

The room emptied, with most of the Rebels glancing back over their shoulder to look at Ben.

Ben was calmly folding and tying a cammie bandana around his forehead.

He looked at Colonel Gray. "Let's do it, Dan."

Thirty-five

The news cut through the camp like a bullet. Even though no member of the Rebel Army that was present when Ben appeared out of the grave had spoken of it, somehow the other Rebels knew.

The somber cloud that had invisibly covered the camp lifted and a fresh new spirit filled the men and women of the Rebels.

Cecil and Dan had already received orders from Ben as to how the attack was to be carried out, and they had informed their people long before Ben made his exit from the grave. Now the camp hummed with a new, fresh melody; a warlike song to be sure, for war was all that many of these Rebels had ever known, many of them having been with Ben since back in '89.

Ben walked among the Rebels as they feverishly broke camp, moving out to preassigned positions. He spoke to as many as possible, stopping to chat with a few of them.

"This time we finish Sam Hartline, Charlie."

"You bet, General!"

"Kick-ass-and-take-names time, Wes."

"Right, General!"

"Watch your butt now, Claire. It's time for you and Eddie to be thinking of having some babies."

"Oh, General!" she blushed. One of Dan Gray's Scouts, Claire was as good a soldier as any in Ben's command.

"Bob, you got your lucky coin with you?"

"Damn right, General! This time we finish Sam Hartline once and for all, right?"

"That's right, Bob. Simon, you were wounded about two weeks ago. What the hell are you doing with this bunch?"

"Gettin' ready to kick the hell out of that schtoonk, Hartline, that's what."

Ben laughed. "Give him hell, Simon."

And so it went, up and down the lines of trucks and Jeeps and the lines of tiger-stripe or lizard cammied men and women who made up Raines's Rebels.

A thin line, the thought came to Ben. How few of us there are. But we have grown, he thought, his eyes finding the two Georges from Red Bluff and Chico. Harris and his people from Redding. Pete Ho and his bunch from Ukiah. John Dunning and several hundred fighters from Santa Rosa.

Some of the newer fighters would be mixed in with Ben's regular Rebels; others would be held in reserve, just behind the lines, to take the place of any Rebels wounded.

Ben watched his people move out. The tanks and artillery had moved out early that morning, when the first news of Hartline's advance reached the base camp.

Lora walked up to him and kicked Ben on the shin.

"Oww! Jesus Christ, Lora. What was that for?"

"It isn't nice to have people think you're dead and gone, Ben Raines. I cried a whole bunch over you."

"Yeah? Well, you just brought tears to my eyes, too. I guess that makes us even."

"Oh, yeah. Well . . . guess so. Ben?"

"What, Lora?"

"I never did liked Sylvia. Never trusted her." She slung her carbine and turned to go.

"Wait a minute! Where are you going, Lora?"

"To join my friends. There's a fight coming up, Ben Raines."

"I *know* that, Lora. How about staying here with me?"

She smiled, and as she did, Ben saw the wisdom in her young eyes. "It don't pay to get too close to people, Ben. More likely than not, you're gonna get hurt when you do that. "You really liked Sylvia, didn't you, Ben?"

"Yeah, I did, kid."

"Lots of times, Ben, the people you want, don't want you. Ain't that the truth?"

"That's the truth, Lora. You be careful out there."

"Oh, I'll be careful, Ben." She walked off, a very small and very brave Rebel, her black beret cocked to one side of her head.

Ben felt eyes on him and turned to look at Dr. Chase. "Lamar."

"Goddamned shame when kids have to fight wars, isn't it, Ben?"

"Yes, it is, Doc. You want to be the one to tell those kids they can't fight?"

321

"I think not. How's your shin?"

"It hurts."

Chase chuckled then looked at Ben. "I rather like that bandana tied around your head, Ben."

"Oh?"

"Yes. Makes you look more like the damned roguish pirate I know you are."

He walked off, leaving Ben sputtering.

Hartline abruptly halted his column halfway between Yreka and Mount Shasta. He had suddenly developed a very uneasy sensation in his guts.

"What's up?" one of his company commanders radioed to Sam's APC.

"Bad feeling," Sam radioed back. "Check the communication truck. See what they've been receiving the past few hours."

In a few moments, Sam got his reply. "Nothing."

"*Nothing?*"

"Not a peep, Sam."

"I don't like that worth a shit!"

"Hell, Sam. The Rebels are in mourning! They don't even know we're on the way."

"Don't be a jerk, Benny. Raines may be dead — and I'm still very dubious about that — but the Rebels aren't stupid. They might relax their guard some, but not much. I got a feeling we're heading into a trap. Put out guards. You guys meet me up here pronto."

Hartline's field commanders gathered around his APC. All but one.

Sam looked around him. "Where in the hell is that goddamned Harrison?"

No one had seen Harrison.

"He was in the drag, wasn't he?" Sam demanded.

"Last time I saw him he was."

"Don't just stand there. Go check him out."

Ralph came back, his face a bit pale. "He's gone. His driver's gone. Everything is gone."

"What do you mean, *everything* is gone?" Hartline yelled. "Where's his Jeep!"

"I'm tellin' you, Sam. It's gone!"

"That goddamned Ben Raines has done it to me again," Sam bitched. "That sorry, no-good, low-life, sneaky son of a bitch has screwed me again!"

"Sam!" the excited yell came from the middle of the long column. "Sam!"

But when Sam turned around and yelled, "What?" no one answered.

Angry, Sam ran back to the center of the well-spaced main column. He had split the column up into three parts. With a mile between each column.

Sam jogged up to a mercenary. "All right, asshole! What do you want? What'd you yell for?"

The merc looked at him. "Huh?"

"I said, what did you yell for?"

"I ain't yelled jack-shit, Sam!" the merc protested.

Sam looked around him a bit nervously. He began edging his way back to his APC. There, he crouched down, his back to the steel place. "Raines is playing with us," he said.

"Ben Raines is *dead*." one of his senior commanders said, exasperation in his voice. "Goddammit, Sam, you're paranoid about Ben Raines."

"Yeah, a ghost can't hurt you," another merc said.

From deep in the timber, there came a hollow-sounding laugh.

One of the younger mercs looked around him, his eyes wide, his face pale.

"Get the column outta here!" Sam yelled.

No sooner had the words left his mouth when an explosion to the north of them rocked the land.

Sam jerked up his mike. "What the hell was that? Rear column, answer me!"

"Bridge is blown," came the weary reply. "Next road leadin' anywhere is 97 to the north. And scouts reports that road is closed. Next highway is 89. And that ain't gonna do us a damn bit of good."

"If I want a goddamned scenic route mapped out, Ira, I'll ask you for it!" Sam snapped.

He tossed the mike to the seat. He rubbed his face, deep in thought. He frowned as laughter once more came from the dark timber.

Sam frowned and once more picked up the mike. "Ira?"

"Right here, Sam."

"Are you cut off from Battalions One and Two?"

"All by my lonesome, Sam."

"Dig in and hold what you've got, Ira."

"Do I have a choice, Sam?"

Hartline chose not to reply. He picked up a map. "Chances are, Raines sent the sambo north with one battalion. Ira can keep him busy. We've still got Battalion Five east of us and Battalion Four to the west. We've got Raines outgunned and outmanned. Smart-assed bastard may have planned this too carefully. He may have cut it too fine for his own good this time."

Once more, from the dark timber, came that taunting laughter.

"I know what that is now," Sam said, visibly relaxing. "The underground people. They don't use guns. They have bows and arrows and spears and shit like that. Long as we don't get in the deep timber, we're all right."

"Sam? We're sittin' ducks out here in the middle of the damn road."

"Yeah, I know. Tell Battalions Four and Five to hold what they've got. Advance only at my orders. What's in the next town?"

"Nothing. It's deserted."

"You hope," Sam said sourly.

Thirty-six

Ike and his personal team had entered South Carolina just north of Mount Carmel, where the Georgia-flowing Broad River merged with the Savannah River. In typical Navy SEAL fashion, Ike and his people entered enemy territory at night, by water.

"Damn alligators probably in here," one team member bitched.

"Beats the hell outta 'Nam," Ike put an end to it. "Let's go."

Dawn found Ike and his team hiding in a deserted house near what had once been the small town of Bradley. They would spend the hot daylight hours resting, then move out again at night.

The Rebels' main problem — other than staying alive — was that they were not sure exactly where Nina was being held.

But Ike knew how to find out.

"We grab some IPA dude and get the information out of him," he said.

"That could get bloody," a Rebel said.

Ike's smile was as savage as the IPA. "I'm sure it will," he said.

Nina listened to Colonel Khamsin's talk, her face impassive. She hurt, but not as badly as a couple of days ago. She could hobble about, with the aid of canes. She could not wear shoes or sandals, because of her swollen feet—where her toenails had been removed with wire-pliers.

The savages of the IPA had broken parts of her body, but not her spirit. Nina did not think they could do that. She really did not know why there were torturing her. For she knew very little about the Rebel movement. She knew there were Rebel outposts scattered throughout the Southeast, but did not know exactly where they were.

And she had told her interrogators as much.

That alone did not cause the pain to stop. Rather, it increased, for they felt she was lying.

And, of course, they had raped her. Nina had endured it silently. She had been raped before. Before she met Ike, and had fallen in love with the man.

Ike! she thought, staring at Khamsin's dark, evil face. Where are you, Ike?

" . . . So you see, Miss," Khamsin was saying. "The men and women of the IPA are not that different from your Ben Raines and his Rebels. We both strive for the same things. Peace, productivity, law and order. Don't you see?"

"BLIVET!" Nina said.

"I beg your pardon?"

"BLIVET. It's something Ike taught me. It's an old military expression."

"I'm not familiar with it. It means? . . . "

"Ten pounds of shit in a five-pound bag!"

Khamsin's eyes turned even more dark and evil. He rose from behind his desk and calmly walked around to Nina's side. He slapped her out of her chair.

Khamsin reached down and grabbed Nina's bandaged feet. He squeezed her toes, laughing as she screamed from the pain.

"Scream, little bird," Khamsin said, his voice taunting. "Perhaps your Ike McGowen will hear you and come to your rescue."

"Wrong," she whispered. "Rebels are expendable. No matter how much Ike cares for me, he won't risk people coming after me." Nina knew that was not true, but maybe she could give Ike a fighting chance to get through to her.

She felt he was on the way. Perhaps very near. But she would never tell that to this camel-humper.

Khamsin stepped back, regained his composure, and gestured for her to get back into the chair. She did, slowly and painfully, almost falling as she fought the pain in her tortured feet.

She sat and stared up at him, defiance in her eyes.

Khamsin watched the woman. He knew, from years of active terrorism, that anyone and everyone could be broken. But sometimes, one had to weigh carefully what would be gained by it.

Khamsin believed the woman knew very little about the Rebel movement. So therefore there was little use in continuing her physical discomfort.

Khamsin felt a stirring in his groin as he stared at the fair-skinned woman. He felt himself begin to thicken as passion took him.

He walked to her and picked her up effortlessly,

placing her on a bunk. "I will not hurt your feet, little bird."

I won't die from rape, she thought. Come on, Ike — hurry!

Ike wiped the blood from his knife, sheathed it, and tossed a ragged blanket over what just vaguely resembled a human body lying on the dirty, rat-droppings-littered floor of the house.

He look at the two remaining IPA members. They stared at him with something very close to horror in their dark eyes.

And something else, Ike picked it up. Fear.

"What are you thinkin', partner?" Ike asked the younger of the captives.

"That you are a savage!"

Ike laughed at him. "Me, a savage? You simple son of a bitch! Bastards like you have been waging a war of terrorism since before you were born, boy. You've killed innocent people, men, women, kids, all over this world. You've raped, kidnapped, tortured, maimed, and killed; and like some of those nuts that used to wage war in Ireland, you don't even know what you're fightin' for."

"Our homeland," the young IPA man said.

One Rebel laughed. Like Ike, he was old enough to remember the terrorism of the 1980s. "Why in the fuck don't you go back to your homeland, then, and leave us the hell alone?"

"We are claiming this land in the name of Allah."

Ike knelt down in front of the young man, his knife in his hand. "You wanna meet Allah, boy? Okay. But

I guaran-damn-tee you, boy, the journey's gonna be a long and painful one."

The IPA man spat in Ike's face.

"Gag 'im," Ike ordered.

"This is as far as we go," Hartline radioed. "We form battlelines here. And here we stand and slug it out. Dismount and dig your holes. Tanks and artillery, station up."

And that decision was to be Hartline's last and fatal one. The mercenary had the Rebels outnumbered three to one. He could have rammed through almost any point in Ben's thin lines. And by doing that, could have had the Rebels in a box, closing it with flanking movements.

But his caution overrode his solid military background.

And as he dug in, Sam Hartline wondered what had happened to those remaining loud-mouthed warlords.

Sonny Boy, Grizzly, Skinhead, Popeye, Plano, and the others were camped far from the battlelines. At this juncture, they wanted no more of Ben Raines. They all knew they would rebuild their ranks; the battered nation was full of sorry people who wanted something for nothing, and who would be more than willing to join the outlaws.

They had never gotten around to voting on a top general. Running for their lives from the Rebels, that had slipped their minds.

For now, the warlords and outlaws would simply wait. And stay far away from Ben Raines and his Rebels.

"Ben?" Cecil radioed. "Looks like you were right — again. We're going to stand and slug it out with Hartline."

"Not yet, Cec." Ben radioed his reply. "What we're going to do is annoy the hell out of Hartline. We've got the time; it's on our side in this operation. So we're going to pick and prod at Hartline and his men. We're going to put the needle to them. All day, and all night. A war of nerves. They're not going to get much sleep, Cec. And some of our people will be so close to them, that when they relax their guard, they get their throats cut."

Cecil's chuckle was grim. "Ben, you are a real bastard, you know that?"

"Yep."

"Doesn't bother you at all, does it?"

"Nope." Cecil laughed and signed off.

Hartline's people dug in, deep and solid. They waited.

And waited.

The long hot days began to melt into each other. Every fifteen minutes, on the dot, a round from mortar or tank or artillery would crash into or very near some position manned by Hartline's men.

And with every hour that passed, Ben's Rebels became more secure and dug-in; moving several yards closer, tightening the deadly ring around the mercenary's bunkers.

Hartline's men could only move about at night, for Rebel snipers had the range, and they were dead-accurate.

Some people might have questioned Ben's tactics, wondering why, if he had Hartline boxed, didn't he just starve the mercs out?

In terrain such as both sides were holding, that's only done in the movies. Hartline and his men could have slipped out during the night, with many of them making it. But they would have been forced to leave their artillery, their vehicles, their heavier machine guns and larger mortars.

Hartline had dug himself into a safe hole, but not a very enviable one.

And the waiting game was beginning to tell on Hartline's men.

"What the hell are they waiting on?" one mercenary CO asked Hartline.

"For us to screw up," Sam replied calmly. "Once we show the first signs of cracking, Ben's people will be all over us like ants to honey."

"Well . . . why don't we pull something like Raines done? Fake it?"

"Because Ben wouldn't fall for it," Sam grudgingly conceded. "He's too goddamned smart for that."

A sniper round blasted into the log-enforced bunker of Sam Hartline. The CO winced; Sam stood impassive, his eyes staring at nothing.

"Jesus!" the CO whined. "Them people are tough with them rifles."

"Yeah. XM-21s."

The young CO looked at him, waiting for explanation.

"Accurized M-14s, using an ART scope. Back in 'Nam, 800, 900-yard first-round kills were common with that weapon. They're good."

Dusk was spreading her dark skirts over the land. Sam called for as many section leaders as could make the run to his bunker to come on over.

"Boys," the mercenary admitted, "I screwed up. Staying in this place is like fucking for virginity. I hate to say it, but we're gonna have to bust out. Raines is not going to stand and slug it out with us."

Even though the risks were awful, the mercenary section leaders knew what Sam was saying was the only way any of them were going to survive.

"Where's the bust-out point, Sam?"

Sam pointed south. "Straight ahead. As near as I can figure it, Raines's people are spread pretty thin all around us. The nigger's up north with Third Battalion. They can keep the nigger busy. I'll take First Battalion and cut west, link up with Fourth Battalion. You take Second Battalion and cut east, link up with Fifth Battalion. As soon as that's done, we'll start inching back toward the border. With any kind of luck, we can hook up with Ira's boys."

"When do we bug out?"

"Midnight."

Thirty-seven

"Something wrong, Dad?" Tina Raines asked, walking up to Ben's side.

Ben shook his head. "Nothing tangible, Daughter. It's just that I think we've held Hartline in a box just about as long as we're going to. He's an arrogant prick, but a good soldier. He'll admit he made a mistake in digging in."

"And then? . . ."

"Well, if I were in his shoes, I'd order a bust-out. Question is, where and when."

Tina waited, knowing her dad had given this considerable thought.

Ben said, "Sam's got a battalion to the west, one to the east, and one that's pulled back into Yreka. He's got his battalion and one other dug in. Now, he could do any number of things. He could retreat back to Yreka and bust through Cec's lines, linking up with that battalion. But he'll quickly reject that because of those blown bridges.

"Sam could bust out to the south, then swing around and join the western group. But that would put his back to the sea. He won't do that. If he moved

335

both his battalions to the east, that would mean he'd sacrifice the western battalion. And he won't do that because he needs those people.

"If I were Sam, I'd split my forces, one battalion to the west, one to the east, link up, and begin retreating back toward the Oregon border."

"Then you think he'll be coming straight out of the chute, heading south, then split east and west?"

"That's what I'd do."

"And you want us to do? . . ." She left the question open-ended.

Ben grinned. "Why, open the gate, dear. Just give him all the space he needs." Ben's smile broke into a wide grin.

"Until he splits his forces, that is," Tina said. "And then we hit them hard."

"That's it, dear."

"But you don't know for certain when he'll try to bug out, do you, Dad?"

"No, not for sure."

"But you have a feeling it'll be soon, right?"

"Like . . . tonight, daughter."

"What else do you have up your sleeve, Dad?"

Dan Gray had joined the group, standing quietly and listening. The Englishman began to smile.

Ben looked at Dan. "You finish it, Dan."

"I never presume to know what is in another man's mind," the ex-SAS man said primly.

"Horseshit!" Ben replied.

"You've been hanging around Ike too long, General. How crude. Very well. I would draw the Rebels back several hundred meters; put them deep in the timber. Then just as soon as Hartline's people passed,

336

and I mean within seconds, I would move the Rebels into the abandoned bunkers, reposition the mortars and other artillery, and use the mercenaries' own weapons against them. That's what I'd do."

"But suppose Hartline has booby-trapped his bunkers and artillery and tanks?" Tina asked.

"No time," Ben said. "This would be a snap decision on Sam's part. I know he called a meeting early this afternoon. In his bunker. I ordered a double bino watch. Those behind the long lenses report no unusual activity. Any type of behavior other than what we've grown accustomed to would be a dead give away on Sam's part. Dan, start pulling the Rebels back. Give Sam a chute to use. He may fall for it, he may not. I'm betting he will."

"Yes, sir."

Nina fought away her feelings of suicide. She had been a survivor all her life; she was not going to quit now.

She had thought once Khamsin had his way with her—how long had it been?—a week, she guessed—then he would leave her alone.

It was not to be.

The man was worse than a goat. She had endured the assaults as silently and stoically as humanly possible.

The only thing about her that had improved was her feet. Most of the pain was now gone, but her tortured toes were still very tender.

She heard footsteps in the hall. A guard knocked on her door. Nina swung her feet off the bed and carefully slid her feet into house slippers. "Yes?"

"The colonel is ready for you, woman."

"Charmed, I'm sure," Nina muttered. Ike! she thought. Where are you, Ike? Please, Ike—hurry!

Ike was less than two miles away. He and his team had been in the Columbia area for several days. They had slipped in at night, moving carefully, and just as carefully mapping out Colonel Khamsin's headquarters, where Nina was being held.

The last member of the IPA patrol that Ike had questioned had broken under Ike's knife, spilling his guts—literally.

Ike and his team had moved out for the Columbia area before the terrorist's body had cooled.

"Okay, gang," Ike said. "It has to be tonight. We've already pushed our luck too hard. One more recon of the area is not only useless, but risky. We go in at midnight."

Ike and his team were on the second floor of an old warehouse. Ike knew how they were going to get Nina out; but then getting away was quite another matter.

Ike looked at his radio operator. "You got the other teams on the horn, scrambled?"

"Yes, sir."

"Tell them at *exactly* midnight, on the dot, I want diversion strikes all along the borders, as many as possible. I wanna shake Khamsin's people up. For fifteen minutes, minimum, get our people on the borders to throw everything they've got into South Carolina. That's all the time we're gonna have, people. Fifteen minutes to get in, grab Nina, and get out."

Ike glanced at his team. "Let's take it from step one, people."

"I'm at the gate," a Rebel said.

"I drive the truck," the second Rebel said.

"I carry Nina," a big Rebel said. "In case she's been tortured and can't walk."

"I start the fires," a woman Rebel spoke quietly.

"And you and me," Ike said, looking at another Rebel. "We bust her out."

The radio operator was busy transmitting Ike's orders.

Ike glanced at his watch. "Let's go."

Ben glanced at his watch, then at Tina. "Everybody pulled back, girl?"

"Yes, sir. Hartline's got a hole wide enough to stampede cattle through."

He should be making bug-out any second."

His walkie-talkie crackled.

"Speak," Ben said.

"Bugging out, sir," came the whispered report. "And traveling pretty light."

"Keep your head down," Ben ordered.

Up and down the lines of pulled-back Rebels, the scouts radioed in to Ben. Sam Hartline and his men were bugging out.

Ben looked at his daughter. "It won't take Sam long to realize he's been had. But by then, I'm hoping, he'll be past the point of no return. But either way, we can still kick the shit out of him."

"Gonna finish him this time, Dad?" Tina asked.

"I'm going to give it my best shot, girl."

"Too easy," Hartline whispered to his aide. "That goddamned Ben Raines is up to something. But damned if I can figure what it is."

"I feel like I'm being watched," one of his men whispered. "And I heard something move behind me about a mile back."

"Yeah, me, too," a mercenary said. "But it sounded like they, whatever it was, was movin' back the way we come."

Then the light bulb of full understanding clicked on in Sam's head. "That sneaky son of a bitch!" he growled.

He halted the snakelike column and stood for a moment, listening. He could just detect the sounds of breeches opening and closing; the sounds of tank-mounted howitzers being raised.

And Sam Hartline *knew*, Ben Raines had bested him—again.

"Matt?" Sam called softly.

"Right here, Sam. What's up?"

"Every man for themselves," Sam Hartline gave the orders. Gave them with a bitter, copperlike taste in his mouth. The taste of defeat.

And Sam Hartline took off running, running as if the hounds of Hell were snarling and biting at his ankles.

Ben Raines lifted his walkie-talkie. "Guns facing east?"

"Yes, sir," came the quick response.

"Guns facing west?" Ben asked.

"Yes, sir. Locked and loaded."

"East and west," Ben said. "Have your forward observers pinpointed your targets?"

"Yes, sir," came the dual reply.

"Commence firing."

Ike's team hit the gates of Khamsin's command post fifteen seconds after midnight. They had slapped C-4 onto doors and buildings and operational vehicles as they made their way to the compound.

The charges began blowing just as Ike and his team opened fire and began tossing firefrag grenades about the compound.

The news of the attacks along the border had just been rushed to Khamsin when Ike's team began their assault. The compound erupted in confusion and smoke and explosions and gunfire.

A team member had driven two deuce-and-a-half trucks into the only street that had not been blocked off. The Rebel backed off, rolled a grenade under each truck, then ran like hell back to the compound to join in the fight. The transport trucks blew, blocking the street with fire and hot metal and smoking glass.

The attack had been so sudden, so totally unexpected it had caught the IPA with their pants down—, or off, as the case was, with many of them sleeping.

Ike tripped a running IPA troop. With the blade of his knife against the man's throat, he snarled, "The woman prisoner? Where is she?"

The man spat in Ike's face.

With the point of his knife, Ike dug out one of the man's eyes. Ignoring the screaming, Ike repeated the question.

With his eyeball dangling down the side of his face, and the blood spurting, the IPA troop answered Ike's question.

"Shoulda told me that in the first place, stupid!" Ike kicked the man on the side of the head, knocking him out, but allowing him to live. For a time longer.

Ike ran up the outside stairs of what had once been a walled office complex and kicked in the door. He grinned at Nina.

"Hello, baby! Ready to go home?"

Thirty-eight

Ben hated to do it, knowing that unless his people set backfires to check the burning woods, half of California might well be wiped out. He hesitated, then called for WP rounds.

The night sky erupted in flames as the white phosphorus rounds exploded, as the fires caught, the sap in the trees ignited, burned, and exploded. And Hartline and his men were caught smack in the middle of the raging maelstrom, with absolutely no place to run.

Sam literally stumbled into a lifesaving hole in the ground. The soft earth under his boots gave way and he fell about five feet into a slanting cave. He slid another twenty-five or so feet before reaching bottom. He carefully put out his hand, feeling the rocky surface beneath him. No bat shit. Good. Sam hated bats. Filthy fuckers.

Using his flashlight, Sam inspected the cave. About ten feet high at the widest point, perhaps eight or ten feet wide at the widest point, narrowing down to no more than several inches wide.

One way in, one way out. Fine with him.

Then he wondered why the smoke from the fires was not entering the cave. He crawled as far as he could deeper into the cave. Air fanned his face, coming out of the small crack. That explained that. The updraft kept the smoke out.

Sam curled up on the floor, making himself as comfortable as possible, and went to sleep.

Khamsin had hurled himself to the floor when the first explosion sounded. When automatic-weapons fire began raking the compound, he crawled under his desk. But he left his ass exposed.

A grenade blew just outside his main office, sending ragged shards of glass flying in all directions.

A long jagged piece hit Khamsin square in one cheek of his buttocks, penetrating several inches. Khamsin howled in pain and rage and frustration. When he reached back to pull the glass out, he sliced his hand open, to the bone.

On his knees, the Libyan cursed America, Americans, and especially Ben Raines.

By everything that was holy, Khamsin swore to someday kill Ben Raines.

But the pain in his ass overrode his prayers and he wondered where in the shit his medics might be hiding.

"You won't want me no more, Ike," Nina said. "I'll leave and let you find yourself a whole woman when we get back."

"Girl," Ike said, looking at her. "What in the holy

billy-hell are you talking about?"

"That camel-humpin' bastard used me pretty bad, Ike."

Ike grinned at her in the darkness of the canvas-covered bed of the truck. "You reckon he wore it plumb out, baby?"

"Ike!"

"Then don't worry about it, baby. Tell you what. When we get back, how's about you and me gettin' hitched?"

"Ike?"

"Yes, baby?"

"I love you."

"Is that a fact? Well, dip me in shit and call me stinky!"

"If you folks will quit all that romancin' up there," a Rebel called from his post by the tailgate. "Here comes a whole bunch of those camel-jockeys."

"Ridin' camels?" Ike called.

"I wish!"

Ike picked up his CAR-15 and joined the guard. "How about us start rollin' out some surprises for them folks, Ed?"

The Rebel grinned and held up both hands full of firefrags. "Like these?"

"How did you guess?"

"Cease fire!" Ben ordered. "Cease fire!"

The night became eerily quiet, except for the popping of trees as the sap exploded. Fires ringed the interior of the battleground.

And the cloudy skies cracked just a bit and a light

mist began falling. After only a few moments, the mist changed into a sprinkle, then a downpour. Ben looked up, the rain streaking his face, and smiled.

"Thanks," he said.

Dan Gray came to Ben's side. "I've ordered the troops to start mopping up, General."

"Fine. Have you any prelims on troop loss?"

"We lost no one. It appears that Hartline suffered approximately ninety percent loss of his battalions. We'll probably never know for sure."

Ben nodded. "I'm going to get some rest. Take over, Dan."

"Yes, sir."

The Englishman watched as Ben walked away, back to his command post for some much-needed sleep.

A Rebel approached Dan. "Sir?"

"Yes, son?"

"General Jefferys was just on the horn. He reports that his people are kicking ass north of here. Your people have engaged the other battalion and have them on the run. Looks like we won, sir."

"Thank you. Keep me informed and don't disturb the general."

"Yes, sir."

"Carl?" Dan called.

"Here, sir!" the batman said.

"A bit of tea would be nice. Perhaps a cracker or cookie to go with it."

"Right away, sir."

Dan sat down on a log and rested, waiting for his early morning refreshment. He wondered how Ike was doing?

"Sir!" the shout came from the cab of the truck.

"Go ahead!" Ike hollered.

"Our teams have smashed across the border and put the IPA on the run. They're waiting for us just five miles up this road. As soon as we pass, they'll blow the bridges over the Little Lynches and Lynches Rivers. After that, we're home free."

"Right!" Ike leaned back and let the weariness flow over him. Nina was lying on a blanket, looking up at him through the darkness. "We made it, babe," he said.

She winked at him.

Khamsin lay on his stomach and endured the pain as the doctor stitched up his buttock.

"I simply cannot believe that many Rebels made it across our borders, penetrated our security, and successfully executed this raid," Khamsin spoke through gritted teeth.

Khamsin's XO had dreaded this moment. "There weren't that many Rebels, sir."

"There had to be a full battalion," Khamsin said.

"Six, sir," the XO said.

"Six *battalions*!" Khamsin cut his eyes to the XO, disbelief in the evil darkness.

"Ah, no, sir. Six . . . people."

Khamsin began roaring his rage. "Six! Six men did all this?"

"Five men and one woman, I believe, sir."

Khamsin began pounding his clenched fists on the operating table, screaming his fury.

347

The XO waited until his colonel had exhausted his fury — hopefully. "They were led by Ike McGowen. That's the former U.S. Navy SEAL, sir."

Khamsin said some very uncomplimentary things about Ike McGowen.

General Georgi Striganov was awakened from a sound sleep by an aide.

"Sir? A great many confusing radio reports from California. It seems some great battles have been taking place there."

Striganov looked at his bedside clock. It was time to rise anyway. In the few weeks he had been in Canada, Striganov was feeling better than he had in months. He had placed himself in the capable hands of Vasily Lvov and had followed the doctor's orders to the letter.

He dressed and walked out to where the aide was waiting in the hall. Striganov followed the aide to the radio room, took a seat, and began listening.

It soon became apparent that Sam Hartline was finished. Now Ben Raines's Rebels were mopping up, and Georgi Striganov knew what the Rebels did when they "mopped up."

They took no prisoners.

Sam Hartline was through.

But had Sam escaped?

The radio reports gave not a clue. And Striganov knew Ben Raines well enough to know that the commander of the Rebel Army did not boast. If the reports said one thing, take it as fact, for it was.

Striganov listened and sipped hot tea until the

radio messages became repetitive. He left the radio room and went to his office. He sat down behind his desk and allowed himself a few moments of quiet meditation.

He would stay in Canada; God forbid crossing the border back into America for a long, long time.

If ever.

Lvov entered his office and sat down before the commander of the IPF.

"Something, Vasily?"

"Intercepted radio messages from South Carolina, Georgi. Some of Ben Raines's Rebels struck hard at the command post of the IPA. Heavy damage was inflicted. Colonel Khamsin escaped serious injury."

"How many Rebels struck?"

Lvov smiled. "Six," he said softly.

Georgi laughed, this laugh holding real mirth. "Khamsin is learning just how vicious the Rebels can be, correct?"

"It would appear that way, Georgi. Have you considered Khamsin's proposal?"

"Yes. And I have rejected it."

Lvov sighed with relief.

"I am weary of it all," Georgi said. "Tired of war. Tired of fighting General Raines. And tired of constantly being bested by the man. No matter where he goes, the man gains strength. I am weary of letting slip the dogs of war."

"Georgi?"

Russian eyes met, locked.

"I have ordered a halt to all human experimentation. I have instructed my people to focus on nonaggressive experiments. A way to produce better crops, medicines. How do you feel about that?"

"I feel a load lifting from my back, Vasily. That's how I feel. I do not wish to make enemies of those Canadians remaining. We shall work with them, be friends with them — as we should have done with the Americans."

"I have destroyed those mutant babies, Georgi."

"God forgive us all, Vasily."

"I wonder if it's too late for that, old friend. And believe me, I have given it much thought of late."

"As have I."

"Ben Raines?"

"In time I shall approach him, by radio," he added drily. "And extend the dove of peace to him. I can only hope he will accept."

"He probably will. But if you do that, bear this in mind: Ben Raines makes peace with no force who will not fight side by side with him."

"I think it's past time we did something decent for a change, Vasily."

The two men rose and shook hands.

"To a new way, Georgi."

"No, Vasily. Just a better way."

Thirty-nine

By late afternoon, it was apparent to all that Sam Hartline's mercenaries were no more. Those remaining were running in wild-eyed panic from the troops of Ben Raines. Panic because they knew they could not surrender; fear because they knew there was no place to run; terror because they each knew death was all that awaited them.

They engaged the Rebels in spotty combat, and died. Even though the mercenaries and the Rebels were just about equal in numbers, the Rebels were fighting for a just cause, with a definite goal in mind; the mercenaries fought only for booty and rape and torture and joy in killing.

And they died for it.

Ben left the camp and walked the battleground, his usual complement of Rebels surrounding him. He could still find grim amusement in all the attention paid him.

Better get used to it, Ben, he thought. This is the way it's going to be—from now on.

The rain had put out most of the fire; some trees still smoldered and smoked. And the Rebels were soon filthy from the soot and ash.

Ben removed his camo headband, poured water on it from his canteen, and washed his face and neck, retying the camo bandana around his forehead. His Thompson was on sling.

Broken bodies littered the forest. Some had died from gunshot wounds, others from the heavy shelling of the night before, still others had no marks on them. Either smoke got them or they died of fright.

Ben's walkie-talkie crackled. "Go," he spoke into the mouthpiece.

"Ike made it back across the border, General. Nina is okay. Reports are that Khamsin got shot in the ass."

"Good," Ben laughed the reply.

They walked on, their boots making little noise in the ashes of fire and war. A slight noise turned Ben's head. He waved the patrol quiet and down. Ben walked toward the source of the small noise. Crouching down near the mouth of a hole in the ground, Ben could hear the sounds of someone climbing up, clawing at the rock and dirt beneath the surface of the earth.

Ben signaled for his patrol to remain where they were. He squatted and waited.

Sam Hartline's head popped out of the hole, his eyes darting left and right.

Like a large rat.

Sam turned in the hole, and Ben placed the muzzle of his Thompson between the man's eyes, the metal pressing against flesh.

"Hello, Sam," Ben said. "I can't tell you how I've looked forward to this day."

"Wish I could say the same, Ben."

"Very slowly, Sam—very slowly, pull yourself out of that hole. And there better not be anything in your hands except skin."

"I'm not a fool, Ben." Hartline pulled himself out of the hole to stand before Ben. "You going to give me a fighting chance, Ben Raines?"

Ben laid his Thompson aside and smiled. "Oddly enough, Hartline, I am."

"You're a fool, Raines! You can't take me with your hands."

"We're about to find out, Sam."

"Mind if I limber up a bit, Ben? It's been sort of cold and cramped sleeping on rock."

"Help youself, Sam. I'm feeling rather magnanimous this morning."

Neither man noticed when a Rebel lifted his walkie-talkie and spoke very quietly. Since neither man took his eyes off the other, they did not notice the woods filling with Rebels until several hundred had gathered silently.

Sam stretched and did several deep knee bends, flexed his arms, and shadowboxed for several seconds.

"How's it going to be, Raines?" Hartline asked.

"Rough-and-tumble—anything goes, bare-handed."

"And if I win?"

"You won't," Ben said flatly.

"Let's assume."

"One of those Rebels will shoot you dead."

"Well, goddamn, Raines! You're giving me a hell of an option, aren't you?"

"I've giving you a last chance to do something

353

you've never been able to do before."

"What?"

"Best me in anything."

That stung Hartline. He flushed, then grinned. "Rani had some good gash, Raines. You should have heard her scream when I took her like a dog."

Ben did not change expression.

"I heard another of your women turned on you, Raines. Made a deal with the Libyan. What'd you do with her, slap her on the wrist and tell her she's been bad?"

"I shot her between the eyes—personally."

Hartline narrowed his eyes. "*You* shot her, Ben? You killed a broad? I thought you were the last of the great romantics . . . women on a pedestal and all that shit."

"You pays your money you takes your chances, Sam."

Hartline grinned. "Yeah, I guess you're right, Ben." He studied Ben for a moment. "You'll never beat Khamsin, Raines. I know him from years back. He was Abu's right hand. Until the world blew up."

"I'll beat him, Sam."

Hartline nodded his handsome head. "Maybe. We gonna talk all the damn day, Raines?"

"No," Ben said, then took a quick step forward and hit Hartline flush on the jaw with a hard right cross. The blow knocked the man backward and down into the soot and ashes. Ben stepped forward and kicked Hartline in the side with his boot, sending the man rolling on the sooty earth.

Hartline sprang to his booted feet quick as a big cat. He grinned at Ben, the blood leaking from a cut somewhere inside his mouth. "Sneaky bastard, aren't you?"

"Yep," Ben agreed, and ducked a roundhouse swing from Hartline. He grabbed the man's arm and flipped him. Hartline landed on his back on the earth, sending great clouds of ash and soot billowing. Just as he was getting to his feet, Ben kicked him low, just above the left kidney. Hartline squalled in pain and rolled, coming up on his hands and knees.

Ben stepped in to give the mercenary a knee in the face and Hartline grabbed Ben around the knees and dumped him to the ground. Sam was immediately on top of Ben, straddling him, pounding at Ben's face with both fists.

Ben worked one arm out from under Sam's leg and grabbed Sam's genitals in one strong hand, clamping down hard and twisting with all his strength.

Hartline screamed like a panther and dropped both hands to Ben's wrist.

Ben rolled over, still holding on, and worked his way to his knees. He lifted Hartline's buttocks and legs off the ground and then suddenly released his hold and stood up. Sam was huddled on the ground, in a painful ball.

Ben stood for a moment, blood leaking from his mouth and nose. He caught his breath just as Sam slowly got to his booted feet. The two men went at each other with fists, hammering at each other, all thoughts of their many skills in the martial arts forgotten.

This had once been known — back when the nation was whole, before — as Oklahoma oilfield, bare-knuckle, slug-it-out type of fighting.

Hartline hit Ben in the wind with a solid left that staggered Ben. Ben responded with a vicious hook to Sam's jaw, the punch driving the man back. Ben stepped in and hit the man in the face with both fists, a jumping type of punch. Hartline went to the ground, spun, and kicked Ben on the knee with a boot.

Ben fell to the earth and rolled, narrowly missing Sam's boot aimed at his face. Ben grabbed up a handful of ash and soot and flung it into Sam's face, momentarily blinding the man.

Ben got to his feet and went to work, slashing at the man with both fists, left and right combinations, to the body and to the face. Sam was staggering now, his eyes glazed. He backpedaled, shook his head, and came up with a knife in his hand, jerked from the sheath on his web belt.

Ben stepped back and pulled his own Bowie-type blade. He feinted with his left hand and Hartline swung his blade in that direction. The blades clanged and echoed through the charred woods. Each man was as good as the other with the blade, and it did not take either of them long to realize that.

Sam stepped in close and tried for a gut cut. Ben sidestepped and swung his heavy knife, cutting Sam from temple to point of jaw. Sam yelled and dropped his guard for just one second.

That was all Ben needed.

Ben drove the point of his knife into Sam's stomach, driving it into the hilt. Ben stepped back.

Sam's fingers opened, his knife dropping from suddenly numbed fingers. Sam Hartline sank to his knees, his eyes mirroring his disbelief that this could happen to him.

"You . . . you killed me!" Sam said, blood pouring out of his mouth.

"Sure looks that way," Ben panted.

Sam tried to pull the blade from his mangled stomach and guts. But he did not have the strength. He lifted his eyes to Ben. "You gonna bury me right, Ben?"

"Nope."

"You owe me that much. We're . . . soldiers and all." His voice was getting weaker.

"You're a disgrace to the profession, Sam. I'm just gonna let the buzzards have you."

"You . . . !" Sam never got to finish it. He fell forward on his face and chest and stomach, the force of his fall driving the knife blade deeper into his guts.

His fingers dug into the soot and ash, clawing as life began leaving him.

"You . . . !" Sam once more whispered.

Ben waited.

Sam Hartline never spoke another word. His legs trembled and his body jerked in spasms of pain. Blood poured from his mouth, staining the dirty ground.

Ben walked to Dan, standing by Tina. He winked at his daughter and shifted his eyes to Dan. "Give the orders, Dan. Let's go home."

Forty

"You people don't have enough numbers to sway what will happen one way or the other," Ben told the civilian freedom fighters from California. "So it would be best if you stayed out here. But that doesn't mean I might not call on you."

"We'll roll as soon as you call, General," John Dunning assured Ben.

Some of the materials taken from the Russian and from Hartline were given to the new Rebels in the west. Much of it was tied down on trucks and readied for the trip back east, to Base Camp One.

Ben ordered the miles-long column out in sections, with ten miles between each section. It was an awesome sight in the early morning mist, this eastward trek of Raines's Rebels. Thousands of men and women, hundreds of trucks and Jeeps, APCs, tanks, gasoline transports, motorized artillery.

In Utah, Ben ordered the column to halt for repairs and rest. The newest vehicle among the many was fourteen years old; that was the last year the United States of America had ever produced anything. Parts for the vehicles were no problem, millions of them lay all over the nation; but the vehicles did break down often.

Ben set up his command post in what remained of a motel, after having it cleaned free of rat shit and other debris. He ordered his radio operator to make contact with Base Camp One and got Ike on the horn.

"Ike? Congratulations. How's Nina?"

"She's fine, I think. The IPA used her pretty badly, Ben. Physically, she's okay."

"What are we going to be up against, Ike?"

"More than we've faced since the government assaulted the Tri-States, Ben.* The IPA are all seasoned fighters. From what I got out of prisoners, fighting is all they've been doing for ten to twelve years."

"Do you have any hard intel on the warlords and outlaws still alive?"

"Only that they've pulled in their horns and are somewhere up in the midwest, gathering strength. They won't be as easy to take the next time, Ben."

"I know. There is always something to contend with. But it's Khamsin and his people that I'm concerned with at the moment."

"Ben? Remember Sister Voleta?"**

"How could I ever forget her? Don't tell me she's popped up again?"

"Oh, yes. With her son. You ready for this? Ben Raines Blackman."

Ben's reply was a grunt.

*Out of the Ashes

**Blood in the Ashes

"Yeah, I knew you'd be thrilled. Anyway, Sister Voleta and son have a commune up in Michigan. Accurate intel is hard to get, but it was reported to me that she's got about a thousand or so people."

"You're just a regular fountain of glad tidings, Ike."

Ike's laughter boomed over the miles. "Yeah, I know. Sam Hartline is really dead, Ben?"

"He's dead."

"That's good news. His men?"

"Most of them destroyed. I'm sure a few of those remaining will pop up around the country, but Sam's army is only history."

"I wish I could tell you something about the Russian, but he's keeping low."

"I'll see you in about ten days, Ike. Hold the fort."

"What's the word?" Grizzly asked the trail-worn biker who had just roared into camp.

"This kookie Sister Voleta's got a hell of an outfit, Griz. She claims to be religious, but man, she's one mean bitch. She and her son run the place. Ben Raines Blackman."

"Are you serious?"

"She claims the guy is Ben Raines's son."

Grizzly and the other warlords smiled. "Let me guess. This Sister Voleta is claimin' that her son, Ben Raines Blackman, has some of the powers that the real Ben Raines is supposed to have, right?"

"You got it."

"And she wants us to join her group. I gotta ask,

Why?"

"Protection. That's it simple. If we wanna link up with her, all we gotta do is abide by her rules. We don't have to pray with them or any of that shit. And the rules is easy. We'll be her army—or at least part of it. Griz? Don't sell this bunch short. They did better fightin' Ben Raines a couple years back than we just done."

"So I heard," Grizzly said, scratching his bushy beard, his fingernails seeking, unsuccessfully, a flea. "We'll vote on it."

Two hours later, the outlaws were riding toward Michigan.

"We should strike *now*!" Khamsin's XO was unusually blunt with the commander of the IPA. "We could easily take Ben Raines's Base Camp in Georgia."

"Nothing worthwhile is ever done easily," Khamsin reminded the man. He tapped a huge pile of papers on his desk. "After studying all this intelligence about Ben Raines, I have discovered that in battle, for every Rebel killed, five of the opposing side are destroyed. Rebels do not surrender. They might, rarely, be overrun and taken, but they never surrender. They fight to the death. They are fanatics. We all saw, or heard, firsthand, what the Rebels can do." Khamsin shifted uncomfortably on the pillow beneath his ass. He grimaced in pain. "No." He made his mind. "We shall wait." He mopped his sweaty face with a handkerchief. Silently, he cursed this miserable climate. "Those are my orders."

"Yes, sir," the XO said, and left the room.

Ben and his Rebels made their way slowly eastward. And once more, Ben was amazed at the number of survivors they encountered along the way. He was forced to upgrade the number of people who had survived the war, the disease, and the savagery and barbarism of the past decade.

But the majority of those Ben saw were not *doing* anything. They were not striving to rebuild, were doing nothing—that Ben could see—to struggle out of the ashes. He knew that there must be thousands of men and women, living off the beaten path, so to speak, who were rebuilding the country and their lives. Their own personal little part of the country, that is.

But how to pull them all together?

A question that Ben and the Rebels had been attempting to answer for years.

And sometimes Ben felt he was no closer to the solution than when he had started.

But he knew that was not true.

With a sigh, Ben knew he would have to postpone his dream of a chain of outposts stretching coast to coast. The first step in rebuilding.

Someday. Always someday.

For now, his Rebels had to face the dark, evil threat of Khamsin. The Hot Wind.

The Hot Wind now blew over the cooling ashes, finding a spark in the ashes. Igniting it.

And only one thing stood between the Hot Wind and total enslavement of the survivors of war.

Ben Raines and his Rebels.

THE LAST GUNFIGHTER SERIES BY
WILLIAM W. JOHNSTONE